Pink panties.

Hot-pink panties.

He'd gone into the store on high alert, hovering near Nina and watching to make sure that nobody else got close to her.

What he hadn't realized was that shopping with a woman could be such an intimate experience. He'd been fine as she'd grabbed several T-shirts and sweatshirts, some jogging pants and a nightshirt. His close presence next to her had felt a little more intrusive as she'd shopped for toiletries.

He'd finally managed to snap himself back into professional mode when she'd headed to the intimates section. It was when she tossed that single pair of hot-pink panties in the cart that his head once again went a little wonky.

Nina was the witness to a vicious crime and a victim of arson. She was here to be in his protective custody, not to be an object of his sexual fantasies. Speaking of protective custody, he pulled himself off the bed, grabbed his gun and went in search of his houseguest.

Dear Reader,

Chief of police Flint Colton has his hands full in the small town of Dead River, Wyoming: two fugitives on the loose, a missing heirloom ring and a beloved grandmother deathly ill from a mysterious virus that has the town shut down by the CDC.

When pretty Nina Owens, the owner of the local diner, witnesses a murder and then has her house burned down, Flint further complicates his life and takes her into his home under protective custody.

Flint is a traditional man who wants a wife and a family, while Nina has decided long ago that she wants to live her life alone. It doesn't take Flint long to realize Nina is the woman he wants. Now all he has to do is convince her that they belong together.

Her Colton Lawman is filled not only with exciting danger and sizzling desire, but also with the growing love of two people with wounded hearts that must heal in order to embrace that love.

I hope you enjoy!

Carla Cassidy

HER COLTON LAWMAN

—

Carla Cassidy

Ⓗ **HARLEQUIN**®ROMANTIC SUSPENSE

Special thanks and acknowledgment are given to
Carla Cassidy for her contribution to
The Coltons: Return to Wyoming miniseries.

Recycling programs
for this product may
not exist in your area.

ISBN-13: 978-0-373-27893-0

Her Colton Lawman

Printed in U.S.A.

Books by Carla Cassidy

Harlequin Romantic Suspense

Silhouette Romantic Suspense

Other titles by this author available
in ebook format.

CARLA CASSIDY

is a *New York Times* bestselling and award-winning author who has written more than one hundred books for Harlequin. In 1995 she won Best Silhouette Romance from *RT Book Reviews* for *Anything for Danny*. In 1998 she won a Career Achievement Award for Best Innovative Series from *RT Book Reviews*.

Carla believes the only thing better than curling up with a good book to read is sitting down at the computer with a good story to write. She's looking forward to writing many more books and bringing hours of pleasure to readers.

Chapter 1

Chief of Police Flint Colton jammed on the brakes of his patrol car and with a quick flip of the steering wheel, squealed to a halt along the side of the gravel road.

He slapped his black cowboy hat more firmly on his head and jumped out of the car, closing the door as quietly as possible behind him. He pulled his gun and headed into the woods that formed a perimeter on one side of the small town of Dead River, Wyoming.

He entered the heavily wooded area with his adrenaline pulsing through him. He'd seen something moving among the nearly bare trees…not just something, but rather someone on two legs, someone who definitely didn't belong there.

It could be either one of two people, a cold-blooded killer who was on the loose or the stupid kid who had left Flint's cousin, Molly, at the altar, but not before he'd cleaned out her bank accounts and stolen Flint's grandmother's heirloom ring.

Right now he didn't much care which man it might be; he only knew he'd seen the flash of a red jacket running through the woods that might mean an arrest, and he was desperate for something positive to happen.

He'd lost sight of his prey, but raced in the direction he'd last seen the person running. All of his senses were acutely alive. The scent of November surrounded him with smells of withering leaves and the pleasant odor of a wood-burning fireplace coming from somewhere in the distance.

He not only heard the snap and crackle of dead tree limbs and the crunching of leaves ahead of him, but he also heard the nearby scurry of wildlife disturbed by his presence in their home.

A desperate need drove Flint forward. The town needed something good to happen after the past month of nothing but bad news and abject fear. He hoped the man he chased was Hank Bittard, a murderer who had nearly killed a deputy when he'd escaped from custody last week. Getting that man back behind bars would at least ease some of the worries of the people of the small town.

He muttered a curse as he tripped over an exposed root, nearly going down on one knee. He straightened up and then paused and listened.

Nothing. He didn't hear the noise of somebody crashing over dried brush or the snapping of twigs as anyone ran away. He heard nothing to indicate that he wasn't completely alone in the woods.

Had Flint only imagined the flash of red, the motion of a person running in the woods? Or was the person he pursued also standing perfectly still now as well, waiting for Flint to make a move and give away his position?

He tightened his grip on his gun, hearing his own heartbeat echoing in his head. Bittard wouldn't think twice about putting a bullet through Flint's heart. He was a ruthless killer who had initially been arrested for the murder of his boss. Flint would love to get him back into custody. But Flint also didn't know for sure if the man had a weapon or not.

He moved forward once again, a dose of reality taking the edge off the initial adrenaline rush that had gripped him. He had to admit that whoever he might have been chasing was gone now, and he had no idea in what direction to proceed.

He continued walking and veered slightly to his left, attempting to move as quietly as possible. His breath caught in his chest as he came gun to gun with a man in a white HAZMAT suit.

Flint instantly raised his hands and slowly backed away, grateful that he was clad in his black police uniform and that the sun caught and glinted off his badge.

Flint knew there was only one reason the man in the HAZMAT suit would shoot him and that was if Flint tried to get by him and step out of the perimeters the CDC had set up. Whoever Flint had been chasing wouldn't have a way out of town, not with the quarantine in place.

"Did anyone come this way before me?" Flint asked.

The man in the suit shook his head.

Discouraged, he slowly continued to back away from the man and then turned and headed to his car.

The opportunity to catch the person in the woods had been lost this time.

It was just after noon. He'd check in with his men at the station and then head to the diner for some lunch. He still believed that Hank was hiding out in the woods, a place where he'd often go with his buddies for target shooting. The woods would continue to be a focal point for Flint to hunt for Hank.

As he drove onto Main Street and into the center of town, he was disheartened by the lack of people on the streets, the eerily deserted air of what had been a thriving little town until the mysterious disease had struck.

He clenched his hands around the steering wheel, acknowledging that at the moment there was nothing that could be done about the quarantine preventing people from entering or leaving the town.

The entire town of Dead River was trapped by a deadly disease with no cure so far and shut in with a desperate killer who had no place to run and had yet to be apprehended.

The police station was in the middle of town, a one-story brick building with two small jail cells in the basement and a larger general holding cell. The two cells had seemed adequate for such a small town when Flint had been voted in as chief of police, but he wondered now if, because of the quarantine, they'd have to figure out a way to cobble together more cells as tensions rose and tempers flared. Already occupying the general holding cell was Doug Gasper, a stalker who'd recently been apprehended at his brother Theo's ranch.

The pair of cells in the basement were reserved for the likes of of Hank Bittard and Jimmy Johnson, the young man who had taken advantage of sweet Molly, and it was anyone's guess who might go around the bend and become a danger to others due to the stress and anxiety of the quarantine.

He parked his car and got out, hoping that one of his deputies might have some news about the two missing men, or perhaps an update about the mystery illness that had struck and forced the CDC to quarantine the town.

Kendra Walker greeted him from behind her desk in the small reception area. She worked during the day as both receptionist and dispatcher.

"Hey, Chief," she said and then the phone rang, taking her attention away from him.

He gave her a wave and pushed through the doors that led into the area where the officers had their desks. His private office was at the back of the room, along with a single room that was used for interrogations or staff meetings.

Flint was thirty-two years old but at the moment he felt closer to sixty. The weight of the events of the past month sat heavily on his shoulders, and even heavier in his heart.

"Have you been rolling around in the woods?" Officer Patrick Carter stepped in front of Flint and picked out a twig that had been trapped beneath his collar. He tossed it in a nearby trash can and then turned back and looked at Flint expectantly.

"I was patrolling near the woods on the west side of town, and I thought I saw somebody running. I got out and gave chase, but I didn't manage to catch whoever it was," Flint said, unable to help the frustration that edged into his voice.

"Hmm. That squares with a report we got earlier

this morning. Walt Jennings called in to say that somebody broke into his shed overnight. Whoever it was,
they stole some rope, a fillet knife and some canned
goods that Walt had stored in there. Mike and Larry
went out to talk to Walt and check out the shed to see
if maybe they could pull some prints."

"Sounds like one of our fugitives is getting desperate," Flint replied thoughtfully. "This makes three
break-ins in homes around the perimeter of those
woods. It was a gun and food that was taken last week.
I'd like to know if it's Bittard or Johnson who now has
a gun and a knife."

"Let's hope it's Jimmy. He might be able to charm
a young woman right out of her life savings and break
her heart, but I don't think he has it in him to shoot or
stab anyone," Patrick replied.

"Let's hope," Flint said. "I'm going to head over to
the diner for some lunch. You want to join me?"

"Nah, I grabbed a burger earlier. I'll stick around
here and hold down the fort."

"If you need me just give me a call, and let me know
if Mike and Larry discover anything useful at Walt's
place," Flint said and with Patrick's nod of assent, Flint
left the building.

The diner was two blocks from the sheriff's station, and he decided to walk it. The November sun was
warm on his back although there was a definite bite to
the air that portended winter's imminent appearance.

Winter in Wyoming could be rough, but this winter
would be particularly tough on the town if they had to
spend Christmas still under quarantine, if a desperate
killer was still trapped in the town and not in custody
and if more people got sick and died.

The Dead River Diner was like diners and cafés in hundreds of small towns across the country, with red booths lining the walls, square tables in the center and a long counter where Flint usually sat whenever he came into the place. There was even an old working jukebox that played ancient country songs for a quarter, and it was played a lot.

As he walked the sidewalk, he passed the post office, a dress boutique and the grocery store. Across the street was the Blue Bear Restaurant, popular for special-occasion dining. There was also the Dead River Café and a hardware store.

He waved at the old man who sat on a bench in front of the hardware store. Eighty-five-year-old Harvey Watters had lost his wife three years ago.

Since Harvey's wife's death, the old man ate breakfast each day at the café and then sat on the bench until lunchtime. He'd return to the café for lunch and then resume his seat on the bench until just before dark, when he finally headed home. The only days Harvey wasn't on the bench was when it rained.

Harvey lived two houses down from Flint's house in the center of town. The two men had struck up an unlikely friendship, and it wasn't unusual for Flint to stop in at Harvey's house for a quick game of chess or a couple of beers on an occasional evening. Unfortunately, over the past month there had been little time for that kind of pleasant socializing.

He took off his hat and shoved open the door to the diner and was greeted by the scents of burgers frying and sauces simmering, an olfactory assault that was pure pleasure.

Even more pleasurable was the sight of Nina Owens,

the diner's owner, behind the counter. He'd been attracted to Nina since the moment he'd moved back to town, but with his brother Theo's health issues and the fact that he'd suddenly found himself chief of police, there had been little time to pursue anything resembling a romance.

And now, with the additional pressures of a murderer loose and the virus that had people afraid of their own shadows, this definitely wasn't the time for him to think about a relationship.

In any case, he was fairly certain Nina wasn't particularly attracted to him. Although she was always friendly when she served him, she rarely stuck around to chitchat, and he'd always felt a distance, a wall rising up whenever she interacted with him.

She stood at the far end of the counter, her pretty face lit with a warm smile as she poured more coffee into a cup for Jeff Cambridge, a muscular, dark-haired man who worked as a teller at the bank.

Her thick and wavy auburn hair was captured with a red tie at the nape of her neck, but he knew that when it was loose, it was a glorious mane of burnished reds and gold that fell to just below her shoulders.

The black slacks that were part of the diner uniform fit perfectly on her slender legs, and the white blouse showcased a slender waist and full breasts.

She finished pouring the coffee, put the pot back on the burner and then turned and saw him. He wasn't sure if he imagined the slight narrowing of her hazel eyes, but by the time she reached him, she smiled at him in friendliness.

"Good afternoon, Flint," she said. "What can I get for you?"

"A burger and fries and a cup of coffee," he replied. Before she turned to place the order, he quickly spoke again. "How's business these days?"

"Not great, but I suppose I can't complain. At least we still have customers coming in." She looked around the diner, which on a Saturday afternoon would usually be packed but now only held a handful of people. "I almost feel as if I'm on vacation since we're opening at 9:00 a.m. now instead of five-thirty, but business has dropped off enough that I couldn't justify the early hours anymore. I'm planning a big Thanksgiving feast for everyone in town, a free traditional turkey dinner. I'm hoping to have a big crowd that day. I think we could all use a day of community and mutual support."

"That sounds great. It's a generous gesture." He knew through the grapevine that Nina was known as a positive force in town. She was a Search and Rescue volunteer and had a reputation for being cheerful and optimistic no matter what the circumstances.

He frowned thoughtfully. "Aren't you afraid of getting sick? You work here with the public every day, and if you're inviting the whole town to a feast, there's really no way to know who might be sick with the virus and who isn't."

Her eyes sparkled, and her lips curved into a smile that fired a hint of heat in the pit of his stomach. "If I was going to get the Dead River virus, it probably would have already happened by now. Besides, I refuse to live my life being afraid of friends and neighbors."

She didn't wait for him to reply, but instead twirled on her feet, placed his order with the kitchen and then wandered back down to the opposite side of the counter.

Flint drew a weary sigh. It was obvious she didn't feel any spark of interest in him. It was probably a good thing because with a killer to catch and his own grandmother suffering from the mysterious illness that had the town quarantined, the last thing he needed to entertain was any idea of a romance with the hot owner of the local diner.

Nina Owens was acutely aware of Chief of Police Flint Colton at the opposite end of the counter. As she'd served him his meal, she'd tried not to notice the richness of his dark brown hair or the almost electric green of his eyes. She tried to ignore his handsome, chiseled features and the commanding aura that radiated from him.

His shoulders were broad, his legs long and his waist slender. She'd been physically drawn to him since the very first time he'd walked into her diner around a year ago, but at the same time she'd been faintly repelled by the uniform he wore and the job that he did.

She knew her distaste for any officer of the law was irrational and that she should have grown out of her belief that all police were bad, but it was a vague uneasiness that she'd never been able to overcome when encountering any law-enforcement person.

She knew Flint was a highly respected man, known for his sharp intelligence, his sense of fairness and the seriousness with which he took his job.

She remained overly conscious of his presence at the counter until he'd eaten his lunch and left. Only then did she fully relax. She'd been in Dead River for the past three years, and it was a cruel fate that had made the first man she felt any attraction toward a law-enforcement official.

She'd seen enough dirty cops while growing up to never want to see one again for the rest of her life, not that she'd heard anything to indicate that Flint was anything close to a dirty cop.

It was just after the dinner rush that she went into the kitchen and found one of her waitresses, Flint's cousin Molly, crying.

"Hey, what's going on?" Nina asked as she draped an arm around the young woman's slender shoulder. Even though Nina asked the question, she knew what probably had the pretty redhead weeping.

"I'm sorry," Molly said as she gazed at Nina and quickly swiped the tears from her cheeks. "I know it's stupid, but I just started thinking about what a fool I was with Jimmy. I can't believe I let him talk me into putting his name on all my bank accounts and credit cards. I can't believe I gave him my grandma's ring to give to me at our wedding and most of all I can't believe that I fell in love with him and didn't realize he was such a slimy creep." She drew a tremulous sigh as tears once again filled her bright blue eyes.

"Listen, honey, you aren't the first woman in the world who fell in love with a creep," Nina replied as she gave Molly a hug. "Just be grateful that you found out what his real character was like before the wedding actually took place." Nina pulled a napkin from a nearby container and handed it to Molly.

"Flint says he can't go after him for the money Jimmy stole because his name was on all the accounts, and that means he had the legal right to take it. I don't care so much about the money, but I'm so sick that he took my grandmother's ring." She dabbed at her eyes with the napkin.

"And didn't Flint tell you that once they find him, he will be arrested for the theft of the ring?"

"Yes, but I'm afraid he pawned it or something, and I'll never get it back," Molly replied.

Nina patted Molly's shoulder. "If he pawned the ring here in town, then Flint will find it, and since he can't get out of town, the odds are good that he still has the ring with him. Are you okay to work or do you need to go home?"

Molly sniffled and wiped her cheeks once again. "No, I'm fine. I just had a momentary mini-breakdown. Besides, I'm helping Helen close up tonight."

"And I'm leaving a bit early to take dinner to Grace," Nina said.

Molly's blue eyes deepened in hue. "Aren't you afraid that she has the virus?"

Nina smiled gently. "All I know for sure is that Grace went home sick yesterday. I don't know if she has a bad cold, the common flu or the Dead River virus. I'm sure she won't feel like cooking tonight so I'm fixing up a care package, and I'm taking it to her and Billy."

She gave Molly a shove toward the dining area. "Now get back to work and stop beating yourself up over that jerk Jimmy, and stop worrying about me."

"Yes, ma'am." Molly gave her a saucy salute and left the kitchen.

Nina was grateful to see Molly back to her cheerful sweetness. At twenty-one years old, Molly was probably going to kiss a lot of frogs before she finally found the man meant for her.

Nina had certainly kissed a lot of frogs in her life, but she wasn't looking for any special man to share her life. She was perfectly content alone, always had been, always would be.

With the dinner rush finished, Nina got busy filling a large Styrofoam take-out container with slices of meat loaf and mashed potatoes, green beans and two dinner rolls. There was not only enough food to feed Grace, but also her eight-year-old son.

Grace had left work early the day before with a bad cough and complaining about a bad headache. Nina had called her this afternoon, and Grace had confessed she still didn't feel well at all.

Nina had told her to stay in bed, drink lots of fluids and had promised she'd stop by this evening with dinner for both her and her son, Billy.

Just before she finished packing up the food, she threw into the bag a couple of her special double chocolate chip cookies, knowing that they were one of Billy's favorites.

Billy was almost a daily visitor to the diner. Grace worked an eight-to-five schedule, and Billy would come in after school during the weekdays and take a two-top table in the corner to wait for his mom's shift to be over.

He was a cute kid with shiny brown hair and blue eyes like his mother. He was also a good kid, who sat quietly and did his homework, never bothering anyone while he was there. Nina had taken to him immediately, as she did most of the younger diners who came in with their parents.

Darkness had already fallen when Nina finally stepped out of the back door of the diner where her car was parked. Clad in a long-sleeved white blouse and a pair of black slacks that all the waitresses wore, she wished she'd thought of bringing her coat with her that morning as the night had brought with it a nip of a wintry chill.

She got into her car and placed the bag of food on the passenger seat and then turned her key to start the engine. She frowned at the sound of the familiar *whir-whir* of her battery refusing to catch. She turned the ignition off, waited a minute and then tried again, grateful to hear the engine finally roar to a start.

Gus at Dead River Auto Body had put in a new battery for her last week, but had warned her that the problem might be her alternator.

She waited for the heater to begin to blow warmth, trying to decide when she could take the time off to get the car back in for Gus to fix. Most days and evenings she was at the diner.

She supposed she could drop it off on the way to work one morning and pick it up on the way home. She could get either one of the cooks or a waitress to drive her from the auto shop in the morning and take her back there in the evening.

As she waited, she thought of all the recent events that had changed the town she had come to love and call home.

It was hard to believe that it was just a month ago that Mimi Rand, a local socialite, had returned to town with a baby she claimed was Flint's brother Theo's, the result of one night the two had spent together.

She'd arrived at Theo's house, introduced him to the three-month-old little girl and then collapsed.

Dr. Lucas Rand, the head doctor at the Dead River

Clinic had worked desperately to save the woman, who was also his ex-wife, but she had died anyway. By the time of her death, another man was dead along with two children, also suffering from the same mysterious symptoms.

When Flint's grandmother, Dottie Colton, had fallen ill along with a teenage boy, the town was shut down by the Centers for Disease Control and Prevention.

Overnight the town had transformed from a small tight-knit community to something out of a science-fiction film. CDC trailers and equipment now surrounded the Dead River Clinic, and National Guard and other security forces, who looked like space men in their HAZMAT gear and guns, formed a perimeter around the town. Nobody in...nobody out.

With warm air finally blowing out of her car's heater vents, Nina pulled out of the parking lot and headed toward Grace Willard's small home.

She hoped her words to Molly proved true, that Grace had a simple cold or a common case of the flu and not the Dead River virus, of which the initial symptoms were very similar but then escalated quickly until the patient was deathly ill with severe respiratory issues and a high fever.

Nina wasn't afraid for herself by going to Grace's house. She figured she'd already been exposed to the virus day after day with the stream of people who came into the diner to eat. Of course, as a waitress, Grace would have the same kind of exposure and so would Billy.

There had also been the escape of a hardened criminal and Molly's heartbreak, and all of these issues had changed the very heart and soul of Dead River.

Everyone regarded everyone else with suspicion, wondering who might be sick with the mysterious illness or who might be some sort of carrier. Then there were the suspicions of who might be helping the two fugitives in town, killer Hank Bittard and Molly's jerk, Jimmy Johnson.

She desperately hoped that the Thanksgiving feast she had planned would bring people together, bring back a sense of community and remind everyone that they were all in this mess together, but the holiday was still weeks away. Unfortunately, it didn't seem likely that a cure would be found by then.

Just before turning onto the side street where Grace lived, she frowned and slowed as she saw a couple near the streetlamp just ahead. As she drove closer, a sense of horror swept through her.

In the spill of illumination from the light, she could now see that it was a man and a woman. The man had a rope around the woman's neck, and although Nina couldn't hear a scream or a single indication of the woman's terror, she felt it ripple through her blood.

Nina stopped her car, unsure what she should do but knowing she needed to do something and fast. It would take her too long to dig her cell phone out of her purse and call for help.

Still, if she didn't do something quickly she knew that the woman would be strangled to death. She opened her car door and stepped halfway out.

"Hey," she cried out. "Hey, you, let her go!"

At that moment the woman fell to the ground in a boneless drop that made Nina realize it was too late, the woman was definitely unconscious or possibly dead.

As the man raised his head and stared at her, Nina's heartbeat raced with a frantic rhythm.

He started toward her, and she nearly stumbled as she got back into her car and locked the doors. She had to get out of here and fast. Her heart nearly halted as she realized her car had stopped running.

"Come on, come on," she cried as she turned the key and heard the familiar grinding noise. She glanced out the window to see that the man was getting closer... closer.

"Please," she begged as she pumped the gas and tried to start the car again, knowing that if she didn't get rolling she was a sitting duck for a man who had just possibly committed a murder right in front of her eyes.

Chapter 2

Terrified, sobbing gasps escaped Nina, and she cried out in relief as headlights appeared from a car coming from the opposite direction on the road. Maybe the presence of another car, of other people, would stop the man and save her.

Her engine finally started. For a single instant her gaze caught the killer's, his cold and glittering with unsuppressed rage.

She threw her car into gear and spun out, nearly losing control of it in an effort to escape the scene. She sped down the residential road, passing Grace's house as she continued to play and replay in her mind what had just happened, what she had just seen.

She needed to get to the police station. Maybe the woman on the ground wasn't really dead, but had just been strangled to unconsciousness. If Nina got help soon enough, maybe she could still be saved.

Surely the man had run from the scene when he'd seen the other car coming and knew that if he stuck around, there would be more witnesses to what he had done.

A glance in her rearview mirror showed no car pursuing her. She hadn't even seen a vehicle near the corner where the man might have come from, but she'd been riveted to the struggle, not looking for nearby cars.

It took her only minutes to pull onto Main Street and squeal to a halt in front of the police station. She jumped out of the car and raced inside, still crying with shock and fear.

She flew past Glenda McDonald, who worked the night shift at the front desk. "Hey, wait," Glenda yelled in protest as Nina burst through the door that led into the inner sanctum of the station.

Flint appeared seemingly from nowhere and grabbed her by the shoulders. "Nina, what's wrong?" he asked urgently.

"I...I think I just saw a murder." She was once again overwhelmed by sobs as she tried to choke out what had happened. She was vaguely aware of Officer Mike Harriman moving closer to where they stood with Flint still firmly grasping her.

She feared that if he released his hold on her, she'd fall to the floor as her legs shook so badly beneath her, and she couldn't halt the violent trembling of her entire body.

"Where did this happen?" Flint asked, his handsome features tense, and his green eyes piercing as he stared at her intently.

"At the corner of Cherry and Oak Street. I was on

my way to Grace Willard's house when I saw them struggling near the streetlight. I think he killed her, Flint. I think she was dead when I drove off."

Flint gave a nod to Mike, who immediately left, taking with him Officer Sam Blair. Flint guided Nina to a chair and gently pushed her to sit. He knelt down to one knee, his calm demeanor a counter to the terror that still screamed silently inside her.

He didn't speak for several moments, and she finally stopped crying and felt his calm slowly sweeping through her. Even the scent of his woodsy cologne smelled of safety.

"Better?" he asked.

She nodded and released a deep sigh. "A little better."

"Good. I need you to be as clearheaded as possible and answer some questions for me." He stood and grabbed a chair from a nearby desk and pulled it in front of her. He sat close, his knees almost touching hers. "What did the man look like?"

Nina frowned, trying to fight the fear that leaped back into her throat as she thought about the man she'd seen. "He was dressed all in black, and he had dark hair and evil, glittering eyes."

"What color eyes?"

"I'm not sure. I think they were dark, but the lighting was bad."

"Was he young or old?"

"Maybe late twenties or early thirties," she replied.

"What kind of build? Tall…short…skinny?" Flint's gaze never left hers. She hadn't noticed before that his green eyes held a faint touch of gold right in the center, along with a sharp focus that made it appear he was looking not just at her, but rather into her very soul.

She finally broke their gaze, looking down at her trembling hands in her lap. "He was tall and had a muscular build." A sob welled up, and she swallowed hard against it as she remembered the sight of his arm muscles bulging, his taut neck muscles as he pulled the rope so tight against the woman's throat.

"Sounds like Bittard. Was it Hank?"

Nina shrugged helplessly. "I don't know…maybe. It was dark and everything happened so fast. I didn't get a solid look at him. Plus, I've only seen Hank a couple of times and that was before he murdered Donny Gilmore at the gas station. Hank never came into the diner so I only saw him from a distance. That, plus his mug shot."

The conversation was interrupted by the ring of Flint's cell phone in his pocket. He grabbed the phone and stood, walking away from where Nina sat as he answered.

Nina tracked him with her eyes, afraid that if she didn't look at him she'd fall back into the utter terror that had momentarily gripped her and still simmered just beneath the surface.

Flint was on the phone only a minute or two and then he came back to her and sat once again, his face a study in both weariness and a simmering anger.

"It had to have been Bittard. The woman is Jolene Tate, and she is dead."

Nina gasped, and tears rose to her eyes once again. "Why would he kill her?"

"She was Hank's off-and-on girlfriend and was at the Dead River Gas Station the night Hank killed

Donny. She was a key eyewitness to the murder and intended to testify against Hank."

He slammed a fist against his thigh. "Dammit, I should have insisted she go into protective custody when Hank escaped, but she wanted nothing to do with it and refused to even talk about it." He rubbed the center of his forehead, as if attempting to ease a headache. "Did he see you? Did the man you saw strangle Jolene get a good look at you?"

Nina raised a hand to her throat, a new fear searing through her. "I…I don't know. I mean, I can't be sure how well he saw me. He was more in the light than I was, but I'm not sure if he recognized me or not. I'm not sure even if he got a good look at me that he would know who I was."

Tears welled up in her eyes. "I should have done something more. I should have done something to help her."

"You did the right thing in getting out of there and coming right here," Flint said. "We shouldn't take any chances and assume that he didn't recognize you. You need to be in protective custody."

"Protective custody?" She repeated the words mindlessly.

He stood once again and for just a moment his eyes were a haunting deep green that she was sure held deep, dark secrets. "You can stay with me at my place."

"But surely that isn't necessary," she protested.

"Jolene Tate was just murdered, and you're an eyewitness. I don't have the manpower right now to keep you covered twenty-four-seven. With two fugitives on the loose, we're just stretched too thin."

"I'm not even sure how much of a look he got of me.

I was across the street from him, and we didn't have any real interaction before he looked up. It's very possible he couldn't pick me out of a lineup."

She stood, surprised to find herself still a bit shaky. His offer to stay in his house had stunned her. The idea was both a little bit thrilling and a little bit scary. "I'm sure I'll be fine, but I would appreciate it if you'd drive me home. I have to confess, I feel a little too shook up to drive myself."

He frowned. "Nina, I still think it would be best if you didn't go home, if you aren't alone until I get this creep back into custody."

"Flint, I appreciate your concern, but I'm not going to hole up somewhere on the off chance that he actually got a good look at me. It's a dark night, and I only saw him because of the streetlight, but I wasn't in the light." The last place she wanted to be was confined to Flint's home and living in his space.

She had a business to run, a life to live, and it didn't include being in his protective custody. Besides, the more she thought about it, the more she was fairly certain that the man probably hadn't seen her well enough to identify her. The entire incident had only taken mere seconds, although it had felt like an eternity when it was happening.

"Please, if you'll just take me home, I'm sure I'll be fine. I can have one of the waitresses take me to work in the morning and then somebody can bring me by here tomorrow evening to pick up my car." She raised her chin in a show of strength. "Besides, with everything that's going on around here you have more than enough on your plate without worrying about me."

Flint raked a hand through his hair, as if to show a

frustration he didn't want to verbalize. "It's my job to worry about you, but if you insist, I'll drive you home," he finally relented. "However, if you feel threatened in any way by anything, you have to promise me that you'll call me immediately, day or night."

"I promise. In any case I have a security system at my house, so I'm sure I'll be just fine." She frowned as she remembered the reason she'd turned down that particular road in the first place. "Could you do me one favor on the way? I was taking Grace and her son, Billy, some food. It's in my car, and if you could stop by her house and run it into them, I'd really appreciate it."

He stared at her as if she were an alien creature. "You just witnessed a murder and yet you're worried about Grace and her son having dinner?"

"Grace is sick. I promised to bring by a meal tonight. No matter what just happened, she and Billy are still expecting supper from me."

He pulled his car keys from his pocket and grabbed his hat off a nearby desk. "Okay, let's get moving."

Within minutes they were in his car, the bag of food on Nina's lap. "If you think of anything else that might be helpful to me finding Bittard, you call me immediately," he said as they pulled away from the police station.

She nodded, surprised to find a bit of comfort in the fact that the car smelled of his pleasant cologne. She was also grateful that he took another route to Grace's house, avoiding the place where the murder had occurred.

When they pulled into Grace's driveway, Flint turned to her. "You sit tight in the car, lock the doors when I get out and I'll deliver the food to the door."

His voice brooked no argument, not that she was of a mind to. He took the bag from her, opened the car door and got out.

She locked the doors and watched him walk up to the front door, wondering if she'd made a mistake in insisting he take her home. She felt calm enough now that she could have just driven herself.

She frowned and rubbed the center of her forehead as a headache attempted to take hold. Had the man seen her well enough to know who she was? Did he know her name? Where she lived? Would he now come after her in an attempt to kill another witness?

She wished she had family in town. She wished she had somebody who could take her in for a few weeks, but if there was danger she certainly didn't want to bring it close to any of her friends. At least she had the security system that would alert her to anyone attempting to enter her house.

She knew Flint and his team of deputies would be more determined than ever to catch Bittard with this new murder. Surely she'd be fine until they got the killer back in custody.

She watched as the door opened and light spilled out. Grace waved and then took the bag from Flint. As he started back to the car, Nina unlocked the doors.

"She said to tell you she was feeling a little better," he said when he was behind the steering wheel once again.

"Thank goodness. She went home yesterday with a headache and a cough. I was afraid she might have caught…" She allowed her voice to trail off. She didn't even want to speak her fear aloud. "By the way, how is your grandmother doing?" She knew that Dottie Colton had come down with the virus and had been in the hospital for the past couple of weeks.

"According to Dr. Rand, she's stable, but she's still unconscious." He cast her a sideways glance. "Is it easier to talk about the virus than the fact that you just witnessed a murder?"

A chill invaded her despite the warmth inside the car. "I don't want to think about that poor woman. I just wish I could have done something to stop it from happening. I wish I could have done something to force him to leave and run away before she died." She clenched her fists in despair.

"Then I might be investigating two murders, Jolene's and yours. You did the right thing by driving away, by not engaging with the man, especially if it was Bittard. He's a cold-blooded killer and we now think he might possibly be armed again. There's been some robberies in the past couple of days and among the things stolen have been a knife and a gun and rope."

"Rope that he used to strangle Jolene," she said flatly, fighting against another chill that tried to shiver down her spine.

"Forensics will tell us if the rope used to strangle Jolene is the same kind that was stolen. We'll know more in the next couple of days after a full investigation is completed."

In the glow from the dashboard, his handsome features looked slightly haggard, as if he hadn't slept well for weeks. "You'll catch him, Flint. You'll catch him and that little creep, Jimmy, too. The doctors will find a cure for the virus and before you know it, Dead River will be back to normal."

He slid her a wry look. "From your lips..." The

rest of the sentence wasn't spoken as he turned onto her street.

Nina looked out the front window of the car and gasped in surprise. The street was alive with the swirl of red lights from patrol cars and fire trucks that serviced the small city.

Firefighters in full gear ran with hoses toward the blaze that lit up the entire street and licked upward to the sky. Black smoke rolled up, creating a dark cloud in the otherwise clear night.

What was happening? What on earth was burning so fiercely?

Nina stared at it all in stunned disbelief. It was her house. Her house was on fire. A choking sob welled up inside her and released, followed by another...and another.

Flint pulled to the curb behind one of the fire trucks. "Stay here," he commanded sternly. "Lock the doors and do not get out of this car under any circumstances for anyone but me."

She couldn't have moved if her life depended on it as she watched the window of her living room explode outward. She'd bought the house just a little under a year ago and had spent the past months making it into the home she'd always dreamed of, and now she watched as everything she'd worked so hard for went up in flames.

She'd hand-picked each and every item from the bright yellow throw pillows on the sofa to the little water fountain that sat on one of her coffee tables. Gone...they were gone.

She saw Flint talking to a man she recognized as Stan Burrell, the fire chief. She watched the two men for only a moment and then turned her attention back to the house in time to see the roof collapse.

Numb. She was completely numb as she realized she'd lost everything. The flowered pink lamp in her bedroom, the cheerful daisy arrangement that had greeted her each morning on her kitchen table... everything was destroyed.

Had there been a wiring problem? Had she accidentally left on an appliance that morning that had shorted out and started the fire? How on earth had this happened?

Her neighbors stood on the sidewalk. Thank God there was no wind tonight, nothing to aid a spark from finding its way to their homes. In any case, it appeared that the firefighters had given up attempting to save her place and instead worked to make sure the fire remained contained to her home alone.

It was probably easy to contain a fire that had already consumed everything inside, she thought in despair and watched an outside wall fall inward. She wasn't even aware she was crying until she reached a hand up to her cheek and found it wet.

How had this happened? Her life was suddenly a scene from some crazy movie she didn't want to watch. Her mind worked desperately to find the positives. Thank God she hadn't been home and she didn't have any pets.

Thank God she had good insurance. She could use the cot in the diner and live in the back storage room until she rebuilt. Thank God it was just things that had been destroyed and things could always be replaced.

Still, no matter how many positives she tried to make of the situation, she continued to cry silently.

She'd thought she'd left all the bad things behind her when she left home. She'd believed that had been the worst time in her life, but tonight was right up there on the list of terrible things she had endured in her lifetime.

Flint returned to the car, a tense pulse in his jaw working overtime. "I'll have a full report sometime tomorrow, but there's no question in Stan's mind that this was arson. The ignition points appear to be all four corners of the house, and he believes gasoline was used as an accelerant. Somebody intentionally set the fire, either as a warning to you or hoping you would be inside. If I were a betting man, I'd wager that the man you saw kill Jolene tonight definitely recognized you."

She stared at him, the fear so great inside her she couldn't find words to speak. He started the car. "You're coming home with me," he continued. "You'll be staying at my place until I find Bittard and get him behind bars." He said the words not as a suggestion but rather as a statement of fact.

She simply nodded, knowing that even though the last place she wanted to stay was Flint's house, it appeared she was out of options. She couldn't deny the fact that her life was in danger.

Flint stood at his kitchen window, watching the first streaks of dawn beginning to light the sky. He was already working on his second cup of coffee, knowing that with the lack of sleep the night before, he'd need a good caffeine buzz to get him through what promised to be a long day ahead.

Nina had said very little on the drive to his place the night before. She'd also been silent as he'd led her through the house to his spare bedroom. He'd provided her with one of his T-shirts to wear to bed, and she'd immediately closed her bedroom door and hadn't come out for the rest of the night.

He was sure she had to have been suffering from some kind of shock. It was bad enough that she had witnessed a violent murder, but to know that the murderer had then burned her house to the ground had to be terrifying.

At some point during today he'd need to take her to the discount store to pick up some clothing and toiletries. From the scene at her house the night before, he was pretty sure that nothing would be salvageable. Not only did he need to take her shopping, but he also had a new murder to investigate and a new witness to protect.

Even though his officers would have a report for him first thing this morning concerning Jolene's death, he wanted to go to the scene and check things out himself. The murder had occurred on the corner just two houses from where Jolene had been staying since Hank's initial arrest, and even though he trusted his officers, Flint wouldn't be satisfied until he saw the scene for himself.

This attention to detail, checking and rechecking, was what had made him such a successful cop in Cheyenne, at least until the end of his work there.

He frowned and turned away from the window. He didn't want to think about the case that had been his swan song in Cheyenne. Besides, he'd already screwed up here by not placing some sort of protection on Jolene the minute Hank Bittard had escaped custody.

Even with Molly being stood up by her creep of a fiancé, even with the quarantine shaking everyone up and with his grandmother catching the virus, there was no excuse for failing in his duty of protecting Jolene. *Just like Cheyenne,* a little voice whispered in the back of his head.

He sat at the table and instead of getting caught up in his past and the agony of thoughts that brought, he began to mentally prepare himself for a houseguest that may or may not be so temporary.

It all depended on how long it took him to get the murderer back into custody. So far Bittard had managed to be successfully and frustratingly elusive in a quarantine town.

He thought of the fire at Nina's house. There was no question in his mind that it had been set by Jolene's murderer.

He'd need to check out the gas station to find out if a gas can and gasoline might have been stolen. Hank could have stolen a can of gas from anywhere, but the more details Flint could find out about the man's movements, the better his odds of finally getting him back in jail and letting Nina get back to her normal life.

The object of his thoughts suddenly appeared in the kitchen doorway. She was dressed in the same clothes she'd worn the day before, a long-sleeved white blouse and a pair of black slacks, and by the paleness of her face, she hadn't yet finished processing everything that had happened to her in the past twelve hours or so.

"Help yourself to the coffee," he said as he pulled the blinds closed at the windows. The last thing he wanted was for anyone outside to see her movements inside the house. "Cups are in the cabinet over the coffeemaker."

She nodded and moved to get a cup. After pouring her coffee, she carried her cup to the table and sat down across from him.

She took a drink of her coffee and then set the cup back on the table. "I feel like I'm living somebody else's life right now."

"I wish I could tell you that this was all just a bad dream," he replied. Despite the paleness of her features, she looked pretty with the artificial light over the kitchen table dancing in the strands of her hair and highlighting her delicate features.

"This is such a nightmare," she replied with a tremulous sigh. "And I still haven't quite realized that I'm not going to wake up and find out that everything is fine." She took another drink and then looked at him with slightly narrowed eyes. "If you think I'm going to hole up here and not go into the diner today, then you're sadly mistaken."

"I was just thinking about the logistics of this protective-custody position that you find yourself in," he replied. "And trust me, I figured there was no way I could keep you from your work. Besides being here in my house with me, the diner is probably the only other place I think you'll be safe. Bittard wouldn't kill you in the diner when he'd be leaving behind dozens of more witnesses."

He couldn't imagine that her face could have grown more pale, but it did, and he mentally cursed himself for his bluntness. But it was important she understand the severity of her situation.

She wrapped her fingers around her cup and stared down into the warm liquid. "Do you cook?" she asked and looked back up at him.

He sat back in his chair with surprise. Of all the

things he'd expected her to say, her words weren't even close to being on the short list. "Frozen pizza, microwave meals. Cooking has never been a big priority of mine. Why?"

"Then it's not all gloom and doom. If I'm going to stay here then you can expect a home-cooked meal every night. I'll either whip up something here or bring home-cooked meals from the diner. It's the least I can do."

"I'm not going to argue with you," he replied with a smile. He was pleased to see some of the color coming back into her cheeks. "But if you cook all day long, why on earth would you want to cook for me when you're off duty?"

She shrugged. "Cooking is what I do, it's what I love. It makes me happy to cook for other people."

"Then we probably need to work in a stop at the grocery store before the day is done. My refrigerator and pantry aren't stocked with much of anything but canned soups and bologna and cheese."

She took another sip of her coffee and eyed him over the rim of the cup. "This is going to be weird. I'm sure you aren't used to sharing your space with anyone, and I'm definitely not used to sharing mine. I'll try to be as unobtrusive as possible."

"Nonsense," he scoffed. "I want you to feel at home here for as long as you need to be here."

She lowered her cup and flashed him a smile. "I'm sure it will only be a day or two and you'll get Bittard in custody, and we can both go back to our own lives."

With the warmth of her smile swirling around in the pit of his stomach, Flint almost hoped he didn't find Bittard so soon. But it was a wayward, foolish thought.

His first priority was keeping Nina safe. His second was to get the murderer back behind bars where he belonged, and so far Bittard had remained effective at remaining on the loose.

She got up to pour herself another cup of coffee and when she returned to the table, they lined up the schedule for the day. He would take her to work and then he'd go to work. He'd pick her up sometime early evening, and they'd stop to get her some clothes and things she'd need and stock up on some groceries before landing back here.

They left his house at just after seven, and he dropped her off at the diner, comforted that she assured him there were at least three people already there ahead of her and two of them were male cooks who came in at six each morning to prep for the day.

They had exchanged cell phone numbers earlier, and he told her he'd call her before picking her up that evening. From the diner he headed straight to the place where Jolene Tate had been murdered.

Officer Patrick Carter's patrol car was parked next to the corner where bright yellow crime-scene tape marked off the area where Jolene's body had been found.

Patrick got out of his car to greet Flint. "I've been sitting on the scene all night, and Officer McGlowen is at the house that Jolene has rented for the past month as it appears the confrontation between her and Hank started there."

Flint nodded as he focused on the body form displayed on the ground and the markers that noted potential evidence that had already been collected. Jolene hadn't had a stellar reputation in town, but nobody deserved to die the way she had. He gave himself a moment to grieve the dead and then looked around once again.

His team had done a good job, as he'd trusted them to do while he'd dealt with Nina the night before. "The coroner report should be on your desk sometime this morning, but the cause of death was definitely strangulation by rope," Patrick said.

"That's exactly what Nina described. I'm going to check out the house. I'll be right back," he said to Patrick. Flint headed up Cherry Street where two houses from the corner Jolene Tate had lived alone for the past month in a small bungalow.

Officer Dana McGlowen sat on the front porch and stood at his approach, her brown eyes looking like a puppy dog eager to please. She was a relatively new hire but had already shown herself to be highly motivated to do a good job. She had quickly become a valued member of the team.

"Have you been here all night?" Flint asked.

"Yes, sir," Dana replied. "The crime scene boys were here last night and collected some things but intend to be back here this morning. They didn't want to do too much before you had a chance to check things out."

She stepped aside so he could enter the small living room. "It looks like a fight started in the kitchen, and then Jolene managed to run out of the front door in an attempt to get away. The front door was standing wide-open when we arrived last night to check it out."

Normally, Flint would have been at both scenes immediately, overseeing the evidence gathering and leading his team, but Nina's arrival at the station had forced him to allow his men to do their jobs without him. He could have assigned another officer to sit on Nina, and he had to admit that his desire not to had been strictly emotionally-driven. He'd simply felt he was the best man to stay with her.

He followed Dana into the kitchen, where it was obvious some sort of brawl had taken place. A kitchen chair lay on its back near the table, and broken glass littered the floor. A half-empty bottle of cheap wine sat in the center of the table, with a single glass. Flint suspected the other glass was what crunched beneath his feet.

"Any sign of forced entry?" he asked.

"None."

"Then she must have invited him in," Flint said thoughtfully. "If it was Bittard, then why in the hell would she let him inside? Why wouldn't she call for help?"

"They were lovers before he got arrested. Women do stupid things when they're in love," Dana said as if she'd had personal experience in the matter. "He was probably trying to talk her out of testifying against him, making promises to her that she wanted to believe. Maybe he was trying to talk her into going on the run with him, and as soon as the quarantine was lifted, they could get out of town and be together with a fresh start."

Flint shook his head. "She saw Hank kill Donny Gilmore in cold blood. What could Hank possibly say that would make her change her mind about testifying? Make her even think about hiding out or going on the run with him?"

"Apparently, from the looks of the way things went

down, he didn't get her to change her mind. Something went wrong. Jolene tried to escape, but he caught up with her and made sure she wouldn't be a threat to him."

"This is just what we need with everything else that's going on in town," Flint replied in frustration. "Is somebody relieving you here?"

"Mike Harriman should be here within the next hour or so," she replied.

"When he gets here, go home and get some sleep. I have a feeling we're all going to be putting in plenty of long hours until we get Bittard under arrest again."

Flint left the house, his head swirling with everything that needed to be done as far as this particular case. He needed to start at the beginning, reinterview all of Bittard's low-life friends and check out the old haunts where he used to hang.

He had to be getting help from somebody to stay hidden in a town with no exit, and Flint was determined to arrest anyone who was aiding and abetting him.

Approaching his car, his gaze fell on the place where Jolene Tate had breathed her last breath. For just a moment, his mind cast him back in time and instead of Jolene Tate, he saw an older woman with blond hair sprawled on the ground after having been shot in the head.

Madelaine Vasso had witnessed a gang shooting, and unlike so many, she had been determined to put some of the thugs away. It had been Flint's job to keep her safe until she got to the courthouse to testify. They had been walking up the courthouse steps and had nearly reached the front door when a single bullet had pierced her head and instantly killed her.

His utter failure to protect her and the depth of his grief and guilt had eventually made him leave the Cheyenne Police Department and return home, back here to Dead River.

He shook his head to dislodge the memory of Madelaine and instead was punished by a vision of another woman's body lying on the ground, her wavy auburn hair like a lush blanket beneath her head.

Nina.

His heart crashed, and he drew a deep breath, knowing he needed to keep it together. He *would* not have another failure like Madelaine. He refused for Nina to suffer the same fate as Jolene Tate.

Somehow, someway, he had to find Bittard and neutralize him before he got to Nina and before the quarantine was lifted and a killer ran free.

Chapter 3

Nina stood at the front door of the diner, waiting for Flint to pick her up. The talk of the day had been Jolene's murder and the house fire at Nina's. While most of the conversations had been sober, at least it had taken the thought of the Dead River virus out of everyone's head for a short period of time.

Business had been a little better today than in the past couple of weeks as people ambled in to get a bite to eat and soak up the latest gossip. She had been touched by the concern she'd received from customers and her staff. But she knew the uptick in business wouldn't last. By the time all the gossipmongers got their fill, they'd disappear back into their own isolation.

There was no question in her mind that her business had taken a hit because of the disease that kept the town quarantined. It broke her heart to see people shunning each other as fear of catching the virus guided their decisions and movements.

She hoped the big Thanksgiving Day feast she'd planned in less than three weeks would bring people out of their homes and give them a single day to put all their fears behind them and come together with the community spirit that had been sadly lacking since the quarantine.

Wilma, an older woman who worked as a waitress for Nina, moved to stand next to her. "Nina, are you sure you're really okay? I know you with your Pollyanna smiles and your need to make everyone else feel comfortable and happy, but you went through quite a trauma last night."

"I'm fine, really," Nina assured her. Wilma had no idea what kind of trauma Nina had endured in her life before last night. "I won't lie, it was a horrible night, but I'm confident that Flint will find Hank Bittard soon, and he won't be an issue for me or anyone else anymore."

Wilma's eyes darkened. "Everyone in town wants that murdering creep back in jail where he belongs. He was a bully as a teenager, and now he's responsible for two people's deaths."

"And don't forget the officer who is still in the clinic recovering from the injuries he received when Hank escaped," Nina added.

"At least you have one of the most handsome bodyguards in town." Wilma winked slyly. "There are plenty of single women in Dead River who think the chief of police would be a fine catch. They wouldn't mind being in his custody for at least a night or two."

Nina laughed. "Don't go starting any rumors about

my love life, or lack thereof. I have no attraction to Flint, and in any case, he has more than enough on his plate without adding in any time for romance. I imagine that's the last thing he's thinking about right now."

"Maybe, but you've been here in town for a little over three years, and you've never even dated anyone," Wilma said with obvious curiosity.

"In case you haven't noticed it, I've had a fairly demanding business to run. Besides, I'm not looking for anyone in my life. I'm perfectly satisfied alone, always have been and always will be. Now get back to work and stop trying to matchmake for me."

"It's just a darn shame. You're so warm and have such a big heart. You'd make somebody a wonderful wife." Wilma sighed and disappeared into the kitchen.

Flint had called earlier to tell her that he would pick her up at five o'clock, and at precisely that time his car pulled in front of the diner.

She started out the door, but he halted her by placing his hand up to keep her just inside the doorway. He got out of the car and came into the diner and greeted her with a grim smile.

"I'll walk you out," he said. He looked exhausted, as if he'd fought with the day, and the day had definitely won. He took her by the arm and pulled her close against him.

Instantly, she was surrounded by the pleasant scent of him and the solidness of his tall, muscular body intimately close to hers. He kept her close against him until they reached the passenger side of the car and only then did he release her.

She slid into the seat and watched as he walked around the front of the car to the driver's-side door.

He cut a handsome figure in the black uniform that fit him perfectly and with the cowboy hat that added a rakish flair.

She knew he had her safety upmost in her mind, but she couldn't help the faint wariness that mingled with her physical attraction to him.

She had lied to Wilma. She'd been attracted to Flint Colton since the very first time he'd walked into her diner about a year ago, but there was no question in her mind that he could never be the man for her. Besides, what she hadn't lied about to Wilma was that she was fine living her life alone.

She'd made the decision a long time ago that marriage wasn't in her future, and nothing in her thirty-one years of living had come close to changing her mind.

"You look positively exhausted," she said as he got into the car.

"I think that's become my permanent state of being over the past couple of weeks," he replied. The lines of his face that made it interesting, that gave him character, appeared deeper than usual.

"If you don't feel like stopping by the discount store now, I can make do for another night and have one of the other waitresses take me tomorrow," she suggested. "I've got plenty of uniforms at the diner to put on during the day."

He shook his head. "That's not going to happen. I don't want you going anywhere with anyone else but me. We'll swing by the store and pick up what you need and then stop to get some groceries. I haven't forgotten that you said you'd cook for me while you're under my protection." He flashed her a quick smile that warmed her from head to toe. "So, how was your day?"

"I was the talk of the town," she replied. He headed down Main Street toward the store where she could buy whatever she needed to get her through for a week or two. "It's amazing how fast the grapevine works in small towns. Everyone who came in already knew about Jolene's murder and the fire at my house and there were definitely more customers in today than has been in the past couple of weeks."

"I wish somebody had been able to tell you where Bittard is hiding out," he replied. "We worked today interviewing some of his former friends, but nobody professes to have any idea where he might be holed up."

"I wish somebody would have given me some information you could use. I'm used to being independent and coming and going as I please." A sudden knot of emotion pressed tight in her chest. "Now I don't even have a house to come and go from."

Despite the fact that she'd had the entire day to process everything that had happened, it still didn't feel real to her. She felt as if she had stepped into somebody else's life and was just waiting to get back into her own.

"Did you contact your insurance company today?" he asked.

"I did, but unfortunately, the adjustor is not local and so he can't get into town to do anything right now. I can start the paperwork, and I need reports from the fire chief, but there's little else that can be done until the quarantine is lifted."

"You're welcome to stay at my place for as long as you need, even after I get Bittard in custody," he replied.

"Thanks, I appreciate the offer, but as soon as you get Bittard back in jail, I'll either rent a small apartment or just use the back room of the diner until I can figure things out and get the house rebuilt."

His offer confused her. Why would he want to be stuck with her any longer than he had to? She couldn't help the flutter of emotion that stirred in her. She'd never had a man be so protective of her, especially a man she found so attractive.

"Right now you don't have to worry about where you're living. As long as Bittard is loose, you're stuck with me. We issued a press release this afternoon indicating that we have a witness in protective custody and that the investigation into Jolene's murder is ongoing. We didn't name a suspect."

"At this moment, I can't be one hundred percent certain that the man I saw was Hank Bittard," she replied.

"And that's why we didn't name him," he replied.

She was grateful when they reached the store and she could step out of the interior of the car where his woodsy cologne wrapped around her and his nearness was definitely unsettling to her peace of mind.

She didn't want to like the way he smelled. She didn't want to like the way his piercing green eyes crinkled at the corners when he smiled. It was like an unexpected gift on a face that wasn't accustomed to smiling too often.

She waited as he got out of the car and came around to the passenger door. She couldn't help but notice that the snap over his gun was undone, allowing him easy access to the weapon.

This single action alone forced her to face the reality she'd tried to downplay in her head for the past twenty-four hours. Before she'd been a little afraid that she might catch a virus that seemed to pick and choose people to attack at random, but now a real terror simmered deep inside her.

This was a specific threat to her, a man who wanted her dead, and the only thing that stood between him and her was the lawman next to her.

Pink panties.

Hot-pink panties.

Flint closed the door to his master bedroom and began to change from his uniform to more casual clothes to wear for the remainder of the evening.

He'd gone into the store on high alert, hovering near her and watching to make sure that nobody else got close to her. He kept his gaze out for Hank, unsure if it was possible at this time that the man had a car and could have followed them from the diner.

What he hadn't realized was that shopping with a woman could be such an intimate experience. He'd been fine as she'd grabbed several T-shirts and sweatshirts, some jogging pants and a nightshirt.

His close presence next to her felt a little more intrusive as she shopped for toiletries. Peach-scented shampoo joined a bottle of peach-and-vanilla-scented body cream. It was then that things began to get a little wonky in his head.

He imagined her slathering that lotion up and down her shapely legs and rubbing it over her slender shoulders. He imagined the two of them showering together, the scent of peaches filling the steamy air as he washed the length of her glorious hair and then stroked a sponge all over her body.

He'd finally managed to snap himself back into professional mode when she'd headed to the intimates section. He was okay when she grabbed a white bra and threw it into the shopping basket. He even remained calm and cool when the bra was followed by a package of underpants.

It was when she tossed that single pair of hot-pink panties in the cart that his head once again went a little wonky. Pink panties and peach lotion—those things had been all he'd been able to think about as they'd raced through the grocery store to buy food to stock his pantry and fridge with what she needed to cook decent meals.

He now pulled on a pair of his worn, comfortable jeans and a black polo shirt and sat on the edge of his bed to get every inappropriate vision and thought he'd had of Nina over the past couple of hours out of his head.

She was the witness to a vicious crime and a victim of arson. She was here to be in his protective custody, not to be an object of his sexual fantasies. Speaking of protective custody, he pulled himself off the bed, grabbed his gun and went in search of his houseguest.

He found her in the kitchen putting away the groceries they'd bought while the savory scent of frying hamburger and onions filled the air. "Hmm, something smells good," he said.

"Just a simple pot of goulash," she replied.

"Can I help with anything?"

"Absolutely. Sit at the table and stay out of my way. If we're going to make this little arrangement work well, then the first rule is that I'm the sole captain of the kitchen," she said with a slight raise of her chin.

He sat at the table and placed his gun in front of him.

"I won't argue with you on that, but now seems like a good time to discuss the entire set of ground rules."

He couldn't help but notice how cute she looked in a pair of pink jogging pants and a matching T-shirt. He also noticed the slight stiffening of her shoulders, as if she didn't particularly like the idea of rules.

Tough. It didn't matter to him whether she liked them or not. There had to be rules to assure her safety. He refused to have another stain on his soul. He watched her open a can of tomato sauce and add it along with some spices to the hamburger mixture.

"I don't have a security system installed here," he said. "I always figured it would take a real nut job to try to rob or break into a chief of police's home. But that means we need to get a little creative as far as making the house as safe as possible while you're here."

She dropped a handful of egg noodles into a pot of boiling water and then turned to look at him, her hazel eyes narrowed slightly. "Creative how?"

"Your bedroom door stays open at night. There's only two doors that would allow entry into the house, the front door and the kitchen door." He pointed to the door that led out to his fenced backyard. "I intend to sleep on the sofa in the living room, that way I will hear anyone trying to come into any door or window."

"Surely that isn't necessary," she protested.

"I think it is, so the rule is your door is open when you go to bed or are in your room, and I'm on the sofa during the nights. The other rule is that you avoid all the windows in the house unless the blinds are shut." He leaned back in his chair and smiled at her. "Now, that wasn't so bad, was it?"

"What do you mean?"

"You tensed up the minute I mentioned rules."

"I grew up with a father who had a lot of rules. Once I left home I decided I'd make my own rules." She stirred the noodles and then pulled from the refrigerator the makings of a salad.

"Where was home?" he asked as he realized he knew very little about the woman now under his protection.

"I was born and raised in Casper." She offered nothing else and appeared to concentrate solely on finishing up the meal and getting it on the table.

An awkward silence ensued, one that grew as she seemed disinclined to break it, and he felt unusually tongue-tied. Part of his problem was that he was incredibly attracted to her. He wanted to get to know her and what better opportunity would he have than this?

Unfortunately, he didn't get the same vibe from her. He had the feeling that the only thing she wanted to know about him was how fast he could get Hank Bittard behind bars so she could escape Flint's presence altogether.

Once she had dinner on the table and sat across from him, he decided to attempt to make the best of things by indulging in small talk.

"I've been back in town for a little over a year now and from what I've heard about you, you've been in Dead River three years. I eat in your diner several times a week and yet I know almost nothing about you. Is there somebody in particular who you're dating?" He waited for her to fill her plate and then filled his own.

"Absolutely nobody. I don't even have time to own a cat," she replied. She smiled and not for the first time he noticed that she had the kind of open, generous smile that instantly made the world feel right. "Trying to make the diner a success has taken up all of my time and energy."

"What brought you to Dead River in the first place?"

"When I left Casper I knocked around the entire state, staying in small towns and working as a waitress at different cafés and diners. I knew that eventually I wanted to own my own restaurant of some kind, and I considered what I was doing by working in a variety of places as my college degree of sorts."

She paused to add more salad to her plate and then continued. "Five years ago my mother passed away and left me an inheritance that was enough for me to buy something when I found what I wanted. Three years ago I stumbled onto Dead River and the diner. Maggie, the previous owner, wanted to leave Dead River and the diner behind, so I made her an offer she couldn't resist. And now you know pretty much everything about me."

He knew he'd barely scratched the surface of what he wanted to know about her, but as they finished the meal, the conversation remained pleasant but strictly superficial. She offered nothing else personal about herself nor did she ask him any personal questions about his life.

Even though the conversation bordered inane, Flint enjoyed the very novelty of having a beautiful woman seated at the kitchen table in his home. She filled the silence of the evening that he'd grown accustomed to for far too many years.

There had been few women while he'd been in Cheyenne ambitiously climbing the ranks in the police force. There had certainly been nobody special and only rarely had he had somebody in his home.

Right after the two of them finished eating and cleaned up the kitchen, she told him she needed to finish unloading the bags of personal items she'd bought and disappeared into the guest room.

He was glad that she kept the door open, letting him know she intended to take that particular rule seriously. While she was busy in the bedroom, he went to the master suite and checked to make sure all of the windows were locked. The smallest bedroom he used as an office, and after checking the windows in there he grabbed a handful of files from the desk and returned to the kitchen.

He sat at the table with the files and his gun before him. One thick file was Hank Bittard's and the other, thinner file was on Jimmy Johnson, the twenty-one-year-old loser who had left his cousin Molly at the altar, stolen her money but more egregious, had absconded with the Colton heirloom ring.

Flint was relatively certain that Jimmy would eventually be found, as the quarantine kept him from being able to get out of town. He wasn't a seasoned criminal, and he'd get tired of sleeping in the woods and foraging for food, especially as winter set in for real.

He wouldn't be surprised if the dumb kid wouldn't eventually turn himself in before the weather got really cold and the snow began to fly.

Flint opened the thicker file on Hank Bittard. The first item in the file was Hank's mug shot from when he was arrested for the murder of his coworker at the gas station.

At twenty-seven years old, Hank was a fairly handsome man with dark hair and equally dark, soulless eyes. He was six foot two, and with a muscular build, he looked like he'd never backed down from a fight, nor would he hesitate to start one.

He'd had several arrests before the last one, mostly for disturbing the peace and bar fights, but that had been before Flint had become chief of police. His single run-in with Bittard had been on the day he'd arrested him at the gas station for the murder of Donny Gilmore.

Now the man had killed the only eyewitness to that crime, and Nina was a new witness to that second murder, and there was no doubt in Flint's mind that sooner or later Bittard would come after Nina.

What if Bittard changed his hair color? Somehow managed to disguise himself? Would Flint see him coming? He hadn't seen the shooter who had taken down Madelaine on the courthouse steps in Cheyenne. He'd vastly underestimated the risk to Jolene Tate.

Bittard was no Jimmy Johnson. He was hard, accustomed to spending time in the woods. He'd have the kind of survival skills that a kid like Jimmy wouldn't have.

Flint had come back to Dead River for a number of reasons: to help his brother, Theo, in his recuperation after being thrown from a bucking bronco, and to be close to his sister, Gemma, who worked as a nurse at the Dead River Clinic, and the grandmother who had raised them all.

Finally, he'd returned to his home and family to lick the wounds of the job gone wrong in Cheyenne, to enjoy the slower pace of life in the little town. He'd lost his driving ambition in Cheyenne.

He should have never taken the job as chief of police here. After the debacle in Cheyenne, he should have retired from police work altogether.

Evil was loose in the town of Dead River, with nobody getting in to help and nobody getting out, and the truth of the matter was that Flint had lost any confidence he'd ever had that he was the man the town needed to fight the evil.

Dr. Rafe Granger was unsurprised as he made his way down the hallway of the clinic just past midnight and saw the lights on in Dr. Lucas Rand's office. They'd all been working long hours but none more than Lucas.

The man had been working like a maniac to find a cure for the virus that had taken his ex-wife as its first victim. Mimi Rand had been gone from town for some time when she returned with a baby she'd insisted was Theo Colton's. Although Theo was suspicious, the baby had the Colton vivid green eyes, and he'd had a one-night stand with her around the right time for the baby to be his.

Mimi had been on her way to Theo's house with her three-month-old little girl, Amelia, when she'd stopped in to grab a cup of coffee in the café before heading out to Theo's place. Shortly after arriving at Theo's ranch, she collapsed, and within hours she was dead.

Lucas had been inconsolable. He'd known about Mimi's pregnancy and initially had assumed the baby was his. He'd done the stand-up thing and had been financially supportive from the moment the baby was born. It had only been when Mimi had confirmed that the baby was Theo's that Lucas had stepped back from the role of potential fatherhood. Lucas had heard through the grapevine that a DNA test was in the process to assure the paternity of the baby.

Other victims had followed Mimi, and while everyone at the clinic was working nearly round the clock to find the source and a cure for the virus, nobody had taken the illness and deaths as hard as Dr. Lucas Rand.

No place else in the country had the virus shown up. It was as if it had specifically chosen the little Wyoming town to grow and breed.

Rafe gave a quick knock on the door and then opened it. Lucas didn't look up from whatever was in front of him on his desk. It was as if he was unaware that anyone had entered his office.

"Lucas." Rafe walked over and dropped a hand on the man's broad shoulder, and Lucas started and whirled around in his chair to face Rafe.

Lucas Rand was a handsome man, with dark hair and eyes, but at the moment his eyes burned with feverish desperation. "I feel like I'm so close to figuring out a cure that will save everyone, but I can't get it right. There's something I keep missing. I've got to get it right. We've got to fix this before we lose more people."

"I know, and we will, but it's late, Lucas," Rafe said gently. "Why don't you knock it off for a while and get some rest. You've been pushing yourself so hard, and eventually you're going to crash and then you won't be good to anyone."

Lucas leaned back in his chair and ran his hand through his thick dark hair. "Maybe you're right. Maybe a little sleep will bring everything into better focus. I am tired," he admitted.

He rose slowly, as if the mere act of pulling his tall, muscular frame out of the chair was almost too much for him. He appeared haggard, much older than his thirty-two years. "I just feel like I'm missing something, and if I could figure it out I could solve this."

"Surely we'll get the answers we need when the expert from the CDC, Dr. Colleen Goodhue, gets here," Rafe said as the two men left Lucas's small lab.

"If she ever gets here," Lucas said darkly. "By that time everyone in town might be sick. In the meantime, my hope is that I'll find the cure for this scourge before she arrives. Every day it seems like we have a new patient or we lose somebody else." He heaved a weary sigh.

They stopped at the door of one of the closetlike offices the doctors had been given to work in or take a break in while dealing with the virus. "Get some rest, Lucas," Rafe said kindly, knowing the kind of hours Rand had been putting in. "Right now that's what you need more than anything."

"I should be able to save them," Lucas said in frustration. "I'm a good doctor. I'm a smart man. I'm just missing something. I'm afraid if we don't figure this out soon, eventually everyone in town will be dead. This is killing people, and we don't know how to stop it."

His words hung for a moment in the dim hallway, and then he turned and entered his office and closed the door behind him.

Rafe rubbed his own gritty eyes and decided sleep was exactly what he needed, too. He only hoped while he slept no other patients arrived with the virus symptoms. He was already exhausted by the sick and the dead. All the doctors and nurses had been working side-by-side with the CDC personnel since their arrival at the beginning of the quarantine, but so far they'd had little success. He could only pray that when CDC Dr. Colleen Goodhue, a virus expert, arrived, she'd have the advanced equipment and the knowledge to save Dead River before it was too late.

Chapter 4

Flint had barely gotten his feet into his office when dispatcher Kendra Walker stopped him and said she'd just gotten a call of a domestic dispute at the Brown house. Flint grabbed Officer Patrick Carter to ride along and within minutes, the two were in the car and headed to the south side of town.

"Heck of a way to start a new week. Thelma and Ed Brown have been married upward of twenty-five years," Flint said. "They've always seemed as happy as can be."

"It's strange times in the town of Dead River," Patrick replied.

Strange indeed, Flint thought. It had been strange beginning with awakening that morning to the scents of freshly brewed coffee and a peach-and-vanilla fragrance that had momentarily muddied his senses after

Nina had crept by the sofa where he'd slept in the pre-dawn hour.

By the time he'd showered and dressed, she had bacon and eggs waiting for him. As he'd eaten, she'd sat across from him sipping from a mug of coffee.

Once again she'd seemed distant, unengaged or uninterested in anything but him finishing up his meal and getting her to the diner. "What do you know about Nina Owens?" he asked Patrick.

"Nina? She's great. Everyone in town seems to love her. She's cheerful and will talk your ear off. She cares about everyone she comes into contact with." Patrick slid him a sly glance. "Why? Do I sense a bit of a romance brewing between the local chief of police and a material witness in his custody?"

Flint released a dry laugh. "Hardly. I knew she had a reputation for being very social and positive, but apparently, I'm the only person in town she doesn't like much."

"Ah, don't take it too personally. She's out of her element and has been through a traumatic experience. Seeing a murder committed is bad enough but then to have your house burn down is a double trauma."

"I'm sure you're right," Flint replied, although he wasn't so sure those were the reasons Nina seemed closed off and with defenses raised against him. Not that it mattered. He didn't exactly have time to wine and dine a woman at the moment.

His thoughts changed gears as he turned on the street where Thelma and Ed Brown lived in a neat, two-story home with a large wraparound porch.

"How do you want to play it?" Patrick asked as Flint pulled against the curb several houses away.

"Let's go in quiet and see if we can identify what room they're in," Flint said. "You stick to the right side of the porch, and I'll go to the left." The two of them got out of the car and pulled their firearms.

Flint knew as well as any officer of the law that domestic calls could sometimes be the most dangerous. Tempers exploded, and rational people suddenly became irrational. While he knew Ed and Thelma socially and had never been called here for any issue before, he had no idea what he and Patrick might be facing.

They both moved stealthily, hugging the houses they passed in an effort to maintain as little visibility as possible. Patrick stopped at the side of the Brown house and covered Flint while he crouched and moved beneath the windows on the front porch.

The minute he passed the door he heard voices inside yelling, indicating to him that the couple was in the living room. He motioned for Patrick to join him and then moved to the front door.

With weapons still drawn, Flint knocked on the door. "Ed...Thelma, its Chief of Police Flint Colton. We got a call that you two were having a little problem."

"The door is unlocked. Come in, Chief," Thelma cried out. "Ed's gone stark raving mad, and you need to get in here and straighten him out."

"I don't need straightened out," Ed's big voice boomed. "I just need you to get out of this house. You've got the virus, and you aren't taking me down with you. You need to stay away from me and get out of this house."

Flint tried the doorknob and found it unlocked. He tensed as he slowly turned the knob and opened the door. He halted as he saw Ed Brown, a short, slender man with a gun pointed at his wife, an even shorter, slender woman with dirty-blond hair tied back in a messy knot at the nape of her neck.

"Ed, you need to put the gun down," Flint said calmly.

Ed cast a quick gaze at Flint, his blue eyes filled with terror. "I'll put it down when you get her out of here. She's got the virus, and she refuses to leave. I swear she's going to give it to me, and then we'll both die."

"You stupid man," Thelma said in disgust. She looked at Flint and then at Patrick. "I choked on a piece of toast. That's all I did. It went down the wrong way, and I coughed and coughed and my eyes watered and then he started to freak out."

"Coughing and watery eyes…that's the beginning of the virus," Ed replied frantically. "She's probably running a fever, too. Please get her out of here. I don't want to die."

"Ed, we'll take her to the clinic to get her checked out, but you need to put that gun down before something unnecessary happens," Flint said sternly.

"You're going to take her to the clinic?" Ed asked.

"They'll test her and see if she has the virus or not," Patrick said.

Ed slowly lowered the gun and collapsed on the sofa. Patrick took the gun as Flint gently took Thelma by the elbow. "I'm sorry, Thelma. I'm so sorry," Ed began to cry. "I love you, but I'm just so damned scared."

He was still weeping on the sofa when Flint and Patrick escorted Thelma to their car and placed her in the backseat. Patrick had taken the gun with them and they would hold it in custody for the time being.

"He's been plum crazy since Mimi Rand died and all those other people got sick," Thelma said when they pulled away from the curb. "He's stopped going to work and refuses to leave the house. If somebody comes to the door, he won't answer it. I'm not sick. I know I'm not, but he just freaked out when I started coughing earlier."

"We'll swing you by the clinic, and you can get checked out just to satisfy Ed. A simple blood test will give you the answer, and if it comes back okay then hopefully everything will go back to normal," Flint said.

"Normal? I've forgotten what normal is in this town these days," Thelma exclaimed. "We've got a killer running around and men wearing space suits and wielding weapons keeping us all from leaving town."

Flint tightened his hands on the steering wheel. "I can't do much about the space men, but I'm doing what I can to get Hank back in custody."

"You're good people, Flint, just like your brother, Theo, and your sister, Gemma. You were raised with the right values by a good woman. How is Dottie doing?" she asked with concern.

A knot of anxious despair twisted in Flint's stomach. "She's still unconscious so there hasn't been a change, but at least she's hanging on."

Flint couldn't stand to think of the paternal grandmother who had raised him and his brother and sister after their mother had died when they were all young and their father had run off, being victimized by a virus that had kept her in isolation and barely clinging to life.

Although he visited her when he could, it was heart-breaking to suit up to go into the isolation ward and be unable to stroke her forehead or hold her hand as he begged for her to find the strength to beat the illness.

By the time they dropped Thelma off at the clinic and arranged with Gemma to find the woman a ride back to her house after her checkout, it was midmorning and time to start the hunt for the two fugitives in town.

Once they were back at the station, Flint gave out assignments to his officers, tasking two of them to talk to anyone who knew or hung around with Jolene Tate. If anyone had possibly known where Hank was hiding out, it would have been Jolene and maybe she had told somebody else while drinking in the bar or in a little bedtime talk.

Most of the officers would be on regular patrol with the instruction to keep an eye out for Hank Bittard and Jimmy Johnson. After the issue at the Brown house that morning, Flint warned his officers that tensions and fear were rising with every moment that passed, and they should be ready for any situation.

He told Patrick to do a ride along with him to the gas station where Hank had worked. Despite the murder, Flint knew Hank still had friends there, friends who might harbor a fugitive or at least have some idea where Hank had gone to ground.

Normally, Flint rode alone, but he'd cautioned all his officers to work in pairs and intended to take that advice himself whenever possible. Hank was desperate and dangerous, and Flint didn't want any of his men trying to take him down alone without backup.

It was just after ten when they arrived at the Dead

River Gas Station, a two-pump business with a small building that held a cashier and sold the usual variety of soda, coffee and packaged food to fuel a driver passing through.

There was usually only one person manning the station, and Flint was pleased to see Ted Garrett behind the counter. He and Hank had been drinking buddies and had been fairly tight before the murder.

Ted frowned as he saw the two men enter the small building. "I don't have anything to tell you," he said as he straightened his thin shoulders defensively. "I didn't have anything to tell you the last time you talked to me, and nothing has changed since then."

"Things have changed. He's killed again," Flint said with more than a hint of steel in his voice. "Jolene Tate didn't have a chance against him. He dragged her out of her house and wrapped a length of rope around her neck and strangled her to death."

Ted's brown eyes darkened. "I know. I heard. Look, I haven't had any contact with Hank since the day he killed Donny here at the station. Even though we hung out and had a few beers together before then, he wasn't like my best friend or anything, and once I knew he had killed somebody, I definitely didn't want anything else to do with him."

"Who might still want something to do with him?" Flint asked. "Surely you knew him well enough to know what other friends he might have, maybe somebody he could depend on if he got himself into some trouble."

Ted frowned and raked a hand through his shaggy, slightly greasy, brown hair. "Hank didn't exactly have a bunch of close friends. He just had drinking friends.

He was a bully who put people off with his temper and arrogance. But there was one guy who usually hung out with us, a little weasel who works part-time at the auto body place. He seemed to have a little bit of hero worship going on where Hank was concerned."

"What's his name?" A sharp jump of adrenaline filled Flint's veins as this was information he hadn't had before. Of course he hadn't been looking for a fugitive before.

"Ralph Dane," Ted replied.

"I know him," Patrick said. "He's a little pip-squeak who also works part-time as a busboy at the Blue Bear Restaurant. Do you have an address for him?" he asked Ted.

"He still lives at home with his parents. I'm not sure of the exact address but it's someplace on Cherry Street."

Once again, a surge of adrenaline pumped through Flint. Cherry Street...where Jolene had lived and where she'd been killed. What were the odds? Maybe Ralph had been hiding Hank in his parents' basement or up in the attic? At this point Flint believed anything was possible.

"Then I guess we need to go talk to Ralph and see if maybe he's still got fond feelings for his old friend," Flint said. He looked at Ted intently. "You know that if I find out you have done anything to aid Hank Bittard, I'll throw you in a cell and tie you up in the court system for months."

"Trust me, I don't want anything to do with a murderer, especially one who killed a woman," Ted replied fervently.

"So, you'll let me know if Hank tries to contact you in any way." Flint said it as a statement, not a question.

"I swear I will," Ted replied. "I don't want anything to do with Hank, and I won't think twice about turning him in if I get the chance or hear any information about where he is."

"We appreciate your cooperation," Patrick said.

Minutes later they were back in the car and headed down the block to the Dead River Auto Body Shop. "I can kill two birds with one stone here," Flint said. "Since that little creep Jimmy worked here before he ditched Molly, we can question everyone working about both men."

"That jerk should be hog-tied for what he did to Molly. She's one of the sweetest gals in town, and I can't believe he took advantage of her the way he did. It's like trying to understand why people kick puppy dogs...not comprehensible in my world."

"Mine, too," Flint agreed. "But we both know there's all kinds of people capable of all kinds of things. Molly's heart will eventually heal, and she'll make back the money he took from her, but I definitely want the Colton family ring back that he stole."

Maybe after they talked to Ralph they'd swing by the diner for some lunch, Flint thought, and then immediately dismissed the idea. He wasn't particularly hungry for diner food, he just wanted to see Nina's face and smell that dazzling scent of hers.

Fool that he was to be attracted to a woman for the first time in years, a woman who obviously felt absolutely no attraction to him in return. He had to stay focused on all the other issues that faced him, and at the moment he had a date with a weasel named Ralph.

* * *

Nina had spent half the morning trying to forget the very hot vision of Chief of Police Flint Colton tousle-haired and bare-chested on the sofa as she'd crept through the living room and into the kitchen at the crack of dawn.

It had not been an easy vision to put out of her mind. He was hot enough when in uniform with his black cowboy hat topping his head, but the sight of him half-naked in the dawn light had weakened her knees.

She'd been desperate to maintain distance from him, knowing that she was in his home only temporarily for her own protection. She trusted him completely to keep her safe, but she didn't trust him as a man, especially as a man wearing a uniform of power.

From all accounts he was an honorable man who people trusted and respected. The men from her child-hood had shared the same traits, but they'd been mas-ters at hiding their true natures until finally they could hide them no longer. She shoved thoughts of that past out of her head. It was not relevant in the life she had chosen for herself since she'd left Casper behind.

She now stood at the counter waiting for a pot of coffee to brew. Grace walked over to stand next to her. Thankfully, Grace's illness had been a touch of the flu and not the virus.

Nina turned to smile at her. "I'm glad to have you back here. I missed you when you were gone."

Grace returned the smile. "Trust me, I'd much rather be here than home sick. Thankfully, Billy didn't catch the flu from me, and we're back to life as usual."

"I can't wait for him to get here after school. I had Charley bake those cupcakes that Billy loves so much."

"You spoil him too much," Grace chided.

"I love him to death," Nina replied. "He's the son I'll never have."

"Don't talk like that," Grace replied. "Someday you're going to meet the man of your dreams and have children of your own to love and spoil."

Nina shook her head firmly. "Not happening. I'm definitely anti-marriage, anti-family. I can't believe after that fool husband of yours ran off and left you and Billy that you'd want anything else to do with marriage."

"What can I say? I'm just a hopeless romantic. I got it wrong once, but that doesn't mean the next time wouldn't be wonderfully right," Grace replied.

Nina laughed. "You're definitely a hopeless romantic, and I see that booth three looks like they are ready to order."

Grace nodded and hurried to take care of the two people in the booth. Nina looked around the diner, making sure that all the customers appeared satisfied and her staff appeared busy. The jukebox played a tune by Garth Brooks that had her tapping her foot, despite the fact that it had been a slow day.

Once again, her thoughts turned to Flint. She had to confess that both last night and this morning had been awkward as she'd stifled her natural openness in Flint's presence.

She wasn't sure why, but she felt that she had to protect herself from him, from her own attraction to him. He was the absolute last person on earth she would ever want to hook up with, and yet he was the first man in a very long time who stirred something that felt dangerous and exciting in her.

With a frustrated sigh she headed back into the kitchen to check on preparations for dinner. Charley Crane was a tall, thin man who had worked for her since she'd bought the place. Unlike the cook's assistant, Abe Tennant, who would talk to a tree if nobody else was available, Charley was a quiet man who suffered Abe's constant chatter like a benevolent uncle.

She had another cook, Gary Wells, who was less creative than Charley, but equally competent at putting out food she could be proud of. She also had a handful of cook assistants that worked a variety of hours.

She remained in the kitchen until three-thirty when she returned to the dining room and waited for Grace's son Billy to arrive after school.

At precisely three forty-five he came through the door, bringing with him an infectious grin, an undeniable energy and a bright yellow backpack that made his dark brown hair appear even darker and his blue eyes even more vibrant.

He waved at his mother, who was serving a table and then quietly slid into the chair at a two-top table near the end of the counter where he always spent his after-school time. Nina sat across from him. "How's my favorite guy?"

"Good." He smiled, and a smattering of freckles danced across the bridge of his nose. "How's my favorite fake auntie?"

Nina laughed. They had decided months ago that fake auntie would be her title. "Good. How was school?"

"It was okay. Actually, it was kind of boring." He opened his backpack and pulled out several notebooks.

"Lots of homework?"

He rolled his eyes. "Lots of math. I'd rather do science than math homework."

Nina stood. "I'd rather do anything than math homework, but I have a little treat that might help take the bad taste of math out of your mouth. I had Charley bake up some of those cookie dough cupcakes that you like."

"Awesome!" Billy's eyes lit up.

"How about you get to work, and I'll bring you one with a big glass of milk."

"Thanks, Nina. You're the very best," Billy replied.

His words warmed her as she headed to the kitchen. She delivered the cupcake and milk to Billy and then left him to his homework. She went into the office located beyond the kitchen and quickly checked the schedule for the week, making sure the diner was fully staffed each night until closing.

Normally, she would be the one who closed up each night, but with Flint taking her home at five, she had to make sure the evening hours were all covered and somebody responsible was assigned to do the closeout when the diner went dark at nine.

By the time she finished up in the office, it was nearly time for Flint to arrive, and she returned to the main dining area, where she greeted the few guests coming in and visited with those who were there.

She finally moved behind the counter and refreshed Curtis Carpenter's coffee. Curtis was a regular. At seventy-three years old, he'd been a widow for several years and often found himself seated at Nina's counter.

"How's it going, Curtis?" she asked.

"I've been thinking about it a lot lately, and I believe the end times are upon us," he replied with his gray eyebrows furrowed close together.

"Goodness, I hope you're wrong about that. I've made a lot of plans for my Thanksgiving Day feast here, and that's still a couple of weeks away," Nina replied. "Ben Mack is donating fresh turkeys from his farm, and Charley is making stuffing and cranberry salad."

"What about his sweet potato casserole?" Curtis asked.

"We'll have that, too, along with all kinds of goodies."

Curtis took a sip of his coffee and then set the mug back on the counter. "Then maybe the end of times needs to wait. How many people are you expecting to show up?"

"I hope most everyone in town will stop in at one point or another throughout the day. I've planned two serving times, one around eleven and the other one around three, but food will be available virtually all day long. We need this, Curtis, a day to come together and remember what this town is really all about."

Curtis frowned. "I don't know, Nina. If I were you, I wouldn't get your hopes up too high. With this virus, folks are scared to gather in crowds. Heck, these days neighbors aren't even hardly talking to each other."

"You wait and see," Nina replied optimistically. "We're going to have a full house, and it will be a day of laughter and joy and blessings that we all desperately need, especially now."

"Now there's a man I don't envy," Curtis said as he looked toward the front door.

Nina followed his gaze and saw that Flint had entered the diner. He pulled off his hat and plopped it on Billy's head, who giggled and smiled up at the tall lawman.

He approached Nina and Curtis, and the smile he offered them was one of weariness that instantly let Nina know the day had yielded no answers as to the whereabouts of Hank Bittard.

"Nina...Curtis," he greeted them.

"Take a load off, Flint. Let me buy you a cup of coffee," Curtis said.

"Please, sit for a minute," Nina said. "I've got Charley putting together some to-go boxes for dinner, and while we wait for those, you look like you could use a cup of coffee."

He eased down on the stool next to Curtis, and Nina turned to grab a mug and the coffeepot. She poured his coffee, and he gave her a grateful smile that shot straight to her heart.

Drat the man anyway. She returned the coffee carafe to the burner and then excused herself and headed for the kitchen to check on the food she planned to take with her.

That tired, grateful smile he'd cast her had touched her more than she wanted to admit. It had made her feel bad about how distant, how disengaged she'd been with him since living beneath his roof.

He was working his butt off every day to keep this town safe under extraordinary circumstances, and she was allowing a distant, traumatic past to make her treat him differently than she would anyone else, even an unknown customer who might meander into her diner for a meal.

He had taken her into his home, drove her to and from work each day. He was going out of his way to assure her safety. He deserved better than what she'd given to him so far.

With a large white take-out bag in hand, she returned to the dining room where Curtis and Flint were in a conversation about the condition of Officer Mike Barnes, who had been attacked and left for dead when Bittard had escaped. Although Mike was still at the clinic for his injuries, thankfully he was getting better and stronger with each day that passed.

"Ready?" Nina asked Flint.

He drained his coffee mug and stood. "Ready," he replied.

With goodbyes said to Curtis and a final check with the waitresses, she and Flint headed toward the front door. As he walked by Billy, he plucked his cowboy hat off the boy's head and put it back on his own.

Billy grinned at them both. "Cookie dough cupcakes and a cowboy hat, that for sure makes a great day," he said.

Nina and Flint laughed, but Nina's laughter stopped the moment they stepped out the door and Flint's gun filled his hand, and his other arm pulled her tight against him, using himself as a shield against any impending danger.

As always, the close contact half stole her breath away. The worst part of all was that it felt right to be so intimate against his body with his familiar cologne surrounding her.

When they reached the passenger door she slid inside and set the food bag on the floorboard between her feet. She watched him walk around to the driver's-side door.

He wore the black uniform of his station well, and

the sun glinted off his badge and filled her with myriad emotions. His gaze swept the general area with narrowed eyes as if looking for trouble, but finding none.

She had learned almost before she could walk that men in uniforms couldn't be trusted. It had been a lesson that had been repeated over and over again throughout her childhood.

For the first time since she'd met Flint a year ago, she found herself wondering about the man beneath the uniform. Was he different from those she'd known in her past, or did he have a dark side that he hid from others?

Chapter 5

It was after six when Flint and Nina had changed into casual clothes and met in the kitchen for dinner. It had been another long, fruitless day, and Flint fought against a weary defeat that he knew if he succumbed to, would do nobody any good.

He sat at the table as Nina prepared the food she'd brought home with her. It didn't take her long to warm up the homemade chicken pot pie, and corn muffins and to make them each a side salad.

She was quiet as she worked, and he didn't expect anything different. It was obvious he was involved in a one-way admiration society, and for the moment he was content just to watch her work as her evocative scent mingled with the food smells.

She moved with a graceful efficiency, each movement with purpose as the early evening sun danced in the strands of her hair. She appeared at peace as she worked, and some of that peace filled the kitchen and seeped into Flint's tired bones.

Reluctantly, he closed the blinds, halting the drift of sunshine inside. There was no way he'd allow her to sit at the table with the blinds open, allowing somebody outside to have a perfect target to attack.

Finally, the food was on the table, and they sat across from each other and filled their plates. "I was thinking about you today," she said, her words surprising him.

"Thinking about what?"

"I don't know your brother very well. I know Gemma a little better, but I really don't know anything about you. I told you last night about my wandering around the state to finally find my life here in Dead River. Tonight I think it's your turn to tell me all about you."

He looked at her blankly, stunned that she wanted to know anything about him given how distant she'd been for the past two nights.

She smiled, that open gesture he'd seen her offer so many people in her diner. "Don't look so shocked," she said, and the smile slowly fell from her face. "I'm afraid I owe you an apology for my mood the past couple of nights."

"I just figured I was the only person in the whole town of Dead River that you didn't like very much," he replied truthfully.

"I don't know you well enough to know if I like you or not," she replied. "So, tell me about Flint Colton. I already know that Dottie raised you, your brother and Gemma."

He nodded. "My mom died when we were all young, and it wasn't long before Dad took off for parts unknown, so Gram Dottie stepped in. She had her hands full with the three of us, but we adored her…still do."

"Then you had a happy childhood?"

He paused with a corn muffin halfway to his mouth and frowned thoughtfully. "It was happy until I hit those terrible teenage years and then Rafe Granger and I became good friends."

"Dr. Granger from the clinic?" she asked.

He nodded. "Rafe lived in the trailer park on the wrong side of the tracks, and he couldn't wait to get out of town. Although I lived with Gram Dottie, like Rafe, I couldn't wait to leave Dead River behind." He smiled ruefully. "Like most self-absorbed teenagers, I thought I was better than this small town. I wanted big-city lights and excitement. I wanted something bigger than Dead River."

"How old were you when you left Dead River?"

"The day after my eighteenth birthday, I headed to Cheyenne. I worked on a ranch just outside of the city until I turned twenty-one, and then I applied to the Cheyenne Police Department. They took me on and for the next ten years the job was my life. I loved it, and I climbed through the ranks fairly quickly."

"Then what brought you back here?" she asked and took a bite of the chicken pot pie.

Between bites, Flint explained to her about Theo, who had been a champion bronc rider and had been severely injured after being thrown. It was later discovered that one of his competitors had injected the horse Theo had ridden with a serum that made it go crazy. The man, Hal Diggins, had been arrested, and Flint had remained in Dead River to help out with his brother, who'd had major injuries to overcome.

"When I arrived in town, the police department was a mess," he said.

She nodded. "Chief Drucker was dirty, and he and half his officers were fired when Harry Peters came in to clean things up."

"And within three months I found myself moving from officer to chief of police because of my long history in Cheyenne," Flint said. "Just in time for murder, mayhem and a quarantine to take place," he added drily.

"Things could be worse," she said. "You could also have crop circles in the fields to investigate."

Her impish grin coupled with her words forced a burst of laughter from him. God, it felt good. He couldn't remember the last time he had really laughed about anything. His sister often told him he didn't laugh enough, that he was far too serious too much of the time.

"The stress of the virus is definitely making some people in town act like aliens," he replied and told her about the call to the Brown house that morning. "I've never seen a man so scared just because his wife choked on some toast. Thank goodness Edith checked out fine and is back home and all is well."

"I've had a couple of waitresses who have stopped coming into work. They're scared about catching the virus from the customers or somebody else working for me. Thank goodness I have some very loyal employees who are picking up the slack," she replied.

"On another topic, we interviewed a friend of Bittard's today, a guy named Ralph Dane. He's a little pip-squeak who apparently enjoyed being Bittard's sidekick. He swore he's had no contact or anything to do with Bittard since his escape, but I'm not quite sure I believed him."

"So, do you have a plan?" Nina got up from the table and removed their now-empty plates.

"I don't have enough evidence to get a phone tap or any phone records, but Ralph lives at home with his parents, who seemed like stand-up folks, and today they gave us permission to go inside the house and look around. There was no sign that Bittard was hiding out there. I have assigned two of my men to shadow Ralph for the next few days and see if maybe he meets up with Hank somewhere."

"Sounds like a good plan. Hopefully, he'll lead you right to Bittard. I've got apple dumplings for dessert. Are you interested?"

"Definitely," he replied. "But with the condition that we stop all discussion of Bittard and the virus and anything else negative and just enjoy some pleasant talk and an apple dumpling."

"That's a deal," she replied. She zapped the dumplings in the microwave just long enough to warm them and then refreshed their coffee and returned to the table.

For the next hour they exchanged tales, her sharing with him some of the experiences she'd had while working as a waitress in a variety of small towns, and him regaling her with stories of growing up with his brother and sister and his grandmother.

The weariness that had weighed so heavily on Flint slowly fell away as he enjoyed Nina's expressive storytelling, her sense of humor and her obvious caring nature.

She breathed new life into the house, into him and

only made his attraction to her grow deeper. He kept reminding himself that she was only being herself, showing him a side of her that was natural and real but had nothing to do with her having any warm feelings specifically toward him. She was obviously making the best of a bad situation.

There were several times during the evening that he thought they were actually flirting and connecting on a deeper level.

But he reminded himself they were in this together under circumstances beyond their control. She hadn't chosen to be here with him, but he definitely enjoyed her company when her defenses appeared to be down, and she was just being the woman everyone in town knew and adored.

By the time they had finished their dumpling and their conversation it was almost eight. She cleaned up the dishes and then told him she was going to take a shower and turn in early.

Her words instantly evoked a vision of her naked in the shower. As she disappeared down the hallway he cursed himself for having sex on the mind when he should be focused solely on the recapture of a murderer.

But it had been nice to find a respite from everything he had facing him as chief of police. It had been good, if only for a little while, to be just Flint Colton enjoying a conversation with a beautiful woman.

Once Nina was in the bathroom and the shower water was running, Flint went to his bedroom and grabbed a pair of boxers to sleep in for the night. He'd shower in the morning when he felt it would be safer to take a few minutes closed off in the bathroom.

Now that Nina had called it a night, the weariness

that had plagued him earlier returned tenfold. He thought of the files he'd brought home with him, intending to study them yet again, but he ultimately dismissed the idea.

What he needed more than anything was an early night and a good sleep to be refreshed and ready for the following day. Besides, he didn't want to screw up his positive feelings after spending time with Nina by immersing himself back into murder and mayhem.

By nine-thirty the house was quiet. Nina had left the bathroom and gone into the bedroom, and he assumed she was already asleep. With only the night-light in the hallway to guide him, he shucked his jeans and T-shirt and changed into his boxers.

With the house locked up and the lights off, he sat on the edge of the sofa and allowed his thoughts to run wild. In a small, quarantined town, where would a killer hide? Certainly there were lots of wooded areas and some abandoned houses, barns and sheds in those areas, but Flint and his men had checked them out in the first days of Hank's escape.

With the reports of burglaries in the area, Flint's gut instinct was that Hank was there, somewhere in the woods, surviving on primal instincts and whatever he could steal or salvage from the people who lived in the area.

It was very possible that Jimmy was there, too, not only dodging the police but any contact with Hank, as well. There was no way that Flint believed either of them had managed to escape the quarantine. The borders of the town were too heavily guarded for one of them to slip through.

He wasn't even sure if Bittard somehow got the

chance to get out of town, that he'd leave before neutralizing the witness who had seen him kill Jolene Tate.

He finally stretched out and closed his eyes. Talking about his time in Cheyenne with Nina had brought back both good and bad memories. He'd been so eager to be a cop, and he'd been a good one, rising through the ranks quickly, driven by ambition and resolve. He wanted to make a difference in the fight between good and evil, but ultimately he'd lost the battle and had come home with his tail tucked between his legs.

In the past couple of months he'd come to doubt his profession of choice, wondering if he'd be better off... happier buying a little piece of land and doing some ranching. No crimes to solve, no tragedies to deal with; a little less stress definitely sounded good right now.

With the events of the past week so fresh in his mind, self-doubts grew strong in the darkness of night. Maybe he'd never really had what it took to be a police officer, let alone the chief of an entire department.

He knew that now wasn't the time to make any changes. The town had enough problems already, but once Bittard was caught, once the cure to the virus had been found and the quarantine was lifted, maybe it was time for him to think of a new path in life.

He awoke with his gun in his hand and his heart banging frantically in his chest. It took him a moment to orient that he'd fallen asleep and something had awakened him.

What? What had pulled him from his sleep and made him automatically reach for his gun? Tense and completely alert, he remained perfectly still, his hearing tuned to anything in the house that didn't belong.

He heard the faint hum of the refrigerator coming

from the kitchen, a *tick-tick* as heated air expanded the vents to warm the house, all normal noises. Nothing alarming…nothing odd.

He sat up and swung his feet to the floor, his gun still clutched tightly in his hand. His heartbeat had slowed to an almost imperceptible rhythm as he stood. Something had awakened him, and he had to make sure it wasn't danger in the house.

His internal clock told him it was about three in the morning, far too early for Nina to be up and around. He crept slowly down the hallway to her bedroom first as she was his number-one priority.

By the faint night-light in the hallway he could see her beneath the covers, her face turned toward the door. He watched until he saw the slow rise and fall of her chest. He breathed a silent sigh of relief and moved on down the hallway.

Room by room he checked for open windows, anything amiss, any danger that might lurk nearby, but he found nothing. He finally paused at Nina's doorway again, feeling slightly guilty as he stared at her face.

Even in sleep she was beautiful, and her lips were curved into a faint smile as if her dreams were pleasant ones. It was then that he remembered his dream, the one that had abruptly pulled him from his sleep and had him automatically reaching for his gun.

He'd dreamed that Hank had Nina. In the nightmare the two of them had stood beneath a streetlamp and Hank had a rope wrapped around Nina's neck. Flint had been down the block and no matter how fast he ran, he couldn't reach them. It was as if his feet were mired in quicksand.

He could see the rope slowly tightening and the

blood filling Nina's face as she tried to gasp for breath, and he knew that if he didn't do something then, Nina was going to die. But he'd been helpless, unable to stop the horror from happening.

It had been just like Madelaine. He'd been standing right next to her, and yet he'd been impotent to save her life. He raked a hand down his face in ragged agony, both from the dream and from the reality of Madelaine's death.

He finally left Nina's bedroom doorway and went back to the sofa where he placed the gun on the coffee table and tried to swallow the taste of failure…of a faint fear that lingered in his throat…the fear of failing yet again.

She liked him.

She'd known since she'd first seen him that she was physically attracted to him. But she'd finally dropped her defenses and allowed herself to interact with Flint like she would anyone else, and to her dismay she'd found him charming and funny and exceedingly likable. Everything would have been so less complicated if she'd found him to be arrogant and a jerk.

The next morning she awoke feeling refreshed and eager for a new day. She refused to think about the fact that a killer was after her or that the town was under quarantine. She'd spent much of her adult life determined to focus on the positives no matter what the circumstances she found herself in.

"You're very chipper this morning," Flint said when they were in his car and headed to the diner.

"I feel chipper most mornings," she replied. "I'm going to spend the day feeding people great food and hopefully making them feel better when they walk out of the diner than when they walked in. The high point of the day will be when my little half-pint boyfriend comes in after school."

"Grace's boy?"

She nodded. "Billy. He's owned a piece of my heart since his mother first started working for me. He calls me his favorite fake auntie."

"He's a cute kid. I know he's at the diner almost every day," Flint replied.

"Every weekday when his mother works. He comes in after school and does his homework quietly at a table while he waits for Grace to get off work. He's a great kid."

He shot her a quick glance of his amazing green eyes. "And why aren't you married with a couple of little Billy boys of your own?"

"I'm not wife or mother material. I'm content on my own with the diner as my partner and my child. What about you? Why aren't you married with a couple of rug rats running around?" she asked. "You aren't hard to look at, and I'm sure plenty of women in town would be interested in setting up house with you."

"I guess I haven't met the right woman yet." He frowned thoughtfully, a gesture that did nothing to detract from his handsomeness.

"To be honest," he continued, "I hadn't thought much about having a family until lately when I see Theo and baby Amelia and Ellie together." Ellie Parker had worked for Theo as a cook and had become nanny to the baby that Mimi Rand had declared his, and in the past month Ellie had become a special woman in Theo's life.

"So, you're the marrying kind of man. You just need to find your special someone."

"I guess that's about the size of it," he replied and pulled up in front of the diner. "But in the meantime, I'd say I've got plenty to do to keep myself occupied."

As always, he got out of the car and escorted her inside with the promise to return for her that evening at five. Nina greeted the waitresses who had already arrived. There were no customers yet and so she headed for the kitchen.

"Good morning, Charley." She greeted the cook with a bright smile. "I always feel good when I walk in here and see you hard at work."

He flashed one of his rare smiles. "Aren't you all full of sugar and sweetness as usual this morning?"

She perched on a chair near where he was prepping food for breakfast. "The sun is shining, it's a brand-new day and maybe today will be the day that Flint arrests Hank Bittard, or finds Jimmy Johnson or somebody at the clinic finally finds a cure for the virus."

Charley grunted. "And maybe pigs will fly into the freezer already nicely cut up into pork chops and roasts and thick slices of bacon."

Nina laughed. "Now, that would be nice. Speaking of pigs, we are serving ham as well as turkey for Thanksgiving, right?"

"It's on the ever-changing menu," Charley replied drily.

"I admit I've been a little obsessive-compulsive about the menu and the preparations, but I just want that day to be so perfect for everyone," she replied.

"For you, I hope it is as perfect as you are imagining it," Charley replied.

For the next few minutes, despite moans and groans from Charley, Nina discussed with him the plans for the day that was still a little over two weeks away.

"We'll move the stools and serve everything buffet style on the counter," she said. "And I want centerpieces in reds and bright oranges on every table. It's too bad there isn't Thanksgiving Day music like there is Christmas music."

Charley groaned while he cut up peppers and onions for omelets and to add to their specialty hash browns. "That old jukebox playing Patsy Cline singing 'Crazy' seems far more appropriate for what's been going on around town."

Nina couldn't help but laugh again. "Crazy is right," she agreed. And craziest of all was that she had enjoyed talking to Flint last night more than she could remember talking to any man for a very long time.

She definitely felt a physical chemistry toward him, and now she found herself attracted to him on a more personal level. Of course, it could never go anywhere. Even if he was equally attracted to her, they were destined to be star-crossed lovers.

He wanted home and family. She didn't. As much as she liked him, as much as she depended on him for now, she wasn't sure he would ever earn her complete and total trust. No man ever had.

Her childhood had damaged her. She understood that, accepted that trust would always be an issue with her, and that's why she'd made the decision long ago to remain alone. Her feelings toward Flint surprised her, but they certainly didn't change her mind about her path in life.

"You've suddenly gotten quiet," Charley said, pulling her from her thoughts. "You aren't mentally working on the menu again, are you?"

"No, nothing like that. I was just lost in my own head for a few minutes." She got up from her chair. "I guess I'll get out of here and let you work in peace. Abe will be in soon, and any peace you might enjoy now will be shattered."

Charley grinned again. "Abe talks a lot, but I've discovered that ninety percent of the time I can tune him out. Most of the time he's just white noise that I occasionally need to acknowledge with a nod or a grunt."

"White noise like I am right now," Nina said with a smile. "Okay, I'm out of here. I'll go check on things up front."

She left the kitchen and stepped into the dining area where a single customer sat with his back to her at the counter. Dressed all in black and with dark hair and a muscular build, the sight of him instantly shot terror into her throat.

She stumbled backward, cast back in time, back to the place where she'd seen a man who looked just like him strangle Jolene Tate to death. With her brain on fire and her body shaking nearly uncontrollably, she continued to back up until she reached the ladies' restroom.

She fled inside and locked the door, her heart racing with a vengeance she couldn't control.

Was it him?

Was it Hank?

Had he come here to get her?

Her shaking knees cast her to the floor with her back

against the door as she relived that moment in her car when she'd seen Hank Bittard killing Jolene.

Had he come in here early, knowing he would probably be the first customer of the day with the intention of killing her? Maybe he didn't care anymore about other witnesses, or maybe he'd crossed a line where he'd kill everyone in the diner just to neutralize her.

She shivered uncontrollably as terrified sobs nearly strangled her. She was frozen, unable to get out of her own fear, out of her own head.

Maybe if she stayed hidden in here, maybe if he didn't see her, he'd just assume she wasn't in today and would leave without hurting anyone else. Oh, God, she didn't want him to harm any of her staff.

Quiet…she had to stay quiet. She placed a hand tightly over her mouth in an effort to staunch her sobs. She couldn't let him hear her. She just wanted him to go away without hurting anyone.

Over and over again her brain played the vision of the rope twisting around Jolene's neck, her falling to the ground and the man advancing on Nina, his eyes glittering with abject menace.

He'd come for her, and there was nobody to stop him. She didn't even have her cell phone to call for help. There was no way to warn anyone.

She wasn't sure how long she'd been in the bathroom when a soft knock sounded at the door. She jumped in alarm. "Nina? Are you in there? Are you okay?" Grace's concerned voice drifted through the door.

Nina got to her feet, opened the door and pulled Grace inside. She grabbed her friend and employee by the shoulders with trembling hands. "Who's sitting at the end of the counter?" she asked feverishly. "Who's the man there?"

"I don't know. I didn't pay any attention. I'm not working the counter this morning," Grace replied. "Why? What's going on? Why are you so upset?"

"Just go see who it is and come back here and tell me." Nina released Grace's shoulders and pushed her back out the door. Once Grace was gone, Nina leaned weakly against the door and although she was still afraid, she fought for some kind of control, some modicum of composure.

It took Grace only moments to return. "It's Brian Bollinger. He's having a cup of coffee and a muffin."

Nina sagged against the sink. Brian Bollinger...not Hank Bittard. "I thought...from the back he looks just like..." She allowed her voice to drift off as a new sob threatened to escape her.

"Oh, honey." Grace wrapped her arms around Nina and hugged her tight, but Nina realized the arms she wanted holding her right now were bigger and stronger. The arms she wanted wrapped around her were Flint's.

Grace released her but grabbed her by the hand. "Do you want me to call Flint?"

Yes, tell him to come right away. I need him, her emotions screamed. "No, I'm fine now," she said. The last thing Nina wanted was to bother Flint with her crazy, momentary breakdown. "I think I'll just go into my office for a little while. Could you bring me a cup of coffee?"

"Of course. Are you sure you're okay?" Grace asked worriedly.

"I'll be fine now," Nina assured her as her terror began to ebb away.

Nina finally left the bathroom as Grace went back to the dining area. On shaky legs Nina made her way down the hallway, through the kitchen and into her small office where she collapsed on the chair behind her desk and leaned back.

Through all of the years of her life, despite the trauma of her childhood, she'd never had a breakdown like the one she'd just experienced. She'd always been able to rise above any adversity, but she now realized how frightened, how utterly terrified she was of Hank Bittard.

He wanted her dead. He'd burned down her house hoping that her death would be the outcome. She knew he'd do anything to get to her, but at least she had Flint standing between her and Hank's desire for her permanent silence.

She remained in her office for most of the day, dealing with work schedules for the week to come, ordering in supplies and looking at the website of the local Home and Hearth store for centerpieces she could use for Thanksgiving Day.

The work finally calmed her and made her breakdown feel just a little silly in retrospect. Still, for just a moment she'd been so sure it had been Hank.

She was interrupted at just after noon when Grace brought her a club sandwich and a soda. "Are you sure you're really all right?" she asked worriedly. "It's not like you to hole up in here and not be out front with the customers."

"I just freaked myself out for a few minutes, but

I'm fine now," Nina assured her with a forced bright smile. "I've just decided today is a good day to hang out back here and get some busy work done. Today I think I just need the peace and quiet of being closed up in here. I'm confident you all will take good care of the customers like you always do."

"Then I'll just leave you to eat your lunch, and it won't be long before Flint will be here to pick you up." Grace closed the door behind her.

For the first time that Nina could remember, she couldn't wait for Flint to arrive and take her to his house where she felt completely safe. For the first time since she'd bought the diner she didn't feel like being here.

She remained in her office until it was almost time for Flint to arrive, and then returned to the dining room to visit with Billy while she waited for her protective lawman to pick her up.

She finally felt as if she'd put the morning trauma behind her and had her emotions firmly under control, until Flint walked through the door.

The moment he stepped inside, rather than greet him the way she normally did, she rushed to him and threw herself at him. Instantly, his arms wrapped around her, even as he stiffened in obvious surprise.

She had no idea how long she stood, warmed and secured by his embrace, before he finally took her by the shoulders and stepped back to peer at her face. "Nina, what's going on? What's happened? Are you all right?" He looked at her worriedly.

Aware that they had drawn the attention of all the staff and the few customers in the place, she nodded and took a step back from him, suddenly embarrassed by her uncharacteristic action. "I'm fine. We'll talk at home."

She was grateful he didn't press the issue, but instead hurried her to the car and headed toward the place where she knew she would feel safe and protected.

Chapter 6

She was silent on the ride home, and Flint decided not to push her for any answers as to her unexpected greeting of him. Something had happened during the day, but the fact that she was fine and safe next to him in the car let him know whatever had happened was over and she was, at least physically, okay.

"Why don't you get comfortable and I'll whip up something for dinner," he suggested once they were in the house.

She eyed him dubiously. "Whip up what?"

"I've got a decent frozen pizza that I'll pop into the oven."

She frowned a moment and then nodded. "Okay, I'll be back in a few minutes."

As she drifted down the hallway toward her room Flint frowned after her. Something definitely had shaken her up today for her to agree to a frozen pizza for dinner. He hoped that she'd tell him what had happened sooner rather than later.

He unfastened his holster and slung it over the back of a kitchen chair, first taking out the gun and laying it on the table where it would be easily reached.

Next he turned on the oven to preheat and got out the pizza stone he used when baking a pie. The stone had been given to him a couple of years ago as a birthday present by a woman he'd briefly dated. The woman had moved on, but the pizza stone had stayed with him.

Worry simmered inside him as he grabbed the pizza from the freezer and tore off the outer packaging. What could have happened at the diner today that had made Nina throw herself into his arms with such fervency?

In the brief moment he'd held her, he'd felt fear radiating from her, an emotion she'd shown little of since the night she'd seen Jolene's murder and watched her own house burn to the ground.

In fact, she'd shown remarkable resilience and bravery under the circumstances since that night. Most women would still be weeping over what they'd seen, what had happened to their home.

He'd just put the pizza in the oven when she came into the kitchen. Clad in a pair of jeans and a gold T-shirt that did amazing things for her hazel eyes and auburn hair, she looked both beautiful and tired. She sank down into a chair at the table and released a long, deep sigh.

"Do you want to talk about it?" he asked. He pulled a pizza cutter from one of the drawers.

"I totally lost it this morning," she confessed.

He pulled two cans of soda out of the refrigerator

and placed them on the table and then sat across from her. "You lost it how?"

She explained to him about seeing the man at the counter and believing it was Hank Bittard, her rush to the bathroom where she locked herself in and remembered in horror Jolene's murder, the approach of Hank on her car and the terrifying fear that she was going to die.

"I was a slobbering, terrified mess," she said. "It was like I was reliving the whole thing again and again in my mind, and I couldn't get out of it. I was sure he'd come in as the first customer of the day so that he could kill me and, even worse, whoever else might be in the diner. It was only when Grace came to find me and told me it was Brian sitting at the counter that I finally managed to pull myself together."

Flint couldn't help himself. He reached a hand across the table toward her. She didn't hesitate but rather immediately grasped it and held tightly. "I feel so foolish," she said softly. "I've never lost it like that."

"You shouldn't feel foolish at all. It sounds to me like you had an episode of post-traumatic stress. You need to cut yourself some slack, Nina. You've been through a lot and have handled it better than anyone I know. You're allowed to break down. I just wish you would have called me when you were so frightened."

She pulled her hand from his. "I didn't want to take you away from your work of trying to find that crazy killer. Besides, I spent pretty much all the rest of the day in my office doing busy work and getting myself back under control."

"I admire your strength, Nina." His gaze was warm and filled with respect.

She offered him a small smile. "You might not have admired my strength so much this morning when I was on the bathroom floor sobbing and frozen with terror."

The mental vision he got of her so frightened, disturbed him. The fact that she'd gone through it all alone broke his heart. "You get that scared again you call me, no matter what time of the day it is," he said firmly. "Nina, I don't want you going through that all alone ever again."

"And it's bad enough that you are feeding me frozen pizza, but I definitely refuse to eat burned frozen pizza," she replied.

He jumped up from the table, suddenly aware of the scent of the pizza that filled the kitchen. He hurried to the stove, where he grabbed a couple of hot pads and removed the perfectly cooked pie from the oven. "No worries, not a burned edge on it," he said.

He cut up the pizza and then carried it to the table. He grabbed a couple of plates and then sat back down. "Pizza, Flint style," he announced.

"I'm impressed. The slices are even cut almost perfectly," she replied. She pulled a piece onto her plate to cool, and he did the same. "At least something good came out of today."

"And what's that?" He didn't want to dwell on the vision of Nina on that bathroom floor, stifling sobs as terror raced through her body. The vision ripped at him and made him wish he would have been there to protect her from her own fears, from the terrible memories that had plagued her mind. He wished he'd been there to wrap her in his arms and calm her fears.

"I worked on the schedules, did some supply ordering and found the perfect centerpieces for the booths and tables for the Thanksgiving Day feast," she replied.

As they ate she explained the centerpieces she had found and how Charley got aggravated with her for changing the Thanksgiving Day menu each day. The sparkle was back in her eyes, and he was amazed by how easily her optimistic spirit had returned.

He wished he were feeling as optimistic. It had been another frustrating day of dead ends and no leads where both Hank and Jimmy were concerned. Two of his officers had had to break up a fight on Main Street between two men because one of them had accused the other of having the virus and coughing without covering his mouth.

Just another day in paradise, he thought as they began to eat. Still, he found Nina a balm to the long day. Despite her trauma that morning, as they shared the pizza, she talked about various members of her staff and how much she was looking forward to the coming holiday.

"I'll bet you had great holidays with your family," she said.

"We did. Gram Dottie went out of her way whenever there was a holiday. She arranged egg hunts at Easter, made us special Valentine cards and cupcakes, hand-sewed our Halloween costumes and fixed enough food to feed an army at Thanksgiving. Christmas was like every holiday all rolled into one, with more tinsel and toys than any one family should have."

He smiled at the pleasure of those memories, but his smile was fleeting as he thought of his grandmother now, clinging to life with an unknown, so far incurable virus. "What about you? How were your childhood holidays?"

"Stressful. To be honest, since I left Casper, I haven't celebrated any holidays. The Thanksgiving Day at the diner will be my first one in years, and I want to make it as joyous as possible."

She offered no more, and he was afraid to press her for details. He knew there were people who found the holidays intensely stressful. "Do you have siblings?" he asked.

"No, I'm an only child. So, tell me how your day went?" She not-so-deftly changed the subject.

He told her about the frustrations of his day, finding it cathartic to talk to somebody other than another officer, somebody who seemed to care more about his state of mind rather than what had or hadn't happened through the long day.

"Sooner or later one of them will make a mistake, and you'll catch them," she said as she reached for another piece of the pie. "As long as the quarantine stays in place, the odds are definitely in your favor."

"Are you always this good at shifting gears? Going from bad things to reach for the good?" he asked curiously.

"I learned early in life to compartmentalize and rationalize. Bad things get quickly shoved away in my mind to make way for positive thoughts. Dwelling on the bad never fixes anything or makes things better. I just look for the sun and the rainbows instead of the storms."

"That's a nice way to go through life if you can do it," he replied.

She eyed him intently. "It's a conscious choice you

make. Maybe you should try it more often. You told me all about your failures today, but you didn't mention that every place you looked that Hank and Jimmy aren't is a place you've cleared so you can look in other places. You act like each day is a failure, but it's simply a matter of elimination, and each day you're eliminating hidey-holes where Hank or Jimmy could be so that eventually, they'll have no place else to hide."

He grinned at her. "I think you would be nice to have around all the time."

She laughed. "I'm not sure everyone would agree with that. I'm sure Charley thinks I'm a real pain sometimes. He not only thinks I am nauseatingly cheerful, but I also tend to be a bit controlling when it comes to everything at the diner."

"Because that's your baby," he replied.

"That's right." She pushed her plate aside. "I have to confess that wasn't the worst frozen pizza I've ever eaten."

"Unfortunately, I don't have any frozen dessert to offer you."

"I don't need dessert. All I needed was to be here with you where I feel safe." Her cheeks grew dusty with color. "Thank you, Flint, for everything you're doing for me."

He held up a hand. "Please, don't thank me. I'm doing my job, but more important, I like your company. I hadn't realized how quiet and lonely this house was in the evenings before you came here."

"I like spending time with you, too." She stood abruptly and grabbed her plate to carry to the sink. It was as if the conversation had taken a turn too personal, and that had made her uncomfortable.

"Leave that," he said. "I'll take care of the cleanup. Are you a wine drinker? I think I've got some red wine if you're interested."

"Actually, I'd love a glass of wine," she replied.

"Why don't you make yourself comfortable in the living room and I'll bring in the wine?"

"It's a deal."

She left the room, and he quickly attended to the dishes and then strapped on his holster and gun, poured the wine and joined her. She had turned on a lamp on the coffee table and sat in a chair next to the sofa with her legs curled up beneath her.

"I didn't want to sit on your bed," she said and gestured toward the sofa where a sheet was neatly folded on top of a bed pillow on the end.

She took the glass of wine he offered, and he sat on the sofa and placed his glass on the coffee table. "I still feel guilty that you're sleeping there," she said.

"You shouldn't. It's my choice, and besides, it's a comfortable sofa," he assured her.

As they drank their wine they talked about the coming of winter with its snow and ice, the hope that the quarantine would be lifted by Christmas and a variety of topics that were light and easy.

Everything she said only made Flint more attracted to her. He liked the way she thought; he loved the way she smelled and looked. He found it difficult to forget those minutes in the diner when she'd been in his arms, plastered against him so intimately he could feel her every curve.

Although he had been worried about her, he'd also felt a lick of lust rise up inside him, an emotion he'd quickly staunched because it had been so inappropriate under the circumstances.

He felt it now, watching her drink her wine, noting the play of the table lamp glow in her hair. He knew it was equally as inappropriate now as it had been earlier, but it was there nevertheless. He had to admit that he had a healthy dose of lust where Nina Owens was concerned.

By the time they'd drunk their second glass of wine, she was ready to call it a night. She got up from her chair, and he rose, as well.

He walked her to the mouth of the hallway and took her by the arm. "Nina, I meant what I told you earlier. Day or night, if you are afraid, you call me, and I'll come running. I don't want you to ever be alone and afraid again."

She reached up and placed her palm against his cheek, her eyes filled with curiosity. "Are you really as nice as you seem, Flint Colton?"

"What you see is what you get with me, Nina."

She dropped her hand to her side and gazed up at him, and he knew in that moment that he had to kiss her. It was impossible not to. She just looked incredibly kissable.

He took a step toward her and was emboldened when she didn't step away from him. He took her in his arms and leaned his head down to capture her mouth with his. Her lips were soft and yielding, and as he deepened the kiss, her mouth tasted of red wine and fiery heat.

He'd intended it to be a simple, quick kiss, but she wrapped her arms around his neck and leaned into him, and the kiss continued, her lips as hungry against his as his were against hers. He could smell the heady peach-and-vanilla scent of her, taste the faint linger of wine, and his blood fired through all his veins, and he wanted to keep kissing her forever.

He'd fantasized about tasting her lips for what felt like an eternity, and it was far better than any fantasy he'd ever entertained.

It was only when he realized he was becoming embarrassingly aroused that he finally ended the kiss and stepped away from her. "Sorry about that," he said. "You looked way too kissable, and I just couldn't resist."

"Please, don't apologize. There were two people involved in that, and I definitely wasn't protesting," she replied, her voice slightly husky.

"Still, it probably wasn't a good idea," he said, even though he'd repeat it again in a nanosecond.

"Probably not," she agreed. "But it was nice…it was actually better than nice. Good night, Flint." She turned and headed down the hallway and disappeared into her bedroom.

Flint walked back into the living room and sank down on the sofa. *Better than nice*…as far as he was concerned, it had been nothing short of amazing.

The kiss had definitely been a mistake because now he wanted more of her. He wanted her naked in his arms. He wanted her naked in his bed, and she'd already warned him she wasn't interested in a relationship with anyone.

He got ready for bed and stretched out on the sofa, then released a deep sigh and realized for the first time just how hungry he was to have a special somebody in his life forever.

* * *

It had been almost a week since the night that she'd shared that kiss with Flint, and since that time she hadn't been able to get it out of her head.

Worse was that the memory of his warm lips against hers had evoked the desire for more from him…far more. She was definitely working up a healthy dose of lust toward her lawman bodyguard.

They had fallen into a comfortable routine over the past week, eating breakfast and dinner together and sharing the events of their days during the evenings with a glass of wine.

The more time she spent with him, the more she wanted him. She wanted to soothe the lines of stress he so often wore when he came to the diner to pick her up. She found herself wanting to make his time at home away from work as pleasant as possible, to see the smiles he gave her that warmed her.

She knew he wanted more than a kiss from her, too. His desire for her shone from his eyes when she caught him gazing at her. There was a crackling tension between them that she knew was suppressed desire. It was heady and exciting and made her feel like she'd never felt before.

"You definitely look like protective custody is agreeing with you," Grace said Sunday midmorning when the light breakfast rush was gone and the diner was empty of any other customers. "You've been sitting on that stool for the past fifteen minutes with a secretive little smile playing on your face. Tell me the truth, you and Flint are having hot, mad sex every night."

Nina laughed, but felt a guilty warmth fill her cheeks.

"Absolutely not," she replied. "I just really like him, and we're getting along great."

"He's a good man, Nina, and he seems to be good for you."

"He is a good man, but that doesn't change my mind about living my life alone."

Grace eyed her curiously. "I'd like to know who broke your heart so badly in the past."

"No broken hearts," Nina replied. She'd never allowed anyone to get close enough to break her heart. "I just know who I am and what's best for me."

They both looked up as the front door opened and two young men from the Home and Hearth store carried in several boxes. "Where do you want us to put these?" one of the guys asked. "We have several more boxes to bring in."

Nina jumped off the stool with excitement. "Just set them here for now. These are the centerpieces for Thanksgiving," she said to Grace. "We can move them to my office later, but I can't wait to show you what I got."

The two men set down the first load of boxes and then disappeared outside to get the rest of the delivery. Nina pulled open the top of one of the boxes and lifted out something wrapped in brown packing paper. She quickly unwrapped it to reveal a red candle in a delicate gold glass holder surrounded by fall leaves in shades of bright red and orange and yellow.

"These are for each table and booth," she said and set the centerpiece on the counter.

"Oh, they're going to look so beautiful," Grace exclaimed.

"And then I have a huge one with five candles that will be on the counter with the food on either side."

The men returned with two more large boxes, and Nina's excitement for the upcoming holiday buoyed up inside her. She got Charley and Abe to help her drag the boxes into her office, where they would remain until the night before the Thanksgiving Day celebration.

She returned to the dining room and sat next to Grace at the counter, unable to contain her anticipation of the special event only eleven days away.

"It's going to be a great day," she said. "Charley and I have finally finalized the menu, and I've promised him I won't tinker with it anymore. It's going to be a day of good food, good company and community spirit."

"I hope you aren't disappointed," Grace said. "We haven't exactly had any full houses since the virus struck. In fact, I heard last night that Mildred Walker was taken sick and is now in isolation."

Nina frowned. "I'm sorry to hear that, but I just have to believe that the holiday will help people put their fears aside long enough to come in here and enjoy a free meal," Nina replied. "It has to be a wonderful day. Everyone deserves a break from the fear and stress that's gripped this town for too long."

Grace reached out and grabbed her hand and gave it a squeeze. "It's a generous gesture, and I hope it's everything you want it to be."

"I'm having fliers printed up and am going to have them posted all around town announcing the free meal," Nina replied.

"If anyone can bring the people in, it's you, Nina."

The two women got up from the counter as two customers came through the door. Nina's spirits remained positive until later that afternoon when the day turned from pleasant to unexpectedly unpleasant.

With the Thanksgiving Day feast coming fast, she'd tried to line up the staffing for the day, only to discover that half of her waitresses didn't want to work that day.

"If most of the town shows up, we won't know who might be sick and who might not be," Amy Nettles, a young waitress, whined. "I'm just not going to come in that day."

"Neither am I," Sonja Jenkins, another of the waitresses added. "It's bad enough I take a chance catching the scourge every day that I come in here to work, but that day there will be tons of people, and I'm not putting my health at risk any more than I have to."

"But I was depending on you both being here. I'm already short staffed," Nina protested.

"You know I adore you, Nina, but I'm not working your feast," Amy said firmly.

"Ditto," Sonja added.

"Okay," Nina replied in defeat. She should fire the two right on the spot for letting her down, but she was already so short staffed she couldn't afford to let them go permanently.

By the time the day was nearly over, one of the busboys and a prep cook had refused, as well, to work Thanksgiving Day, and Nina couldn't seem to find the optimism that she could normally tap into.

It was almost time for Flint to arrive when Nina sat at the end of the counter, discouraged beyond words. Grace sat down next to her. "We'll make it work, Nina," she said softly. "Even if we are short staffed, the people who are here that day won't let you down. We'll make sure the customers get the same great service they always do, and it will be easier since it's going to be a buffet."

"It's still going to be tough if we have a full house," Nina replied, unable to be placated when she knew the special day might possibly already be compromised. "Aren't you supposed to be off the clock for the day now?" she asked Grace.

"Yes, but I just wanted to make sure you're okay."

"I'm fine," Nina replied, but she felt a ridiculous burning at her eyes. "Take your sweet son and go home and enjoy the rest of the weekend."

Within minutes Grace had left, and Flint walked through the door. "What's wrong?" he asked as if he could instantly read her mood.

"Nothing," she replied. "Everything is fine. I had Charley fix us some to-go food for the night. Let me grab it from the kitchen and I'm ready to go."

With every step she took, her depression deepened. The last thing she'd expected was for valued members of her staff to let her down on her special day. "Beef tips and noodles, corn and a Jell-O salad," Charley said as he handed her the large take-out bag.

"Sounds perfect. Thanks, Charley, and I'll see you tomorrow." She returned to where Flint awaited her by the door.

It wasn't until they were in the car and driving toward home that he cast her a quick glance. "What's going on? I don't see my happy Nina anywhere on that face."

Once again, she felt the sting of tears burn her eyes, tears she quickly held back again. "I'm just not feeling very optimistic or happy right now."

She told him about how her wait staff had wigged out about working Thanksgiving Day and her concern that the experience she wanted her customers to enjoy that day would be compromised.

"I know I'm being a big baby, but I had a vision of what the day would be like, and suddenly the vision has changed, and I can't seem to find anything good about it."

"You aren't being a baby," Flint protested. "You're disappointed by some of the people you thought you could depend on."

"The story of my life," she muttered beneath her breath. By the time they reached the house and had dinner on the table, her mood hadn't lightened, but rather had grown darker.

Her mind cast her back to her childhood, one of broken promises and violence, of holidays ruined and distrust born of circumstances beyond her control.

She rarely allowed herself to dwell in those painful memories, but she couldn't seem to pull herself from the black hole of depression that had sucked her in.

She was quiet through dinner, and she felt Flint's concern for her, but didn't have the energy to attempt to put on a fake happy face even for him.

He filled the quiet with conversation about his day, sharing bits and pieces that had nothing to do with crime or sickness, but rather stories about his coworkers and funny incidents that had happened in the past.

She recognized that he was working hard to cheer her up, and she appreciated his efforts, but by the time they'd finished eating and had gone to the living room with a glass of wine, the press of tears was once again hot in her eyes.

"Come here," he said and patted the space next to him. She rose from her chair and joined him on the sofa. She leaned into him and released a deep sigh.

"I think maybe my mood isn't just about Thanksgiving," she said as she burrowed into his side. "Maybe I'm having a little meltdown about everything that's happened to me, to my life. I've just always been able to bounce back, and tonight I don't feel like I have any bounce left."

"It's okay to be discouraged. I hate to see you like this, but you're allowed an off night." He wrapped an arm around her shoulder and toyed with a strand of her hair.

It was as if his words allowed her emotions to tumble out of her. The tears that had been so close to falling all evening began to trek down her cheeks.

"Hey, don't cry," Flint said, pulling her closer against him.

She angrily swiped at her cheeks. "I never cry unless I'm scared," she said at the same time a deep sob ripped up and out of her. "And I'm not scared so I shouldn't be crying."

"Tell me what to do. Tell me what to say," he said. "I can't stand to see you like this." He stroked down the length of her hair and looked at her with helplessness.

She shook her head and buried it in the front of his shirt and began to weep in earnest. He wrapped both arms around her and just held her.

She cried for the house she had lost that had been burned to the ground. She grieved the child she had been who had never known safety, a child who had grown into a woman who would never know how to trust. She wept because the joy from a day of giving had been stolen from her and finally she was finished, her well of tears finally gone dry.

He continued to hold her in his arms, his hands stroking slowly up and down her back in a soothing rhythm. She became aware of his heartbeat against hers and a new emotion growing inside her.

His body tensed, as if he sensed a different mood emanating from her and wasn't sure what to expect.

She raised her head to look at him. His eyes shone an intensive green that made her want to fall into their depths, to lose herself in the flames that danced in the very centers.

He cleared his throat. "Better?" he asked, his voice slightly husky.

"Much better," she replied.

"Are you ready for more wine?"

"No. I'm ready for you. I want you to make love to me, Flint."

His eyes widened, and he released his hold on her. "Nina…I…"

She reached up and placed her index finger over his mouth. "I want you, Flint. I've wanted you since the night we shared that kiss, and I know you want me, too. We've both been fighting against it, but I'm ready to stop fighting it. I want you."

"Nina, I think I've wanted you since the first day I walked into your diner and saw you standing behind the counter, but I don't want to be your escape from your sadness."

"I don't feel sad anymore," she replied. "And you aren't an escape. You're a desire that I want, that I've wanted." She stood and held out her hand to him. "No promises, no regrets, Flint, just this moment together."

* * *

Flint could think of a million reasons why making love to Nina wasn't a good idea, but he rose from the sofa as if in a trance and took her hand and allowed her to lead him down the hallway to her bedroom.

The window blinds were pulled, and the only illumination in her room was that which drifted from the night-light in the hall, just enough to lend a silvery glow to the room.

He took off his holster and gun and set them on the nightstand, even as he told himself he should stop this before it ever began, but then she was in his arms, and his mouth was on hers, and he knew he didn't want to stop this from happening, not now...not ever.

She wrapped her arms around his neck and melded her body into his, and he was overwhelmed with the scent of vanilla and peaches, undone by the intimate curves of her body against his. She fit so neatly against him, as if they'd been made to match perfectly.

While they kissed, he tangled his hands in her hair, loving the silky feel of the strands on his fingers. He had fantasized about making love to her for so long, had wanted her soft and yielding in his arms for what felt like a lifetime.

She unwound from him only long enough to sit on the bed and pull him onto it with her. They tumbled backward, arms and legs entwined as their lips sought each other once again.

He had no idea how long they kissed, but it didn't take long for him to want more. He wanted to feel her skin against his, he wanted to make her moan with pleasure.

She pulled his T-shirt from the top of his jeans, and

her hands were hot and feverish against his bare chest. He wanted to feel her bare flesh, and he plucked at the bottom of her sweatshirt.

She broke their kiss and moved away from him to the side of the bed. His heart nearly stopped as he thought that perhaps she had suddenly changed her mind about the whole thing.

"I don't know about you, but I'm not into the awkward wrangling off of clothes in bed." She stood and pulled her sweatshirt over her head and threw it toward a chair in the corner.

It took Flint a mere heartbeat to get out of bed, shuck his shoes and socks, his jeans and T-shirt, leaving him clad only in a pair of boxers.

When he gazed at her again she was naked except for the hot-pink panties that had given him such vivid fantasies.

"Wait," he said as she grabbed the sides to pull them off.

She paused, standing perfectly still as he approached her. She was so beautiful with her long, slender legs, her willowy waist and perfectly proportioned breasts.

"Those hot-pink panties have tormented me since the moment you bought them," he said. "All I've been able to think of since then is you wearing them and me taking them off you."

Her eyes glowed a brilliant gold. "Then what are you waiting for?" Her voice was half-breathless.

He felt as if his heart was about to pound out of his chest as he stepped closer to her, close enough to cup her breasts with his hands, close enough to claim her lips with his own. But he stayed focused on the panties that fit so perfectly and rode low on her slender hips.

He looped his thumbs on either side of the silky material. As he began to slide them down, she shivered and whispered his name. When she was completely naked, she quickly got back into the bed. Flint took off his boxers and joined her there and pulled up the sheets that smelled of her around them.

They began the sensual exploration of each other. He trailed kisses down her throat, nuzzled the hollow of her neck and then moved down to her breasts, where he licked and sucked first one pebbly tip and then the other.

She was certainly not a passive partner. Her hands stroked fire down his back as she pressed her lower body intimately against his. He had been fully aroused from the moment she'd told him she wanted him to make love to her.

He was ready to take her now, but he knew his limitations. It had been so long since he'd been with a woman, he knew that if he wasn't careful, this experience would be over almost before it began.

His goal at this moment was to bring her as much pleasure as physically possible and to make her want him again and again. He didn't want to think about the possibility that this was a one-time event driven by her discouraged mood and the fact that she'd had a bad day.

When she reached down to stroke his turgid length, he stopped her. "No," he whispered. "Right now I want this to be all about you."

He maneuvered her onto her back and then rose up beside her as he splayed a hand and caressed it slowly down her stomach. He wasn't sure whose breaths were louder, hers or his own, but they mingled together with the sound of passion unleashed.

He stroked her lower stomach, lightly touched and teased her inner thighs, tormenting her by touching her everywhere but where he knew she wanted him most.

She lifted her hips and moaned impatiently as he found her center, and a deep moan escaped her as he used his fingers to stoke her pleasure higher.

Her eyes widened and then closed and she once again whispered his name as he quickened his movements. He knew the second she spun out of control, her eyes flickered open and closed, and she stiffened and then shuddered in utter release.

He gave her no chance to catch her breath, but quickly donned a condom and moved between her thighs and eased into her moist heat. He fought for self-control as she lifted her legs on either side of him to allow him to go deeper.

Drawing deep, slow breaths in an effort to maintain control, he stroked slowly at first, but it wasn't long before he was lost in her, lost in the exquisite moment of being inside her. They moved in a frenzy and despite his desire to make it last as long as possible, his climax rushed up and drowned him in a sea of pleasure.

She cried out his name, and he realized she'd climaxed once again when he had. Good, he wanted her to remember this night with him no matter what happened in the future.

He collapsed at her side, his heart trying to find a normal rhythm. She rolled over on her side and placed a hand on his beating heart.

"You might not be able to cook, Flint Colton, but you sure know how to please a woman," she said.

"Trust me, the pleasure was all mine," he said with a half laugh.

"Now it's time for the awkward after-sex talk." She rose up on one elbow and gazed down at him, her hazel eyes glowing gold in the dimness of the room. The sheet slipped down, exposing her shoulder and half of her breast.

"Do we really need to go there?" he asked, wondering what on earth there was to talk about while they still basked in the warmth of utter fulfillment.

She reached out and shoved a strand of his hair back from his forehead. "I don't know. You tell me. I certainly don't want this to change things between us. I mean, we're here now but we both know that once Hank Bittard is back in custody, I'm back in my own life, and as I've told you before, it's a solitary life."

She looked so beautiful in the faint light, with her hair tousled and her lips slightly swollen from his kisses. She also looked achingly earnest, as if it was important to her that he understand that this had been about sex and nothing more.

It had been about so much more than mere sex to him. He'd not only been physically involved but emotionally, as well, but he knew she had enough burdens at the moment, and that the best thing he could do was simply agree with her.

"Nina, nothing has changed," he assured her. "Except I've just had a bout of amazing sex with the most beautiful woman in town."

She smiled in obvious relief. "So, we're on the same page. This was definitely amazing, but it's probably best that it doesn't happen again."

"I'm not so sure that I'm exactly on that same page," Flint replied teasingly. He sobered and reached out to stroke a finger down her cheek. "One day at a time,

Nina. You decide what you need and don't need from me and that's exactly what you'll get."

He slid to the side of the bed and stood. Although there was nothing more he'd like to do than spend the night in bed with her, he also knew this moment of intimacy was over.

He was aware of her gaze lingering on him as he gathered up his clothing and his holster and gun. "Pancakes for breakfast?" she asked.

"Sounds perfect," he agreed. "Good night, Nina."

She murmured good-night, and he headed for the hallway bathroom, where he quickly cleaned up, folded his clothes and put on his boxers for the night on the sofa.

He settled in on the sofa cushions, gun nearby and mind racing. His head wasn't filled with thoughts of criminals running amuck in the town like it should be; but rather his thoughts were completely consumed by the woman whose bed he had just left.

If anything gave him hope and confidence that he'd get Bittard in custody and find Jimmy and the Colton heirloom ring, it was Nina and the idea of her always being at his side.

It was a foolish thought, but the truth was he was precariously close to being heart and soul in love with Nina Owens. Just his luck to fall in love with a woman who had made it clear in no uncertain terms that she wasn't wife or mother material.

What he'd like to know was who or what had happened in her life to make her come to that decision? She was a loving, caring individual and seemed meant to love and be loved by somebody special.

She'd shared with him a lot about the time after

she'd left her home in Casper and before she had arrived in Dead River, but she'd spoken almost nothing about her parents or her childhood.

He wouldn't press her to share as it was obvious she didn't want to, or didn't trust him enough yet to give him more pieces of herself. He had a feeling pressing her on the issue would only drive her away from him.

He frowned and closed his eyes. He couldn't make her be what he might want her to be. He couldn't make her love him in the way he might want her to love him.

He couldn't make her be the special woman he wanted to fill his days and nights. The kind of love he wanted for himself couldn't be forced or pressured.

One day at a time, he reminded himself, and his ultimate goal where she was concerned had to be her safety from the killer who wanted her dead.

Dr. Lucas Rand stared at the three syringes loaded with a faint amber serum he hoped desperately was the cure he had sought since his ex-wife had died of the Dead River virus.

The syringes were on a stainless-steel tray in the isolation room that held three patients, Dottie Colton, teenager Tyler Miles and Wylie Simms, a man in his mid-forties. They were three of the first people in town who had gotten sick and still managed somehow to cling to life.

All three of them were unconscious with high fevers and labored breathing, and every day Lucas feared that he'd come into the isolation room and find one of them gone.

There had already been too many deaths to this horrible scourge. He couldn't allow another person to die.

He couldn't wait for CDC expert Colleen Goodhue to eventually arrive. Something had to be done now to save the sick and dying.

This was his clinic, the patients were his townspeople and he couldn't just sit idly by while more and more of them got sick and wound up in yet another isolation room.

He was a smart man, some would say a brilliant doctor.

He'd spent the past week in the lab, studying blood and tissue samples, everything that couldn't be sent out for further study by others because of the quarantine.

He once again stared at the three syringes, hoping against hope that they contained the cure he so desperately needed to stop this plague.

He could be a hero. If he'd managed to find the right mix of ingredients and medication that would not only save the sick, but also make sure that nobody else got ill, then he would be hailed as the hero who had saved the entire town.

Right now all he cared about were the three patients before him. He couldn't save the entire town unless he could save the three of them with what he hoped was the magic serum in the syringes.

Drawing a deep breath, he picked up the first of the three syringes and carried it to the IV line for Wylie Simms. With a steady hand he injected the serum into the line that would carry it into Wylie's blood. He stood for a moment and stared at Wylie's pale, thin face, waiting to see if there would be any instant adverse reaction. There appeared to be none.

Tyler was the second one to get what Lucas hoped was the magic elixir and finally Dottie Colton. When he had finished administering the medication, he left the isolation unit, changed out of the protective suit all staff was required to wear when interacting with patients and then headed to his office.

If his calculations were correct, he would know before noon tomorrow if the serum was the cure he'd been seeking. And if not, he would have to start all over again in the attempt to solve the mystery of the deadly virus.

Chapter 7

It was ten o'clock on Monday morning when Flint left his office to do a foot patrol down Main Street. True to her word, Nina had made pancakes for breakfast, and their conversation had been light and easy with no mention of what had transpired between them the night before.

With her big feast only ten days away, Flint was pleased her optimism had been back in place that morning. She told him she'd had fliers printed that would be put up around town starting today, and as he headed down the sidewalk he saw Abe doing just that.

Flint stifled a mental groan as he saw Trevor Garth approaching him from the opposite direction. There were two branches of Coltons in town, Flint's family, and then the affluent branch that had been under the rule of Jethro Colton, who had recently passed away.

The two branches were not particularly unfriendly with each other, they just didn't have much to do with one another. Trevor had married Flint's cousin, Gabriella, and while Flint found the man decent, he'd been an impatient pain in the butt since the quarantine had fallen down around them.

"Flint." Trevor raised a hand in greeting. "Any news on when any of us will be able to get out of this godforsaken town?"

"No news," Flint replied.

Trevor's nostrils narrowed in a way that instantly put Flint on the defensive. "How long can we be captives like insects under a microscope just waiting to get sick? You know Gabriella is pregnant. She's at risk here. I'd love to get her and Avery out of this town."

"Trevor, there's nothing more I'd like to tell you than that you and your family could leave, but you know I'm not in charge of this quarantine. It's bigger than me, and I have no jurisdiction where the quarantine is concerned."

Trevor raked a hand through his hair and released a deep sigh. "I know. I'm just so damned frustrated."

"We all are," Flint replied. "But right now we're stuck with things the way they are, and we just have to make the best of it. How is little Avery doing?"

For the first time since they'd started the conversation, Trevor smiled. "She's doing great, although she's at that age where she's into everything."

Flint smiled. "You'll have your hands full when the new baby comes."

"It will be a good handful," Trevor replied.

The men exchanged goodbyes and continued on their separate ways. Trevor certainly wasn't the only one in town growing more and more frustrated with the quarantine.

Seeing the joy on Trevor's face as he'd talked about his daughter and the new baby to come had created a small tinge of jealousy that shot through Flint. Was it so wrong for him to want a woman to love and children of his own to raise?

He pulled his thoughts away from Trevor and family and instead turned them to what they should be focused on, the crimes and the escaped fugitives that haunted him.

Nothing had come from their tail on Ralph Dane. He either wasn't in contact with Hank Bittard or the contact was so minimal that the officers tailing him had been unable to pick up anything yet.

Flint had a feeling of time standing still. No leads on the two fugitives he sought and no word from the clinic that any progress had been made on finding a cure for the disease.

The only thing that tempered his frustration this morning was the memory of making love to Nina the night before. He'd felt strong and complete with her in his arms.

Her open, giving smiles as they'd shared breakfast that morning had given him the determination to forge ahead in his duties as chief of police to do everything in his power to find the fugitives and at least give Nina back some semblance of a normal life.

While he'd like to keep her in his house forever, he somehow had to break through and get her to open up to him. He knew she was holding back, that something from her past haunted her. He wanted to help her heal so that she would be open to a real, loving relationship with him.

He smiled as he approached Harvey Watters, as usual seated on the bench in front of the hardware store. "How are you doing, Harvey? I haven't had a chance to see much of you lately."

"I figured you got your hands full right now, and with your cute little houseguest, the last thing you need is my old self showing up for a little social chitchat. But, I was just getting ready to go find you."

"Oh?" Flint sat next to Harvey on the bench. "What's up?"

"I think I've sat on this bench for so long that most people don't even see me. I'm kind of like the old homeless man nobody pays attention to. A few minutes ago a couple of scruffy-looking young men left the café, and as they walked out they were talking about taking some supplies to the old Miller place."

Electricity shot through Flint. "Did you know the men?"

Harvey shook his head. "I've seen them around town before, but I don't have any idea about their names."

"We just checked out the Miller place last week," Flint said thoughtfully. The old house was located in the woods that Flint and his men had searched exhaustively.

He supposed it was possible that Hank or Jimmy had watched the search occur from some hiding place nearby and once it had been cleared and the officers had left, one of them had taken up residency there.

Flint shot up from the bench. "Sounds like something we need to check out right away."

"Don't forget the house isn't the only structure on

the property," Harvey said. "There's also a dilapidated old shed you might want to check out, too."

"Thanks, Harvey." With a distracted wave, Flint headed back in the direction of the police station. If Harvey had heard right, then this might be the break they'd all been looking for.

As he hurried down the street, his mind worked the logistics. The last thing he wanted to do was go in with enough manpower to potentially warn or spook whoever might be there.

"Patrick, Mike, come with me," he said as he entered the squad room.

Officers Patrick Carter and Mike Harriman were the two men he trusted most when it came to an operation like this. They both could move as quietly as cats, and since the restructure of the police department, he knew they were the experienced veterans. They had been his go-to men since he'd taken over as chief.

Neither of them asked questions as they followed Flint back outside and to his squad car. It was only when they were in the car and headed to the woods on the west side of town that Flint told them what Harvey had overheard.

"Too bad Harvey didn't know the names of the men," Patrick said from the backseat.

"I just hope they're meeting up with Bittard." Mike shot Flint a quick glance. "I know you're eager to get Jimmy behind bars to give Molly some closure."

"Trust me, I'd rather get an escaped killer in custody than Jimmy right now," Flint replied. "Molly is in no more danger from Jimmy, but getting Bittard behind bars would allow Nina to know she doesn't have anything to fear anymore. She could get her own life back without looking over her shoulder."

He tightened his hands around the steering wheel. He wanted to make an arrest so badly, he tasted it in his mouth, felt the need surging through his entire body.

He knew an arrest of Bittard would send Nina out of his house, but in this case duty and responsibility far trumped any personal feelings he might have for her.

That killer belonged behind bars. The memory of Madelaine in Cheyenne, of Jolene's broken body on the ground, weighed heavy in his heart. While Hank hadn't been responsible for Madelaine's death, Flint had been. Flint had also been responsible for Jolene's murder. He refused to allow Hank to kill again in his town, especially when he knew the killer was focused on Nina.

He parked about a mile from their destination, pulling his car off the side of the road and into a stand of trees where it would be difficult to spot unless somebody was specifically looking for it.

"So, what's the plan?" Mike asked.

"Mike, we'll give you a five-minute head start. Work your way around to the back of the property. Keep in mind there's two buildings we're focused on, the house and an old shed that's somewhere nearby. Patrick, you go to the left of the house, and I'll take the right," Flint said. "Mike, you stay back and watch the area. We'll check out the house first, and needless to say we go in as quiet as possible, and hopefully have the element of surprise on our side."

With a plan in place, Mike took off, and Flint and Patrick waited silently for five minutes to give Mike enough time to get far enough ahead of them to be able to cover the back of the structure.

After five minutes had passed, Flint and Patrick parted ways and went on the move. As with the last time he'd checked this area, Flint moved slowly, stealthily, and tried to avoid stepping on dead roots or twigs that would give away his presence.

Surprise was the only element they had on their side at this moment, and the last thing he wanted was crunching leaves or broken branches to tip off whoever might be holed up in either the Miller house or the old shed.

His gun felt comfortable in his hand as he made his way deeper into the woods. The Miller house had been abandoned for years. Taken over by wildlife, victim to the elements, the place could only be considered hospitable to somebody who had nowhere else to go.

But the wind that blew through the trees was cold, and anyplace would do in a storm, Flint thought. It wouldn't be long before the wind would be bitter and snow would fly and shelter would be a necessity.

As he crept along, he kept his focus in all directions, knowing that it would be far too easy to be ambushed with all the brush and trees as hiding places.

It didn't take long before he had the Miller house in his sights. He crept down and peered across the area, seeking a flash of the black uniform that would let him know Patrick was in place.

The old listing shed was some distance away. They would check out the house and then head to the shed. Flint saw Patrick through the woods and had the confidence that Mike was also in place. If anyone was inside the house, they would have difficulty escaping all three officers.

The porch was broken down on one side, and the

front door hung askew from one hinge. There was no noise to indicate that anyone was inside, but that didn't mean the house was deserted.

Flint moved forward, conscious of Patrick doing the same. They met just in front of the porch. Flint motioned Patrick to follow him as he stepped up on what was left of the porch and whirled into the house with his gun leading the way.

He fought a fierce disappointment as he realized the living room looked just the way it had the last time they'd checked it out. Old beer bottles and cans hugged one corner of the room, and one wall was spray painted with graffiti, indicating that over the years this had been a party place for the teenagers in town.

The kitchen yielded nothing new, either. Dead leaves had blown through a broken window and pooled on the floor. There was nothing on the counters, nothing in the cabinets to indicate that anyone had used this place as shelter.

It took only minutes for them to clear the rest of the house, finding each room empty except for cobwebs and nature's encroachment. Flint was certain that nobody had been hiding here during the time that Jimmy and Hank had been on the run.

He and Patrick stepped out the back door. He motioned in the distance where the shed was barely visible among the bare trees.

They moved as a unit toward the structure. They were halfway there when a loud crashing sound came from their left, a sound that indicated somebody on the run.

He and Patrick raced after whoever they had flushed

out. They ran together and then split up, unable to discern in which specific direction the person had run.

Desperation drove Flint forward. This was as close as he'd been to catching a perp in weeks. He needed this. The town needed this, and if it was Bittard in the woods, then Nina needed Flint to get the job done.

He dodged around trees, threw himself through brambles and brush and stopped every few minutes to listen for signs that he might be closing in. It didn't take long for him to realize that he had no idea where the fugitive had gone.

He was even more discouraged that he heard no indication that Patrick was in hot pursuit of anyone. The damn woods were too big, and it was as if the runner had managed to disappear into thin air. Flint should have brought an army with him, he thought in disgust as he headed back toward the shed.

Patrick was waiting for him there. "I lost whoever it was," he said in obvious frustration. "Looks like somebody has been staying here," he said as he gestured toward the shed. "I took a peek inside."

"Where's Mike?" Flint asked. "He should have shown up here by now."

"I haven't seen him since we parted ways at the car," Patrick said.

A sick feeling filled Flint's stomach. He pulled his cell phone from his pocket and called Mike's phone. It rang and rang and finally went to voice mail. Flint dropped the phone in his pocket and looked at Patrick. "I think Mike's in trouble. We need to find him."

"He would have headed to the back of the house from the car," Patrick said.

Together the two of them left the shed and headed

toward the house. Flint's heart beat with a dull rhythm of dread. Had he put one of his officers in harm's way?

The person he and Patrick had gone after hadn't run anywhere near the house. So where was Mike? Why hadn't he answered his phone or shown up at the shed?

Dammit, Flint should have brought more help. He should have never allowed Mike to stand on his own in the woods where two fugitives were loose.

They reached the house, and Patrick went left and Flint went right around the structure. "Mike," Flint called frantically as he reached the back of the house.

Patrick echoed him, calling out to his fellow officer. It was only when Flint was about twenty feet away from the back of the house that he heard a low moan and saw Mike sitting in the brush and rubbing the back of his head.

Both Flint and Patrick rushed over to him. Flint knelt down next to him. "Mike, what happened? Are you all right?"

"Yeah, I'm okay. Somebody sneaked up behind me and hit me in the back of the head." Mike touched the back of his head again and winced. "And whoever it was had a hell of a swing."

"Can you get to your feet?" Flint asked.

"I think so." With Flint grabbing his arm, the two men rose. Flint moved around to the back of Mike and checked out his head.

"You definitely have a goose egg," Flint said. "We need to get you to the clinic."

"No, I'm okay." Mike straightened his shoulders. "Let's finish what we came here to do. Did you get to the shed?"

Flint filled him in on them flushing somebody out

and that he and Patrick had given chase, only to lose them. "Whoever we chased couldn't have been the person who hit you."

"What I don't understand is why I still have my gun. Why smash me in the head and then not take my weapon?" Mike asked.

"I don't know. Maybe he stumbled on you and got freaked, then hit you in the head and ran," Flint replied. "Are you sure you shouldn't go to the clinic?"

Guilt rode heavy on Flint's shoulders. He should have never put Mike out there alone. If he couldn't keep one of his own men safe, then how in the hell could he trust himself to make decisions that would keep Nina safe?

"I'm fine," Mike assured him. "I have a slight headache, but I don't feel sleepy or nauseous. I'll check in at the clinic later. Let's get back to the shed and see what's inside."

Flint looked at him with pride. This was why Mike was one of his go-to guys. He was tough, and he was all about the job.

As they headed back to the lean-to structure, Flint continued to berate himself for his lack in judgment in not bringing more officers out here with him.

"We chased one man through the woods while another one smashed Mike in the back of his head. What are the odds that the two perps would be in the same general area?" Patrick asked.

"Maybe they're somehow working together to stay hidden," Mike suggested.

"I don't know. I find that hard to believe. Jimmy isn't a seasoned criminal. He's just a stupid kid. I can't imagine him hooking up with Hank for any reason,"

Flint replied. "And I can't imagine Hank wanting to trust a stupid kid."

By that time they had reached the barely standing structure. Flint bent his head to enter the shed that had collapsed on one side. "Definitely somebody was here." A sleeping bag was on the floor, along with a flashlight and several bottles of water.

"Can you tell whether it was Jimmy or Hank?" Patrick asked from outside.

Flint kicked the sleeping bag to see if there was anything hidden beneath and then noticed several cans of food and a hand-operated can opener nearby. "Can't tell. Whoever it is appears to be living on canned tuna and beans." He stepped out of the shed.

"Maybe Jimmy had made himself cozy here, and Hank was hanging around just waiting for the opportunity to get the kid out and take over the space. There aren't many other places to take shelter out here," Patrick speculated.

"I'm surprised nobody has moved into the Miller house," Mike said.

"Too obvious," Flint replied. "Either man would know we'd be keeping an eye on the place. Put on your gloves and let's get all of this stuff out of the shed and into the car. We should be able to pull a fingerprint off something that will let us know which man was here."

While Patrick and Mike got to work, Flint walked the general area, looking for anything that might provide further clues. They'd found one mole hole, but how many more were there in these woods?

Was Jimmy now so desperate that he'd have the guts to hit an officer over the head? Was it possible the two men were now working together to keep hidden?

They had talked to every friend and acquaintance of both Jimmy and Hank. They'd checked all the abandoned or empty storefronts in town. They'd even begun a search of sheds and outbuildings on properties of the people in town, although that particular search was far from over. But this incident today told him that both fugitives were hiding out here, in the vast woods.

Flint entered a small clearing between the house and the shed, his frustration at a peak. The lead from Harvey had been solid. They should have somebody in custody, and the fact that they didn't burned in his gut.

He looked up at the trees, wondering if whoever had run from them had been in the branches and had seen their approach. He gazed down at the ground, looking for any kind of footprints that might have been left behind.

He froze as he saw a small black box on the ground. It was a familiar velvet box. His heart squeezed tight as he leaned down to pick it up. This was the jewelry box that contained the Colton heirloom ring.

The odds were good that Jimmy had been staying in the shed, and when he'd made a dash for it, he'd dropped the box. At least Flint would be able to soothe Molly's devastation about the missing ring.

By that time Patrick and Mike had gathered up the items from the shed and joined Flint. "What did you find?" Patrick asked.

"The Colton heirloom ring that Jimmy stole. He must have dropped it when he beat tracks out of here," Flint said.

"Molly will be happy that you got it back," Mike said.

"I'm happy to have it back," Flint replied. He opened

the box and his heart fell to his feet. Where there should be the glittering gem of the Colton ring, there was nothing.

"You covered all of Main Street?" Nina asked Abe.

"And up and down Oak and in every storefront along the way," Abe replied. "Trust me, nobody can go five steps without seeing a flier for the Thanksgiving celebration here."

"Great," Nina exclaimed. Despite her breakdown of the night before, she'd awakened with her usual excitement and optimism. Of course, making love with Flint the night before might have had something to do with her exceptionally cheerful mood this morning.

She sent Abe off to the kitchen to help Charley, even though the lunch crowd had already left, and she went into her office where Wilma and Molly were carefully unpacking the centerpieces onto a long table she'd set up so that they could be cleaned and shiny for the big day.

"How's it going, ladies?" she asked.

"These are going to look so pretty on the tables and booths," Molly replied as she unwrapped one of the candle displays from the brown packing paper.

"We've got half of them unpacked, and so far we've only found one candle that's broken," Wilma said.

"Let me know what you find broken when you have them all unpacked and I'll call the Home and Hearth to make sure they replace anything that arrived damaged," Nina said. "You two keep working on this, and I'll watch the front of the house. I'll call you if I need you. You never know when we might have a big rush of customers," she said.

She ignored Wilma's snort as she left the office and returned to the dining room. Today was Grace's day off so Billy wouldn't be coming in after school today.

With no customers, Nina made herself a cup of tea and took a seat at the counter, her thoughts instantly going back to Flint and the incredible experience of making love with him.

She'd known instinctively that he'd be a giving, generous lover, and he had proven that and more. He'd made her feel incredibly beautiful and treasured. What she hadn't expected was the intensity of his passion, the breathtaking abandon of his desire.

She would never be able to wear those hot-pink panties again without remembering the fiery burn of his green eyes as he'd slowly removed them from her. She had nearly fallen to her knees with the very sensuality of that single act.

If she let herself, she could love him, but she wouldn't allow it. A vision of her father's angry face filled her head, and the sound of fists against skin rang in her ears.

Her father beat her mother on a regular basis, and then his buddies would come and take him away for a couple of hours until he cooled down. But he always came back and the cycle continued.

Throughout her years on the road, Nina had dated, but she'd never allowed any man to get close enough to hurt her physically or emotionally. She refused to be vulnerable to any man.

Her father could be charming and loving then brutal, and the lasting effect on Nina was that she wasn't sure if all men had two faces and the ugly, mean face was only shown to those who were closest to them.

She sipped her tea and pulled herself from thoughts of her distant past. She was a here-and-now kind of woman, not prone to dwelling on old history. She was mentally strong and didn't need a mate to fulfill her. She didn't want a man who would demand her complete trust.

And in the here and now, it was much more exciting to think of being in that bed with Flint. She'd almost asked him to stay, to spend the night with her in her bed so she could wake up in his arms as dawn broke.

But she was glad she'd fought the impulse. She and Flint had been playing house for a little over two weeks, and it was beginning to feel far too comfortable, far too normal.

She looked forward to him walking through the diner door to take her home; she loved cooking and eating with him in the evenings. More than anything she enjoyed the time when they sat in the living room and drank a little wine and just talked about anything and everything.

She admired how close he was to his brother, Theo, and his sister, Gemma, and she prayed every night that his grandmother would rally from the virus that had her so ill.

The diner door opened, and she was surprised to see Flint walk in. It was only a little after two, far too early for him to be here to take her home.

"Hey, what's up?" she asked as he walked over to the counter where she sat.

"Is Molly working today?" he asked.

"She's in my office unpacking the centerpieces. Has something happened?" Nina couldn't help but be curious. "Did you catch Jimmy?"

"I wish," Flint replied. "Unfortunately, I need to tell her something that isn't going to make her happy." He sighed and took off his hat and set it on the stool next to Nina. "Should I just go on back?"

"Wilma is in the office with her." Nina slid off her stool. "I'll tell Wilma to take a break and that way you can talk to Molly alone."

"Why don't you stay with me when I talk to her? She might need a little female support."

"Whatever you want," Nina replied. She was surprised when he grabbed her hand as they walked back toward the office. He obviously felt like he needed his own support when he spoke to Molly.

He must have some sort of bad news, Nina thought, and her stomach twisted in knots. Had Dottie died? Was that what he had to tell Molly?

"Hey, Flint," Molly greeted him as they walked into the room. "What are you doing here in the middle of the day?"

"Wilma, could you take a break? Flint needs to speak to Molly."

Wilma nodded and left the room while Molly's blue eyes shot from Nina to Flint in alarm. "Has something bad happened?"

"We almost caught Jimmy this morning," Flint said. He explained about searching the shed and finding the items that indicated somebody had been staying there. "We thought we had him but he managed to slip away, but we know it was Jimmy because in a clearing nearby I found this on the ground."

Flint pulled out of his pocket a black velvet ring box. Molly gasped, an ecstatic smile sweeping over her face, a smile that instantly fell when Flint opened it to reveal that it was empty.

"I'm sorry, Molly. It was empty when I found it," Flint said as tears began to fill Molly's eyes. She shoved a strand of her long red hair behind her ear, and her tears fell down her cheeks.

"I thought for a minute that at least you'd gotten the ring back. That's all I really cared about," she said and began to sob.

Nina quickly moved to place an arm around Molly's shoulder. "Don't you worry, Molly. Sooner or later Flint will get Jimmy in custody, and you'll get the ring back."

Molly buried her head against Nina's shoulder, and Nina held tight as the young girl cried out her bitter disappointment. Flint shifted from one foot to the other, obviously upset that he'd had to bring this news to his cousin.

Jimmy Johnson was just another creep who had managed to put on a good face to fool the soft-hearted, loving Molly. Once he had her believing that he loved her, that he wanted to spend his whole life with her, he'd shown his true face of greed and selfishness.

Nina hugged Molly tighter until finally the young woman's tears halted. She stepped out of Nina's arms and looked at Flint. "What if he's lost the ring?"

"He hasn't lost it," Flint said with certainty. "It's worth too much money for him to be careless and lose it. I'm sure he's got it in a safe place so that once the quarantine is lifted, he can take it with him out of town and sell it."

"I just don't understand how I could have been so fooled by him," Molly said. "I thought he was the man of my dreams, but he wound up being a total night-mare."

Flint threw an arm around her shoulder. "You're young, Molly. You'll find that special someone who will love and adore you. You just have to be patient and not let this experience with Jimmy make you close yourself off."

Molly offered him a small smile. "And what makes you so smart on matters of the heart? You're thirty-two years old and still aren't married."

"Don't you worry about me." Flint gave her a squeeze and then released her. "When I'm ready and I know exactly who I want, I'll go after her."

His gaze lingered on Nina, and it made her feel hot and bothered and a little bit disturbed all at the same time. She didn't want Flint falling in love with her. The last thing she wanted to do was break his heart.

Maybe the look he cast her had nothing to do with anything more than their night spent together in bed, she consoled herself. Certainly she hadn't been able to get it out of her head throughout today.

"Molly, why don't you take a break?" Nina suggested. "Get yourself something to drink and just relax for a little while."

Molly nodded and left the office.

"I can't tell you how much I was dreading telling her about the missing ring," Flint said when it was just him and Nina in the office.

"You're right in that I don't believe Jimmy would be careless enough to lose the ring. When you find him, he'll have it on him," she said with certainty. "He'll need whatever money he can get from it if he manages to get out of town."

He raked a hand through his dark brown hair. "I've got to say, this morning has been one of the more frustrating we've had lately. We were so close to getting him, and I still can't believe he managed to slip away."

"At least you know he probably won't return to the shed. You flushed him out, and now he'll have to find another place to hide. Maybe he'll get sloppy or stupid and make a mistake that will allow you to finally grab him."

"I'd like to grab Hank, but we can't seem to find a source to give us any hint where he might be in town. None of his old friends are talking, and there hasn't even been a sighting of him by anyone that we know of until today." He told her about Mike being attacked and believing that Hank had been the person who attacked him.

"How is Mike now?" she asked worriedly.

"I had him go to the clinic where the doctor basically told him he has a big lump on his head but no concussion. I sent him home for the rest of the day."

"One day at a time, Flint. Sooner or later you'll have them both behind bars."

He smiled at her gratefully. "You make me feel like I can do anything. By the way, I saw posters advertising your Thanksgiving Day event all over town."

She leaned against her desk and smiled. "I had Abe hit the streets first thing this morning to get them up. Hopefully, it won't sleet or snow between now and Thanksgiving so they'll stay in good condition."

"The last weather report I heard was for clear and cold for the rest of the week and into next week. And that reminds me. You didn't buy a coat when we shopped for things for you. I could swing by the store and get one for you if you'll tell me your size and what you want."

She told him her size. "Just a warm black coat, and I'll pay you for it when we get home this evening."

"I think I can manage buying you a coat without you worrying about paying me back," he said. And now I'd better get out of here. I'm heading to the clinic to check on things there, but I should be back here by five."

They left the office together. "If you're a little late in getting back here, don't worry about it. I'm not going anyplace without you."

"And that's the way I like it," he replied. He grabbed his hat from the stool and with a wave of his hand, he disappeared out the door.

"That man looks at you as if you're his favorite piece of pie," Wilma observed from her perch on a chair behind the counter.

"Don't be silly," Nina scoffed, but there was no question that even though she had wanted the night with Flint, she was starting to believe that making love with him had been a huge mistake.

Chapter 8

Flint headed toward the clinic with a heavy heart. It had already been a crappy day. Losing Jimmy in the woods had been bad enough, but having Mike attacked and then having to break Molly's heart all over again about the missing ring had been even more difficult. All he could hope for now was that when he got to the clinic his grandmother would still be fighting, still be holding her own against the virus.

He'd just stepped out of his car when he was met by Dr. Rafe Granger. "I need to get out of here for a while," he said to Flint. "Are you on duty or can you take me to the Dead River Bar where we can get a couple of beers and share a little talk?"

Flint was surprised. While he and Rafe had been close as teenagers, they'd hardly had time to really reconnect since both of them had returned to Dead River.

"Get in. You can get a beer, and I'll grab some of Sally Jean's terrible coffee," Flint replied.

Flint got back in the car while Rafe slid into the passenger seat. "Before we leave, I need to tell you we've had a hell of an afternoon here, and your grandmother's condition has worsened."

Flint gripped the steering wheel and stared at Rafe. His heart squeezed so tight he could barely manage to speak. "Is she going to be all right?"

"I wish I could tell you yes, but at this point, I honestly don't know. We managed to get her stabilized once again, but she's weaker than she's been."

Flint started the car and headed out toward Main Street. "Did something happen to change her condition?"

"Last night Lucas thought he'd come up with a serum that would cure the virus. He decided to test it on three patients—your grandmother, Tyler Miles and Wiley Simms. He gave them each the serum last night and then just after noon today all hell broke loose. Your grandmother's fever spiked, Tyler Miles regained consciousness and Wiley Simms died."

Rafe's voice was heavy with emotion. "The worst part was that we couldn't get Lucas off Wiley. Even after the man had been dead for fifteen minutes, Lucas continued to work on him in an effort to bring him back. It took three of us to finally pull him away and get him out of the isolation ward."

The two men remained silent until Flint had parked in front of the Dead River Bar. They entered the dimly lit establishment, and Rafe led the way to a booth in the back even though there were no other customers in the place.

Sally Jean Mabry, part owner and occasional bartender sashayed her way to the booth. She was an older woman, but you wouldn't know it by the tightness of her jeans or the coquettish smile that greeted them. "Well, if it isn't two of the most handsome men in the entire town."

"I'll take a beer," Rafe said, cutting short any opportunity for Sally to do her usual flirting.

"And I'll have a cup of coffee," Flint added.

Sally, obviously getting the message that neither man was in the mood for any fun, headed back to the bar to fill their orders. It took her only moments to set a cold frosted mug of beer in front of Rafe and a hot cup of coffee before Flint.

"So, Rand's magic elixir killed one, made one worse and made one better," Flint said.

"Which means it isn't the magic elixir we've been searching for." Rafe raised his mug and took a drink and then continued, "Lucas was devastated by Mimi's death. Even though she divorced him, I think he still loved her. He took her death so hard and has been so frantic to come up with something to help. He's in that lab day and night. Sooner or later he's going to crash and burn and be no help to anyone."

"Gemma says the same thing about you—that you're working too hard."

Rafe grinned ruefully. "I might be a little obsessed, but Rand is definitely possessed."

"He's been a doctor here for a long time. I'm sure it's got to be tough on him to be so helpless in this situation," Flint replied.

Rafe shook his head. "He was like a madman, refusing to believe that Wylie was gone. It was like a scene from some awful movie. I just needed to get out of there for a little while," Rafe said and then took another drink. "Thanks for riding to my rescue."

Flint leaned back in the booth and studied his old friend. Rafe still had the same sandy-blond hair and pale brown eyes that he'd had as a kid, but his boyish looks had matured into those of a handsome man.

"How on earth did this happen, Rafe?" he said with a touch of wry amusement. "We were supposed to blow this town and never look back, and now we're both back here and stuck."

"I know you came back to help your brother, but why didn't you head back to Cheyenne when Theo got well?"

Flint leaned forward. "By the time Theo was well, the police department here was in chaos. I decided to stick around, and I found myself Chief of Police." He couldn't tell Rafe the real reason he hadn't returned to Cheyenne. He couldn't confess that he'd run from the weight of failure there.

"And now you find yourself in a situation where a woman is depending on you to protect her life."

Flint nodded.

"I was just supposed to be working here temporarily," Rafe said. "I made a promise to my father that I'd come back here and volunteer some time. I finally made the time to return, and then the quarantine trapped me."

"I was sorry to hear about your father's death," Flint said sympathetically.

"Thanks. After he passed it seemed even more important that I fulfilled my promise to him to come back here and volunteer at the clinic temporarily."

"I heard you've been living and working in New York City. That's a far cry from Dead River."

Rafe smiled. "When I left Dead River I wanted to get as far away as possible. I'd spent so many years being the kid from the wrong side of the tracks that I wanted a big city where I could make my own way and become the man I knew I could be without the emotional chains of my past hanging around my neck."

"I've been toying with the idea that once Hank Bittard is behind bars again and I've got that little creep Jimmy Johnson in jail, it might be a good time for me to get out of law enforcement."

Rafe looked at him in surprise. "What else would you do?"

"I'm not sure. I've been thinking about buying some property and trying my hand at ranching." Even as he said the words, a vision of Nina filled his head.

She could be by his side no matter what he did for a living, but she'd made it clear she wasn't looking for the same kinds of things he ultimately wanted in his life.

"I'd like to find me some sweet honey who adores me and who I love and not just grow some cattle, but maybe a couple of kids, too," Flint said.

The two remained in the bar for another half hour, talking about the past and the friendship they had shared, laughing at some of the antics they'd pulled when bored or just angry at the entire world as only teenage boys could be.

The lightness of the conversation came to an end when Rafe finished his beer. "I suppose I should get back," he said with obvious reluctance.

Flint emptied his coffee and stood. He threw enough money on the table to pay for their drinks. "I need to check in on my grandmother." His heart tightened as he thought of her condition worsening. How long could she hang on? How long before her body just got tired and gave up the fight?

"It's odd that the same serum given to three people would have such a variety of results," Flint said when they were back in his car and headed to the clinic. "One is better, one is worse and one died. How do you make sense of that?"

"We can't," Rafe replied. "We've told Lucas that maybe he needs to stop and just wait for the CDC expert to arrive, but he's like a man possessed."

"It probably doesn't help that it was his ex-wife who was the first victim. Thank God Theo and baby Amelia got a clean bill of health since they were some of the last people Mimi Rand had contact with," Flint replied.

"I just wish we could get a handle on why some people get sick and why others don't. It's as if some people are completely immune, but we can't figure out why." Rafe sighed in frustration as Flint parked in front of the clinic. "At least we got a bit of good news today that Dr. Goodhue should be arriving in the next day or two."

"That is good news. Hopefully, she'll be able to get to the bottom of things," Flint replied.

"Thanks for the break."

"Not a problem," Flint said in return.

Both men got out of the car and when they reached the clinic, they said their goodbyes and parted ways. Rafe headed for his office, and Flint went in search of his sister.

He found her coming out of a patient room and at the sight of him, her eyes welled up with tears, and she moved into his embrace. He nearly swallowed her petite frame as she hugged him for a long moment without saying anything.

She finally stepped back from him and swept a strand of her long blond hair over her shoulder. "Have you heard?" she asked, her green eyes simmering with emotion.

He nodded. "I just spent some time with Rafe and he filled me in."

"We almost lost her, Flint. She was on the very brink of death before we finally got her stabilized again."

"But she is stabilized again and still hanging on," he replied. "You know she's a tough one."

"I know, but this afternoon it got really scary. Rafe told you that Wiley Simms passed?"

"And that Tyler Miles regained consciousness," he said. "Are you doing okay?"

"As well as can be expected," she replied. "I was pretty upset earlier but I've calmed down some in the past hour or so."

He tipped her chin up with a finger. "Keep that pretty chin up, Gemma. You're a strong woman. We're all going to get through this."

She gave him a small smile. "I can't believe my serious, intense brother is actually offering words of optimism."

"Must be the company I've been keeping lately," he replied. "I'm heading into the isolation unit to see Grandma. I'll talk to you later."

Flint's footsteps slowed as he headed for the isolation unit where his grandmother had been for so long. He loved her deeply, but hated coming to see her here.

He wanted to visit her at her house. He wanted to

smell the scent of home, not the biting smell of anti-septic and sickness.

His desire to leave Dead River had never been about escaping his grandmother. It had simply been a young man's need to find his own way in the world.

He suited up in protective gear in order to enter the unit that now held only one bed. Wylie's body had apparently been taken out, and Tyler must have been moved to another area.

Once in protective gear, he stepped into the unit and approached his grandmother's bed. Monitors and machines and IVs were all hooked up to her, but what broke his heart was how small, how very fragile she looked in the big hospital bed.

Dottie Colton had always seemed bigger than life to Flint. Although loving and kind, she had a will of steel. Even at seventy-five years old, she'd always had her short gray hair perfectly coiffed and her makeup impeccable.

Now her hair was a ratty mess, and her skin had a fragile pallor that was alarming. He stepped up to the side of her bed as his heart squeezed so tight he could scarcely breathe.

"Gram, you have to keep fighting this," he said softly. "You have to get well. We all still need you here with us." Emotion choked up in the back of his throat.

He wanted to touch her, to stroke his finger down her cheek or touch her arm to let her know she wasn't alone, but he didn't. With all the protective gear he had on, it wouldn't be like touching her at all.

He wanted to tell her he was sorry for being such a handful as a teenager, that he was grateful to her for giving him the tools to become the man that he'd become.

He needed her to know that she'd been the best surrogate parent and loving caretaker that he and Theo and Gemma could have ever wanted.

He finally left the unit, knowing there was nothing he could do here to help. Besides, it was almost time to pick up Nina, and he still needed to stop by the store to buy a winter coat for her.

The lack of judgment he'd shown today by leaving Mike alone in the woods made him worry about his ability to keep her safe. It would only take one false move, one inattentive moment for tragedy to strike.

He was determined not to let that happen. Her safety had to be his number-one priority right now.

It was just after nine when Gemma left the clinic. As she stepped outside into the darkness of the night, she breathed a sigh of relief that this dreadfully long and traumatic day was finally over.

All Gemma had ever wanted to be was a nurse to help people, but she'd never dreamed that she'd be in an impotent position of fighting to help keep people alive because of a terrible, unknown virus.

She was bone weary from the emotional toll of the day, but the brisk, cold night air invigorated her for the walk home. Unless the weather was terrible, she almost always walked home after work, finding the quiet time and the exercise a way to unwind from the day's events.

It wouldn't be long before full-blown winter would be upon them, and then she would no longer be able to enjoy the walk home from work. She pulled her blue coat closer around her as she hit the edge of Main Street where the wind was more prominent.

The storefronts were all dark. Dead River had closed for the night. She'd never been afraid walking the deserted street to get to her house.

She'd grown up in this town and was as familiar with the streets as she was with her own heartbeat. It broke her heart that even during the day, the streets had a forlorn, deserted feel of a ghost town, an effect of the virus.

But good news was on the horizon. Word had it that in the next day or two CDC expert Dr. Colleen Goodhue would be arriving with advanced equipment and her years of experience in fighting mysterious viruses. Despite the horror of the day, the news of her imminent arrival had filled everyone with new hope.

She paused in front of the Home and Hearth store, gazing into the window at the attractive autumn display. Gram Dottie used to love to shop here. Gemma used to tease her that if she could, she'd buy at least one of every item in the store.

How Gemma wished she could tease with her grandmother now. Seeing her grandmother so still and so lifeless each day broke Gemma's heart. Gemma had seen enough people succumb to the disease now to know that there were no guarantees Gram Dottie would ever walk out of the clinic again.

Hopefully, Dr. Goodhue would find the answers that would save not only Gram Dottie but also all the people who were sick with the virus.

She moved away from the store and continued down the street. She hadn't gone far when she thought she heard footsteps behind her. She halted and listened.

Hearing nothing, she glanced over her shoulder and saw nobody on the street.

She was tired and besides, if somebody else was out walking, it wasn't as if she owned the street. Still, as she continued forward, she picked up her pace just a little bit.

In the distance she could see the light of the single business that still remained open. The café was the one establishment on Main Street that remained open until ten.

She had only walked a few feet more when she felt a rush of wind behind her. She was struck from behind and swung into the alley between two stores.

Before she had a chance to scream, a muscular arm wrapped around her neck, and she was pulled tight against a solid male form. Shocked by the unexpected attack, she was momentarily frozen.

However, as the arm tightened, cutting off her air, she tried to stomp on his feet, kick back at his legs in an effort to get free. Her hand scrabbled at the arm that was threatening to render her unconscious or dead. She was frantic, unfocused, like a wild animal caught in a trap.

She fought not only to break his grasp on her, but more important, she also fought against her own fear. Somewhere in the back of her mind she knew she needed to get past the terror of the moment and think clearheadedly.

She'd taken self-defensive classes, and they'd practiced this very scenario a hundred times. What was she supposed to do? What had she been taught? She dropped her hands from around her neck and instead used an elbow to jab backward with all the force she could muster. Her reward was a deep grunt and a lessening of the pressure around her neck.

She didn't wait but delivered another back jab and at the same time stomped down on the man's foot. The attacker uttered a curse, and suddenly his arm was gone from around her neck. She didn't waste time; she ran from the alley as if the very devil himself was after her.

She didn't look back, but kept her gaze focused on the lighted front of the café. She ran as fast as she possibly could, unaware that she was crying until the lights of the café blurred.

Hearing nobody in pursuit of her didn't slow her down. She yanked open the café door and nearly fell inside. A young woman stood behind the glass display that offered pastries and muffins.

Gemma twisted a dead bolt on the front door and then turned to the startled woman. "Call the police. I've just been attacked." She collapsed into one of the few chairs the small place had to offer and began to weep.

Chapter 9

Flint and Nina had just finished with their evening wine when he got the call that Gemma was at the café and had been attacked. He quickly buckled on his holster, grabbed his hat and together he and Nina got into his patrol car. He'd rather be handling this situation alone, but there was no way he could leave Nina by herself in the house.

He peeled out of his driveway, questions filling his mind. He'd gotten far too little information from Shelly Maxwell at the café, who had made the call to him and had only told him that his sister was in the café and that she'd been attacked while walking home from the clinic.

Attacked.

What did that mean? Had she been beaten? Raped? His gut twisted in knots. God, he couldn't imagine why anyone would want to hurt his sister. She was one of the sweetest, most caring young women in the entire town.

"If it was really bad, Shelly would have called for an ambulance and had you go to the clinic," Nina said, breaking the tense silence.

Flint took some comfort in her words, but not much. The idea of anyone accosting Gemma in any way both terrified and enraged him. He just needed to get to the café as quickly as possible and find out exactly what had happened and Gemma's condition.

He sped down Main Street and pulled to a halt in front of the café. His heart felt like it might explode out of his chest as he and Nina left the car and raced to the café door. Shelly unlocked it and let them in, and Gemma jumped out of the chair where she'd been sitting and ran to Flint.

As she burrowed herself against him, weeping into his chest, he ran his hands down her arms, over her back, to assure himself she had no obvious wounds.

Only then did he wrap his arms around her and hold her close as she continued to cry. Nina sat on a chair nearby, her features radiating worry.

"Gemma, I need you to calm down so you can talk to me," Flint finally said. He led her to the chair next to Nina and disentangled her from him and physically sat her down.

He pulled a chair up before her, much the way he had the night Nina had run into the police station, hysterical and crying after witnessing Jolene's murder. He waited for Gemma to catch her breath. "Now, tell me exactly what happened," he said.

"I was just walking home from the clinic, and he came from behind me." Gemma drew a deep breath as if mentally attempting to calm herself. "He shoved me into an alley and tried to choke me." She reached a hand up and touched her throat where Flint could see the skin was already bruising.

"Who was it?" he asked as he tightened his fists at his side.

"I...I don't know. I never saw him. He was behind me the whole time with his arm wrapped around my throat. I was so scared that for a minute I froze, and then I remembered my defense classes."

Her green eyes glittered with a sudden fierceness. "I used my elbows to jab him in his gut, and when he released his hold on me, I ran as fast as I could here."

Pride filled Flint at his sister's courage, pride and a gratefulness that she'd managed to get away. "Did you get any sense of him? Smell anything unusual? Did he say anything to you?"

She shook her head. "He didn't say a word. All I can tell you is that I got the impression he was tall and well-built." She wrapped her arms around her shoulders and shivered as if reliving those moments of sheer terror.

Nina moved her chair closer and grabbed one of Gemma's hands. "Thank God you managed to get away," she said.

"I've never been so scared in my entire life," Gemma confessed.

"Trust me, I know what that feels like," Nina replied.

"What alley was it? Between what stores?" Flint asked.

"Next to the hardware store and the dress boutique," Gemma replied.

Flint got up and pulled his cell phone from his

pocket. Within minutes he'd contacted two of his officers to head to the alley and look for evidence.

"Do you all want coffee or something?" Shelly asked awkwardly. She hadn't moved from behind the display counter.

"No, thanks, Shelly. You do whatever you need to close up for the night, and we'll be out of here as soon as possible," Flint replied. He returned to the chair next to Gemma.

"Have you been having any problems with anyone at work? Has anyone in town threatened you in any way?" Flint asked.

"No, nothing like that," Gemma replied. She and Nina still clutched hands, and neither appeared eager to break the contact. "I can't imagine who did this. Who might want to hurt me? Maybe it was just somebody who has the virus and a high fever that's driven him crazy."

"When you managed to run from him, did he pursue you?"

Gemma frowned. "I'm not sure. I didn't look back, but I don't think so. I didn't sense anyone behind me when I was running away. I just want to go home now," she said miserably.

"Would you rather come home with us for the night?" Nina asked.

Flint's heart expanded at Nina's generous offer and the fact that she obviously considered his home her own. He was also grateful at the obvious support she offered his sister, just as she had Molly when he'd had bad news to deliver to her.

Gemma shook her head and finally released her hold on Nina's hand. "Thanks, but I'll be fine at my own house. Maybe it was just some creep who thought I was an easy target since I was a woman out walking alone in the dark."

"Maybe," Flint replied, although he remained unconvinced. The man hadn't tried to steal her purse. He hadn't tried to rob her. He'd pulled her into that alley and tried to strangle her. "Are you sure you want to go home?"

"Positive. I'll be fine there." Gemma lifted her chin as if to prepare to battle her older brother. "I know now to be on guard."

Flint sighed, knowing how stubborn Gemma could be. "Okay, we'll take you home, but I'll have an officer do regular drive-bys of your house for the rest of the night and the next couple of nights."

It took them only minutes to be in Flint's car, Gemma riding shotgun and Nina in the backseat. "If you think of anything else that might help me find your attacker then you call me day or night," Flint said to his sister.

"You know I will," she replied. "I just can't imagine it being personal. I will tell you one thing. Starting tomorrow I'll be driving to and from work. My nightly walks home are finished for now."

"That sounds like a smart idea," Flint replied. He pulled up in the driveway of Gemma's house off Main Street. "Maybe this guy dropped something in the alley that will give up his identity."

"I hope so. With Dr. Goodhue coming in either tomorrow or the next day, I don't want to think about some attacking creep. I want all my focus to be on helping her find the answers to curing the Dead River virus."

"For now keep your self-defenses high. You know the drill, be aware of your surroundings, don't put yourself in a position of vulnerability and trust your instincts," Flint said. "Now, I'll walk you in and check out the house. Nina, you stay in the car with the doors locked, and I'll be out as quickly as possible."

"Take as long as you need. I'll be fine," Nina replied.

Flint walked his sister to her front door, and a knot of anger twisted in his stomach. She was so tiny and petite next to him. Clad in a pair of pale blue scrubs and a royal-blue coat, with her long blond hair loose around her shoulders, she definitely would have looked like a perfect victim as she'd walked home alone in the dark. But who would want to victimize her?

He quickly cleared the house, finding nothing to give him concerns. He returned to where she stood by the door and kissed her on the forehead. "Are you sure you're going to be okay?"

"I'm fine now," she replied. "I'm just going to chalk this up as one of the longest, worst days of my life and hope that I don't have another day like this for a very long time."

Flint gave her a quick hug and with the reminder for her to call him if she remembered anything else or if she just got scared, he left and hurried back to the car.

He got back behind the wheel, and Nina moved from the backseat to the passenger seat. "Is she all right?" Nina asked worriedly.

"She insisted she was fine." Flint backed out of the driveway. "But I'm not fine. I'm beyond angry. If she hadn't managed to get away then she wouldn't have been found until somebody stumbled over her body in the morning."

They rode for a few minutes in silence. "Her description, as minimal as it was, makes me think of Hank Bittard," Nina finally said.

The knot in Flint's stomach tightened. "That's the first thing I thought, too. What I can't imagine is why he'd go after Gemma? She's no threat to him. She doesn't know anything about his crimes and can't hurt him in any way. It just doesn't make sense to me."

"It's hard to make sense of anything that's happening these days," Nina replied.

By that time they had arrived back at Flint's house. He pulled into the garage, and they got out and entered into the kitchen. "It's late. You can go on to bed if you want. I'm putting on a pot of coffee and staying up until I hear from my men who are checking out that alley."

"I wouldn't mind a cup of coffee before heading to bed," she replied. "Unless my presence would bother you."

"You never bother me, Nina," he said honestly.

"Good." She sat down at the table while he fixed the coffee. As it began to drip through the carafe and fill the kitchen with its fragrant scent, he leaned a hip against the counter and frowned thoughtfully.

"I keep trying to think of a logical motive if Gemma's attacker was Hank," he said.

"Maybe his motive is nothing but sheer madness," she replied. "If what you believe is true, then he's probably been living in the woods like some crazed survivalist. Maybe he only wanted to choke her into unconsciousness and then steal whatever she had in her purse that might be useful to him."

"I don't know. It seems to me if all he wanted was her purse, he could have just grabbed it from her and run. He didn't have to pull her into the alley and try to choke her." Flint turned to the counter and pulled two mugs from the cabinet.

"Is it possible it was some sort of revenge against you?" Nina asked. "I mean, you are trying to hunt him down."

"If his intention was to threaten me and get me to back off, then he tormented the wrong man," Flint said intently. "Gemma told me this was the longest, worst day of her life," he said as he poured the coffee and carried the mugs to the table.

"It sounds to me like it hasn't exactly been a stellar day for you, either," she replied, her hazel eyes filled with soft empathy.

"I've had better days, and I've had worse."

She tilted her head and looked at him curiously. "What could be worse?"

He leaned forward and cupped his hand around his mug, his thoughts taking him back to Cheyenne and Madelaine. He stared for a long moment at Nina, wondering if he wanted to share that day, his utter failure, with her.

He hadn't spoken about it with anyone here in Dead River. It had been a tear in his heart, a stain on his soul that he'd kept to himself. But now, with her soft gaze locked with his and knowing his desire for her to share all that she was with him, he felt the need to tell her.

"What could be worse is being responsible for a woman's safety, to have the duty to get her into a courthouse where she was set to testify against members of a gang and to have her shot dead while she's walking right beside you on the courthouse steps."

He waited for her to flinch, for a hint of disgust to

darken her eyes, but neither happened. Her gaze never left his. "This happened in Cheyenne?"

He nodded. "It's part of why I came back here. I couldn't live with my failure to perform my duty properly."

"And it was all your failure alone?"

He looked at her in surprise. "What do you mean?"

"Who shot her?" Nina asked, initially not answering his question.

"There was a punk gangster hiding up in a tree. It was a perfect sniper attack." He took a drink of coffee, as if it could wash away the taste of failure, of guilt that had lingered inside him since that day.

"And it was your job to check the trees? To guard the entire perimeter? You were the only officer on protective duty?"

"Of course not. We had a team in place."

"And yet it was your personal failure alone?" She offered him a small smile. "How arrogant you are to take all of the blame. How about you cut yourself a break? It wasn't your personal failure, it was a system fail that ended in tragedy, but you can't carry the guilt of that around in your heart."

"I have, for over a year now. It haunts me and what haunts me even more is now that you're under my protection, I'm somehow going to fail you, too." His voice rang with a hollowness that his heart had owned for so long.

Nina reached for his hand. He took hers, clinging to it as if it were a pathway through the jungle of his emotions. "It's time to let go, Flint. You did the best you could, but circumstances weren't completely in your control. It's way past time for you to forgive yourself."

He squeezed her hand. "I couldn't forgive myself if I allowed anything to happen to you."

"Nothing is going to happen to me," she replied with a firm commitment he wanted to believe. "Flint, whatever happened in Cheyenne has nothing to do with what's happening here. You're a good chief of police working under incredibly stressful circumstances. It's amazing you and your men have managed to keep the peace as well as you have in a town gone crazy."

"I'm not sure what I'm going to do when you aren't here with me anymore," he said truthfully.

Before she could reply, his cell phone rang. He plucked it from his pocket and answered. The news that was delivered was both frustrating and yet somehow not unexpected.

"My men found nothing in the alley that they believe is related to the attack on Gemma," he said as he dropped the phone back into his pocket. "I just feel like we can't catch a break on anything."

Nina stood and carried her cup to the sink. "Hopefully, Dr. Goodhue will arrive tomorrow and be able to find a cure for the virus soon."

Flint felt the tick of a clock where his heartbeats should be. "I want Hank Bittard behind bars before the quarantine is lifted."

"You'll get him, Flint. I have every confidence in you. And now I'm heading to bed." She left the sink, and to his utter surprise stopped next to him and dropped a soft kiss on his forehead. "On your worst day you couldn't be a failure, Flint Colton," she said and then left the kitchen.

Flint reached up and touched his forehead where the warmth of her lips lingered. He knew at that moment she was his special woman, the one he wanted by his side through the rest of his life.

His love for her was undeniable, and his desire to have her as part of his life forever was an aching need inside him.

Now all he had to do was catch a killer, trap a thief and get whoever assaulted his sister, and in his spare time try to convince a woman that her place in life was not being alone, but rather sharing life with him.

Ten days had passed since the night of Gemma's attack. Ten days filled with frustrations and disappointments. The imminent arrival of Dr. Colleen Goodhue had been postponed once again, and Flint and his men had run into dead end after dead end in the hunt for Hank and Jimmy and the man who had attacked Gemma.

All of Gemma's coworkers had been interviewed, along with any of her friends and like Flint, nobody could believe that anyone would want to harm his sister in any way. She just didn't make enemies.

It was the day before the big feast at the diner and while Nina knew her thoughts should be consumed with the preparations, instead she found herself sitting at the counter and thinking about Flint.

It had been just over three weeks ago that she had witnessed Jolene Tate's murder and her house had burned down. It had been three weeks ago that she had found herself a reluctant houseguest in Flint's home, but if felt like a lifetime ago.

More than that, being in his house with him felt like a normal life she'd never thought possible for herself. She liked starting her mornings sitting across from him at the table and talking about their plans for the day or the cold front that had moved in a couple of days ago.

She loved cooking for him. She'd quickly discovered that there seemed to be nothing she made that he didn't like, and he was always appreciative and complimentary.

More than anything she loved their evenings together when they kicked back with a glass of wine and unwound. The only difference between them and any married couple was the fact that after their wine and conversation they didn't go to bed together, but instead went their separate ways.

The sexual tension between them had once again risen to levels that were impossible not to feel. She wanted him again, and she knew he wanted her, too.

There were moments when she was in bed alone and he was on the sofa that she wondered why she was denying him, why she was denying herself what she wanted. What harm could come from making love with him again?

At any single moment of any day or night, Hank Bittard could be captured and her time with Flint would be over. Why not take advantage of every minute she had with him before that happened?

Still, they'd managed to fight their attraction and keep everything aboveboard, but it grew more difficult with each passing night.

"I figured you'd be buzzing around today like a fly at a picnic," Grace said, pulling Nina from her thoughts as she sat on a stool next to where Nina had been perched since the lunch rush had left.

Nina smiled at her friend. "I think I overmanaged

things so much in the past week or two that today I'm finally all managed out."

"This is the calm before the storm," Grace observed.

"Exactly," Nina replied. "You know I'll be back to being the usual maniac tomorrow."

"It's your big day. You're allowed to be a maniac," Grace replied with an easy smile.

"Since I'm not opening until eleven tomorrow, I wasn't sure how Flint intended to get me to work a little later than usual, but he insists that he's taking the holiday off and will be here with me all day."

"That's nice. He deserves a day off. He's been working seven days a week since Bittard escaped custody. And Wilma and Molly are going to clean up and set out the centerpieces tonight after we close so that everything is holiday ready in the morning," Grace said.

"And Charley and Gary will both be here way before dawn cooking up all kinds of goodness." Nina took a sip of the tepid tea she'd been nursing while she'd been seated at the counter.

"By the time we walk in here tomorrow morning, the place is going to smell like heaven on earth," Grace said.

"Speaking of heaven on earth, how's my pretend nephew doing?"

Grace's face beamed with a smile. "He's doing great." She checked her wristwatch. "You'll see him for yourself as usual in about an hour."

"Of all the kids who come in here, he's my very favorite," Nina confessed. "There's such a sweet innocence about him."

Grace laughed in obvious amusement. "You might

rethink that if you spent some extra time with him. Trust me, he's a great kid, but he's definitely no angel."

"That's okay. An angel might be too boring," Nina replied.

Grace gestured toward her cup. "You want me to make you a fresh cup of tea?"

"Thanks, that would be nice," Nina agreed.

Grace got up and as she fixed a new drink, Nina tried to dig for energy to get up and do something, do anything, but all her frantic energy had been expended over the past couple of days.

She'd overmanaged, overprepared and now found herself with nothing to do but wait for her big day to arrive. It was a day she hoped would make up for every bad holiday she'd ever spent as a child. She wanted it to be a day of community and counting blessings despite everything that had happened to the town.

Grace returned to her stool next to Nina and set the cup of hot tea before her. "How's Flint doing? He's got to be so frustrated that he still doesn't have Bittard under arrest."

Nina's heart fluttered as she once again thought of her housemate. "Frustrated is an understatement."

She remembered what he had told her about what he considered his personal failure in Cheyenne, and far too often lately she believed she saw a hint of new failure in his eyes. It was only as they talked during the evenings that she saw that haunting emotion eventually disappear.

"If he could just catch one break, either arrest Jimmy or Hank or find out who attacked Gemma, it would help," she finally said. She wrapped her hands around the warmth of her cup.

"Does he still think it was Hank who attacked Gemma?" Grace asked.

"That's what his gut instinct is telling him, but there's no hard evidence to positively prove it, and he's having trouble coming up with a reasonable motive for Hank to go after her."

"The whole thing is so scary. I can't remember a time when anyone was ever attacked just walking down Main Street, day or night," Grace said. "Those kinds of things never happened in Dead River before."

"Flint's biggest fear is that he won't get Bittard and Jimmy behind bars before the quarantine is finally lifted."

"There doesn't seem to be any reason to believe that's going to happen anytime soon," Grace replied drily. "We can't even get the expert from the CDC here."

"According to Flint, the latest news is that she's due to arrive in the next week. Let's hope there isn't another postponement of her getting here," Nina said.

"Then Flint must feel like he's working against a ticking time bomb to accomplish what he wants to before a cure is found and the quarantine is lifted."

Nina nodded, thinking of the tension that she could see building in Flint every night, a tension that even a hot meal and soothing words couldn't dispel.

She ached for him, for his pain and weariness. She wanted to somehow make his world right, but she knew there was nothing she could do to help him with the issues he faced. All she could really do was to provide him a soft place to fall each night when another fruitless day had passed.

She whirled on her stool and looked around the

empty diner. "I hope everyone is building up an appetite to come in tomorrow," she said. "I think today has been the slowest we've had since the virus first struck."

"Maybe people will wander in around dinnertime. This is always the slowest time of the day," Grace replied.

"The lunch crowd was nearly nonexistent," Nina said.

Grace looked at her worriedly. "I know it's really none of my business, but with the virus and the lack of customers, are you in financial trouble?"

"Not yet, but if this continues for another couple of months, I'll be singing a different tune," Nina admitted. Thankfully, over the past two years she'd managed to squirrel away some profits to give her a bit of a cushion, but the cushion wouldn't last forever.

"Surely this can't last another couple of months," Grace replied. "If it does I think we'll all be crazy."

At that moment the door opened and a couple came in and took a booth next to the windows. Grace got up to serve them, and Nina sipped her hot tea and tried not to think about how difficult it would be when the day came that it was time to leave Flint behind and get back to her own life.

She'd never dreamed she'd settle in so comfortably with him, and it scared her more than a little bit. She'd always been so clear on what her path should be through life, but when she was with Flint, her vision of her future got a little fuzzy.

When Billy came through the door at his usual time, Nina was ready for him with a plate of oatmeal cookies and a big glass of milk. "Mom says you spoil me," he said as she sat in the chair across from him.

"I work at it when I can," Nina replied lightly.

Billy grabbed a cookie from the platter and munched it as he gazed at her thoughtfully. He chased the cookie with a drink of milk. "You should be a mom," he announced.

"I'm okay being a favorite fake auntie," she replied.

"But you should be a mom because you'd make a really good one," he replied. "I know about these things. You're nice, and you care and you have good mom eyes, like my mom has."

Nina laughed. "And what exactly are good mom eyes?"

"They have love in them."

Billy reached for another cookie as a sudden, unexpected rush of emotion rose up in Nina. She visited with him for a few minutes and then went into her office and closed the door.

She sat at her desk and fought against the alien emotions Billy's simple observations had managed to evoke inside her. She had never, ever considered having a child before, but Billy's words had pulled forth a deep yearning she'd never experienced.

What would it be like to carry a life inside you? To give birth to a baby and have such love in your heart for another human being? For the first time Nina realized she had the capacity to love a child, and if she closed her eyes and envisioned what that child might look like, she was somehow unsurprised to see rich brown hair and the vivid green Colton eyes.

Chapter 10

Nina was like a frenzied comet from the moment she woke up the next morning. Flint watched in amusement as she buzzed around the kitchen, making a breakfast big enough for a dozen people.

"Are we expecting company this morning?" he asked.

She refilled his coffee cup and then hurried back to flip the bacon she had frying. "No, why?"

"Aren't we having a big feast later today?"

She paused with a fork in her hand and looked at the stack of pancakes that was tall enough to nearly tumble over, the bowl of eggs she had ready to scramble and the tower of toast that had already been buttered. "Frenetic energy," she finally said with an impish grin.

"I think this means we'll be enjoying the later meal rather than the lunchtime meal at the diner."

"Sounds like a good plan to me," she replied and turned back to the sizzling bacon.

Flint leaned back in his chair, content to drink his coffee and just watch her burn off energy. They'd never be able to eat everything that she'd prepared, but that didn't matter. They'd eat leftovers tomorrow for breakfast.

Today he intended to let nothing bother him. He wasn't going to dwell on the weeks of failures and disappointments. He didn't intend to think about the virus or the missing Colton ring. He didn't want to dwell on the missing fugitives or the attack on Gemma. Today he just wanted to exist in the glow that was Nina.

He and his men had been working around the clock for weeks without much time off. Today he'd given the day off to as many of his officers as possible so they could enjoy a day of thanks and blessings with their families. The town was staffed with a skeletal crew who had volunteered to work the holiday.

This was Nina's day, and he planned to spend it all with her at the diner, enjoying watching her feed and visit and laugh with those who came in to indulge in the free feast.

He hoped the day went exactly as she wanted, exactly as she'd planned, and there would be lots of people who, for a single day, managed to put everything negative behind them and just be thankful that things weren't worse.

By the time she got all the food ready and sat across from him, she looked at the table and then at him. "This is ridiculous. You should have done something to stop me."

He grinned. "As I recall, one of the first rules laid

down was that you were captain in the kitchen, and my only power in here was to sit at the table and keep my mouth shut until it was time to eat."

"There should be exceptions to rules," she replied.

"I wasn't willing to go there," he replied. "Besides, we can always wrap up the pancakes and some of the bacon to eat tomorrow."

She nodded absently, and he knew he'd lost her to whirring thoughts in her own brain. He filled his plate with a couple of spoonfuls of eggs, a few pieces of bacon and several pieces of toast.

"I've already called Charley to check on things at the diner four times this morning," she said and snagged a piece of bacon. "He said if I call him again he's turning off his cell phone and will burn all the pies."

Flint smiled. "I'm sure he and the others have everything under control."

She crunched into her bacon and chewed, her brow wrinkled in thought. "Don't let me walk out of here this morning without the aprons we bought last night," she said.

On the way home from work the night before, they had stopped at Home and Hearth, and she'd bought black half aprons for the waitresses that were decorated with colorful turkeys.

"I won't let you get out of here without them," he replied.

She frowned. "Maybe they're too tacky."

"They aren't tacky, they're fun and festive," he assured her.

She smiled at him gratefully. "You know I might be having a mini meltdown."

"I know," he replied easily. "I can handle it. Now,

eat something besides that piece of bacon. I'm not convinced that you'll take time to eat a meal later today."

She dutifully filled her plate, but it was obvious breakfast was the last thing on her mind. "I hope I have enough food. It's hard to plan right when you don't know for sure how many people are going to show up."

"I'm sure you planned perfectly," Flint replied.

She fell silent as they ate, although Flint knew her head was still spinning with thoughts and hopes for the day. She'd told him last night that she wanted to be at the diner by nine to make sure things were all ready for the eleven o'clock opening.

There was no way, Flint knew, she'd be able to wait until nine. It was just after seven now, and he had a feeling the minute the table was cleared and they'd officially dressed for the day, she'd be chomping at the bit to head out.

Sure enough, when the leftovers were put away and the table had been cleared, she didn't linger, but instead headed to her room to dress in the diner uniform.

Flint hurried into his master bedroom. Having already showered, he picked out a pair of black dress slacks and a dress shirt that sported the colors of black and brown and rust. A suitable choice for the day, he thought.

It seemed almost sacrilegious to add his holster and gun to wear to a Thanksgiving celebration, but he certainly hadn't forgotten his number-one role was as chief of police and protector of Nina.

It would be nice if either Hank or Jimmy would be lured to the diner for a turkey dinner. It would be nice if driven by hunger one or the other or both would show up and turn themselves in.

"Yeah, right," he muttered drily. Like that would happen. The last thing he did before leaving the room was grab a small brown bag off the dresser top, and then he left the room and headed back to the kitchen to wait for Nina.

The air now smelled of her scent of vanilla and peaches and stirred the desire in him that was never far from the surface where she was concerned.

He was just about to sit down when she came into the kitchen. Even though he had seen her what seemed like a thousand times in the slim black slacks and the white blouse that all the waitresses at the diner wore, today something about her half stole his breath away.

Maybe it was the exceptional sparkle in her beautiful eyes, or the way her hair tumbled across her shoulders with just a little more wave than usual, whatever it was evoked desire for her that heated his blood.

"I know it's early but…"

"You're ready to go," he finished her sentence.

"Do you mind?" She looked at him pleadingly.

"Nah, I figured. Didn't you have aprons?"

Her eyes widened, and she whirled on her heels and left the kitchen. She returned a moment later with the aprons in hand. "Thanks for reminding me."

"Before we leave, I've got a little something for you," he said and grabbed the bag he'd set on the table.

"Something for me?" She set the aprons on the table and looked at him curiously.

"Don't get too excited," he warned as he pulled from the bag a turkey lapel pin. It was fat and colorful and definitely tacky.

"Oh, Flint! I love it." She took it from him and pinned it onto her blouse.

"Punch the stomach," he said.

She looked at him dubiously and then hit the fat brown turkey belly. "Gobble, gobble, gobble!" The sound came from the pin and set Nina into a fit of giggles.

Flint's day was already a success, especially when she threw her arms around his neck and kissed him on the cheek. The kiss was quick, but managed to warm him from his head to his toes.

Unfortunately, she quickly danced away, grabbed the aprons and looked at him expectantly.

"Okay, we're out of here," he said with a laugh.

It was just after eight when they got in the car to head to the diner. "At least the weather is cooperating," Flint said. The day was clear and bright and just cold enough to be invigorating.

"Thank goodness," Nina replied, squirming in the seat like a child eager to arrive at a birthday party.

When they got to the diner, Nina used her key to unlock the front door while Flint hovered just behind her, his hand on the butt of his gun. It might be a holiday, but that didn't mean criminals took the day off.

When they walked through the door, they were greeted with the scents of roasting turkeys, of cooking ham and the sweet fragrance of cinnamon and apples.

"The centerpieces look just like I envisioned," Nina said with enthusiasm. She placed the aprons she'd carried in over the back of a nearby chair.

Charley stepped out of the kitchen area and into the dining room. He looked at her in mock disgust. "I knew you'd be here early. You just couldn't help yourself even though I told you I had everything under control."

"Short of hog-tying her, I couldn't keep her home another minute," Flint said.

"Nothing wrong with a little hog-tying," Charley muttered and then disappeared back into the kitchen.

"He's just afraid I'll go in there and mess up his creative process," Nina said. "But I have no intention of going into the kitchen at all."

Flint took a seat at a nearby booth as she began to walk around to each table and make sure the centerpieces were exactly in the middle and the foliage was perfect.

He could sit and watch her forever. He loved the way she moved, her attention to detail. Her burnished-shaded hair seemed to shine particularly brightly among the fall colors of the decorations.

She paused in her table-check to make a pot of coffee and when it was finishing brewing, Flint helped himself to a cup and returned to his seat.

At nine o'clock the waitresses began to arrive. Molly was the first, followed closely by Wilma. Grace and her son, Billy, walked in soon after.

They all oohed over the aprons, and each one tied one on while Flint invited Billy to join him at his table. "You know it's going to be a long day," Flint said to Billy.

"I know. Mom already told me, but I'm ready for it. I brought my video game with me to keep me busy," Billy said.

Nina gave instructions to her staff and then came over to the table and dropped a kiss on Billy's forehead. "How about a cup of hot cocoa for my favorite little man?" she asked.

"That sounds good," he replied.

She went around to the back of the counter, and it took her only moments to place a cup of cocoa in front of Billy. She then leaned across the table and instructed him to punch the belly of her turkey pin.

As the pin gobbled, Billy giggled and shook his head. "That's so dumb, it's good," he exclaimed.

"And that's why I love it," Nina said with a warm gaze at Flint.

And then she was off once again, flittering around the dining room, chatting with her waitresses and watching the clock on the wall. Flint knew he'd have little of her attention today, and that was all right.

Today was her day, and hopefully when the doors opened at eleven, people would arrive to enjoy not just the food, but also her company. She was like a bright light in what felt like weeks and weeks of darkness.

At ten forty-five, Charley and his team began to carry food out of the kitchen and fill the top of the counter where electric servers and warming trays awaited them.

Flint and Billy moved to the two-top table where Billy usually spent his time when in the diner after school as several of the young men working in the kitchen removed the stools from in front of the counter.

Nina vibrated like a tuning fork a mere inch from a well of water as the clock ticked down and eleven arrived. "Ladies and gentlemen, we are officially open," she announced and unlocked the front door.

Nobody was waiting to come in, and Nina moved away from the door, her bright smile unwavering. "I imagine we'll see most people show up around noon," she said. "But of course people could start showing up at any time now."

She stood, as if unsure what to do next, and Flint wished there had been a dozen people lined up at the door just waiting for eleven o'clock to arrive.

Flint was eternally grateful when at eleven-fifteen the first people through the door were his brother, Theo, and Ellie, with baby Amelia in her arms.

He got up to greet his brother while Ellie headed for a booth and Nina went to the back to grab a baby chair. Flint grasped his younger brother's hand. "Thanks for showing up," he said.

Theo smiled. "When did you ever know me to miss a meal? Especially one that's free."

"How are you all holding up?" Flint asked. It had only been a month ago that Ellie had been threatened by a stalker who had followed her from her home-town when she'd taken the job at Theo's ranch as cook. Thankfully, the stalker had been caught, and Ellie and Theo were now engaged.

"Despite everything that's been happening here in town, personally, things just keep getting better and better," Theo said and shot a warm, loving glance at Ellie and Amelia.

An unexpected jolt of envy shot through Flint. He was thrilled that his brother looked happier than he had in a long time, and after the near devastating fall Theo had taken from a drug-crazed bronc, Flint couldn't think of anyone who deserved happiness more.

The fact that Ellie's stalker had managed to make love blossom between her and Theo had only been the cherry on top.

"How are things at the ranch?" Flint asked.

"Battened down for the winter. I've got enough firewood split to keep us cozy through the rough months," Theo replied.

The two brothers visited for a few minutes longer, and then Theo left to join his family, and Flint sat down once again across from Billy.

"You know, if you're hungry you can go get a plate of food," Flint said. "It's all ready and waiting."

"Mom told me not to be the first one through the line," Billy replied soberly.

Flint pointed to where Ellie was at the counter filling a plate. "Did she say anything about being second in line?"

"I think second is probably okay," Billy said and with a wide grin he left the table and headed for the counter.

Flint watched as Nina stood behind the counter, chatting with Ellie and helping to serve. Her face was beautiful, wreathed with a smile as she did what she did best…make other people feel important, make other people happy.

There was no question that lunch was a disappointment. There were a total of three groups…twelve diners that showed up. Each group chose a booth far away from the other people. They filled their plates, ate and then left. There was no sense of celebration, no festive laughter to fill the air.

Still, Nina refused to allow her high spirits to be dampened. "A lot of people don't eat Thanksgiving meal until three or so, don't you think?" she asked Grace as the two stood side by side behind the counter.

"When I was married and we all got together as a family, we usually ate around three or so," Grace agreed. "I think my son has found a new hero to worship," she said and gestured to the two-top where Billy and Flint were seated.

Their heads were together as it appeared Flint helped Billy with his video game. As Nina watched, the two males laughed and then high-fived each other. Her heart melted into a puddle of warmth.

Throughout the morning and early afternoon, Flint had kept Billy entertained, and the serious lawman had shown exceptional patience, an ability to connect and a tenderness that merely confirmed to Nina that Flint would make a wonderful father.

Not that it mattered to her. As much as she might yearn to have a child, as much as she'd enjoyed her time in Flint's home, there was still a hard knot in her heart that she believed would never be untied.

In the past week, she'd noticed a change in Flint's behavior toward her. He'd become more flirtatious with her, and he touched her more often, as if unable to help himself. It was almost as if he was courting her, and there was a part of her that liked it and a part of her that was afraid of it.

Two more groups came in, and she busied herself greeting them, shoving thoughts of Flint and fatherhood out of her mind. The two groups, Melissa and Marvin Baker and their two children, and Sam and Ginger Taylor and their three children were all friends.

They took tables next to each other in the center of the room and before long the sound of laughter filled the air.

Nina drank it in. This was what she'd wanted for this day. Hopefully, a little bit later the whole place would be filled with diners laughing and enjoying the food together.

It was about four when she saw Flint make a beeline for the food. She moved behind the counter. "Finally got over that big breakfast?" she asked with a grin.

"That seems like days ago," he replied and began to fill a plate.

"I appreciate you being here with me all day." She spooned a healthy portion of mashed potatoes onto his plate. "I know you must be bored to death."

"Actually, bored isn't so bad. I'm enjoying just relaxing and not thinking about anything too important today." He ladled gravy over his potatoes. "I'm sorry you haven't seen the crowd you'd hoped for so far."

"I think in about an hour or so we're going to see the people really start to pour in," she replied.

"I'm sure you're right," he said.

She thought she saw a hint of concern darkening his eyes, but she refused to dwell on it. She remained optimistic that as the afternoon grew later, people would begin to arrive and before they all knew it, there would be a full house.

For the next hour several more families came in, along with Harvey Watters. "Harvey, I thought you always took your meals at the café," Nina teased.

"Put a nice bench outside of here and I could always change my mind. I might be an old dog, but I can learn new tricks," he replied.

"I never doubted that, and don't be surprised if one of these days in the near future you see a bench sitting right outside my front window. Now, go help yourself to the food and enjoy," she said.

"I intend to do just that," he replied and headed directly for the counter.

Nina looked around in satisfaction. While there weren't that many diners, at least there were some, and the dinner hour was approaching quickly.

Billy had gone back into the large storage area where there was a cot, and when Grace had checked on him she'd returned and told Nina that he was sound asleep.

"I guess he got his belly so full, he's now indulging in another tradition of the Thanksgiving Day nap," she'd said with a laugh.

Flint wandered from table to table, visiting briefly with each guest. Nina couldn't help the way her gaze sought him often.

He looked so handsome in his dress shirt and slacks. She was used to seeing him either in his official uniform or in sweats in the evenings. Even the holster and gun that rode his hips didn't detract from his overall hotness.

He was not only touching base with his constituency, but was also helping to keep the atmosphere pleasant and friendly. In moments like this she found him almost too good to be true.

If she wanted to handpick a man for herself, Flint had all of the qualities she would ever want. It only made it more difficult that there was such an obvious chemistry between them, both sexually and emotionally.

She'd be perfectly content to be his lover until the relationship eventually burned out. Even after Bittard was in custody and the danger to her was over and she'd moved out of his house, she wouldn't mind continuing as his lover.

But she knew that wouldn't be fair to him. She'd watched him interact with his brother and Ellie and had seen a yearning in his eyes. She'd watched him with Billy and recognized his attributes as a potential father.

She already knew by living with him that he would make a wonderful husband, but she was unwilling to be a wife or a mother. Being his lover would only keep him bound and unavailable to find the woman who was exactly right for him, a woman who could give him everything he needed to be happy in life.

Her thoughts shifted from Flint as two more families entered the diner, trailed by Officer Patrick Carter. Wilma greeted the families and got them seated while Nina and Flint joined Patrick.

"Thanks for showing up," Flint said.

"Wouldn't have missed it," Patrick replied.

"Feel free to sit wherever you want," Nina said to the handsome officer. "And of course, fill your plate as high as you want."

Patrick leaned slightly closer to Nina. "Could you point me to a table where Grace is working?" His cheeks grew slightly dusky as Nina looked at him in surprise.

She pointed him to a table next to the window, and as he made his way to the table, she turned to Flint in amusement. "Do I smell a budding romance starting up?"

"Beats me, but Grace could do a lot worse. Patrick is a good man," Flint replied.

"And Grace is a wonderful woman, and she and Billy deserve only the very best," Nina replied. "And speaking of my favorite munchkin," she said as Billy appeared from the back room. She motioned him toward them. "I'll bet after that nice nap you had, you're ready for some dessert."

"Definitely," Billy replied.

"How about you sit down and I'll bring you a big piece of apple pie with whipped cream on top?" Nina asked.

"Awesome," Billy replied and headed toward his usual two-top table.

Nina tapped Flint in the center of his chest. "Sorry, big boy, but you're on your own." She gave him a cheeky grin as she went to take care of Billy.

"Here you are, my little man," she said a moment later as she placed the dessert in front of Billy. "I even added a couple of extra dollops of whipped cream."

"Thanks, Nina."

"You're welcome, squirt," she replied.

When she left his table she snagged hold of Grace's arm. "I think maybe Officer Carter has a bit of a crush on you," she told her friend.

Grace's cheeks grew pink. "Oh, surely not." Her blue eyes grew brighter. "Do you really think so?"

"He specifically asked to sit at a table that you were serving," Nina said.

Grace straightened her apron. "Maybe I should go see if he needs some more coffee."

Nina grinned. "Go get him, girl." Nina punched her turkey pin and laughed as it gobbled. Grace slapped her on the arm and then hurried to where Patrick sat alone.

"I find it slightly ironic that a woman who professes not to believe in marriage and family appears to be indulging in a little bit of matchmaking."

Nina whirled around to see Flint standing just behind her, an amused smile curving his lips. "Just because I don't believe in marriage and family for myself doesn't mean I don't believe in it for other people," she replied.

He looked at her for a long moment. "You're a mystery to me, Nina Owens, and there's nothing policemen like better than to get to the very bottom of a good mystery."

Nina's heart fluttered, but she held his gaze steadily. "No mystery here. Lots of women in this day and age are choosing the option of staying unmarried and not having children."

Before he could say anything, the diner door opened and half a dozen people came in, and Nina hurried to greet them. By five-thirty Nina stood against one wall and watched the diners.

There were probably fifteen families in all and while she'd hoped for at least twice that many, she was happy to see neighbors greeting neighbors and to hear the sound of laughter that filled the air.

It wasn't the huge celebration she'd envisioned, but at least some of the people in town had managed to overcome their fears and show up.

Charley and the rest of the kitchen staff kept the steamers and trays filled with fresh food, and the three waitresses bustled to keep up with drink orders and anything else they could do to accommodate their guests.

"Happy?" Flint stepped up next to where she leaned against the back wall.

She frowned thoughtfully. "Satisfied," she finally replied. "Happy would be twice as many people and three times as much laughter."

"Considering everything that's happened and the

mood of the town, you've had a far better turnout than I expected," he admitted. "I'll be honest with you, I worried that only a handful of people would turn out all day."

"Even though we've had a decent turnout, I'll warn you, you're probably going to be eating turkey sandwiches, turkey pot pie and turkey everything for dinner over the next week."

He smiled. "Thank goodness I like turkey."

The diner door swung open to admit another group, this one all men, and it was obvious they'd spent at least part of the afternoon celebrating the holiday with booze.

The group included Ralph Dane and Ted Garrett and a few others from both the gas station and the auto body shop. With loud laughter and more than a stumble or two, they made their way to one of two booths in the back that seated six.

"That's supposed to be Molly's area, but I'm going to have Wilma wait on them instead," Nina said and motioned toward the older, more experienced waitress.

She quickly explained the change in table duties and Wilma went to tell Molly. "That was nice," Flint said.

"That was smart," Nina countered. "Molly is too sensitive and having to wait on those guys would only remind her of Jimmy. Besides, they appear a little liquored up. Wilma will be able to keep them in line far better than Molly would. And now I think I'll head behind the counter to keep an eye on things."

There were several people there, filling second plates and grabbing dessert. There was no question that she was slightly disappointed by the turnout, but at the moment the diner was almost half-filled and she was grateful for each and every person who had come in throughout the day.

She glanced over to the table by the window where Patrick Carter had spent several hours. At the moment Grace stood next to the table, and it was obvious there was more than a little mutual flirting going on. Good. There was nothing Nina would like better for Grace and Billy than a terrific man in their lives.

She focused back on the people in front of her at the buffet. "John, you don't have enough stuffing on that plate to fill a baby," she said to the man who was slowly working his way down the buffet.

"I've got to save room on my plate for all the other good things," he replied. "There are just too many choices, and it all looks so delicious."

"Don't forget you can always grab a clean plate and come back for seconds or thirds," Nina reminded him.

John laughed. "I think thirds would be out of the question."

Ralph and Ted and their friends made their way to the counter, bringing with them the smell of beer and a touch of belligerence as they jostled against each other for position.

The first of the group who began down the line was a brawny, dirty-blond-haired young man who Nina didn't know by name, but had seen at the auto body shop. He slapped food on his plate quickly and was soon almost shoulder to shoulder with John.

"Hey, man, you breathing on me?" he asked John. "Don't breathe on me. I don't know you. I don't know if you've got the virus or not."

"I'm fine," John replied calmly. "I don't have the virus."

"I told you not to breathe on me and now you're talking to me?" The big guy threw his shoulder against John's.

And that was when all hell broke loose.

Chapter 11

The first indication Flint had that there was any kind of a problem was the splintering crash of a plate to the floor. Seated at Patrick's table, he initially thought one of the waitresses had dropped a dish while clearing a table.

It was only when he saw fists flying between two men at the buffet that he realized there was real trouble. He and Patrick jumped out of their chairs, and by the time they reached the counter, there were more than two men fighting.

It had become a melee that quickly spilled into the people seated at the tables. Food flew and women and children screamed and scurried toward the front door in an effort to get out of the way. It was as if all the stress the town had bottled up for the past two months exploded in a single instant.

Flint was vaguely aware of Nina, backed up from the counter, her face sheet-white as she stood like a frozen statue. He grabbed the back of Ralph Dane's shirt and yanked him back so that he could get to two men exchanging blows nearest the counter.

He grabbed one of the men by the shoulders and shoved him in the direction of the door. "Go home," he yelled. "Just get the hell out of here."

Nobody appeared to pay any attention to him. He heard Patrick shouting the same thing even as a table was flipped on its side and plates and glasses shattered to the floor.

"Everyone go home," Flint yelled again. He had only one pair of handcuffs tucked in his back pocket, not worth anything against a crowd gone crazy. The last thing he wanted to do was pull his gun. It would be downright irresponsible in this particular situation.

This was a brawl, a bar fight misplaced to the diner. Men who had never had trouble with the law were throwing punches to others as yells and obscenities filled the air.

Grace and Billy had joined Nina behind the counter, all three looking shell-shocked as the free-for-all continued. The longer it went on, the clash showed no signs of winding down.

Flint was grateful when the male kitchen staff appeared and began to help Flint and Patrick by breaking up fights and shoving people out the front door.

It felt as if every man in the place had gone mad, and they didn't care who they punched or what they broke. Centerpieces were thrown along with food and uppercuts. It was like every single male who had come into the diner had harbored a simmering impotence that had exploded in unbound rage.

The laughter that had filled the air before was gone, replaced by curses and grunts. Flint took a solid fist to his lower jaw but wasn't sure who had delivered the punch.

He lost track of time as he and Patrick and the men from the kitchen worked to clear the diner. Punch and pull, shove and stop, it became a physical rote in Flint's mind as they worked to clear the diner.

When the last person had finally been shoved outside Flint locked the door and leaned against it to catch his breath.

Patrick collapsed in a nearby chair, his shirt torn and one eye beginning to blacken. Utter silence reigned, and nobody moved. The diner was a disaster with tables overturned, broken dishes on the floor and food everywhere...on walls and underfoot.

Flint looked at Nina, who hadn't moved from her position behind the counter. Her face was completely blank of expression, but her eyes held a hollowness that made his heart ache for her.

Molly was the first person to move. She leaned down and picked up a plate from the floor and set it on one of the tables nearby that was still standing.

"Leave it." Nina's voice rang out sharply and broke the silence. "Leave it all. Charley, divide up all the food that's left over among you all and then everyone just go home. Lock up when you're finished. We're closed indefinitely. I'll be in touch with each of you in the next couple of days."

She turned her gaze to Flint. "Take me home," she said and moved toward where he still stood with his back against the door. She stopped so close to him he could feel her breath on his face. "Just please take me home," she said, her voice holding a hint of desperation he'd never heard before.

He unlocked the door, pulled his gun and then gathered her against his side. It was like trying to embrace a stone. She had no bend, no yield, as he ushered her to the passenger side of his car.

Thankfully, there was nobody lingering on the streets as he hurried around to the driver's-side door. Apparently, everyone who had been fighting inside had gone home or somewhere else.

He started the engine and then turned to look at her. She was curled into the corner of the car, her features still schooled into an utter blankness that he found far more frightening than if she'd been ranting and railing with rage or sobbing and wailing with tears.

He backed out of the parking space and headed for home. His gaze remained divided between the road and her. She stared straight out the window, and he didn't know whether to attempt to force a conversation or just keep his mouth shut.

Her big day had been ruined, and he didn't know how to fix the pain and utter disappointment he knew she had to be feeling at this moment. He had no words to take away the terrible ending of the perfect day she had planned for weeks.

The odd thing was he felt no pain radiating from her. He felt nothing, and that scared him more than anything. It was as if she were a stiff, brainless doll seated next to him.

Was she in some kind of shock? Should he be driving her to the clinic to be checked out by a doctor instead of taking her home? "Nina?" he finally ventured.

She raised a hand as if to ward off any conversation and continued to stare out the window.

Flint was grateful to finally pull into the garage at his house. They walked into the kitchen, and to his dismay she started to head directly for her bedroom.

"Nina, please don't," he said.

She turned and looked at him, her golden eyes holding none of the brilliant light that so defined her. "Don't what?"

"Please don't close yourself off from me. We've come too far together for you to do that." His need to break through her shock or whatever it was that had her so folded inward was beyond overwhelming.

Somehow he had to help her through this. Somehow he had to dig deep and find the right words and the right actions to comfort her, to put her shattered pieces back together again.

She stood for a long moment and then moved to the sofa and collapsed into the cushions. "I don't want to sit around and talk this to death. As far as I'm concerned it was just another disappointing, completely screwed-up holiday. I shouldn't have expected anything less."

There was no bitterness in her voice, just a deep weariness, a lack of spirit that broke his heart. He sat down on the opposite side of the sofa from her, afraid to intrude and yet unwilling not to be near her.

"Your holidays were never good?" he asked tentatively.

"My entire childhood was total hell, but it's the holidays that I remember the clearest." Her eyes darkened, and she stared off in the distance as if lost in memories.

Flint reminded himself that in all the time they'd spent together, in all the conversations they had shared, she'd never told him anything about her childhood; she'd only spoken about the time after she'd left Casper behind when she'd been an adult.

"Tell me, Nina. Tell me about your childhood and those holidays," he urged her. He wanted all of her, both her good memories and her bad. He needed all of her because he was so in love with her.

She ruffled a hand through her hair and released a deep sigh. "My childhood was like a lot of other childhoods, filled with dysfunction, denial and domestic abuse."

Flint leaned forward, a faint anger stirring inside him. "Your father abused you?"

She shook her head. "No, he never touched me, but he used my mother as a punching bag on a fairly regular basis." Finally, her eyes radiated with a depth of emotion...of pain.

"When I was really young, I didn't understand the whole cycle. I loved my father, but when he erupted into one of his fits of rage, I didn't know what to think." She paused and once again raced her hand through her hair, as if she could brush out the painful memories.

Flint moved several inches closer to her, still not invading her personal space but wanting to take her in his arms and banish anything that had ever hurt her in the past. "You said holidays were the worst?"

"My mother lived in some sort of fantasy world when it came to the holidays. It was always her goal to make it the best Easter or Halloween or Thanksgiving or Christmas possible. She wanted perfection. She planned the menus for days, made homemade centerpieces for the table. It didn't matter that it was just the three of us. She put in enough energy that she could have been planning a dinner party for twelve."

It was as if a dam had broken inside her and the words began to tumble out of her without any prompting from him. "Every holiday started with such promise. Mom would be in the kitchen cooking and Dad would be stretched out in his recliner watching television, and for a while I believed the day would pass without something terrible happening."

"But something bad always did happen," he said softly.

"Always." Her eyes were still dark but now held a hint of bitterness, as well. "By noon Dad was watching football and drinking beer and working up a good foul mood, and that mood always exploded at the dinner table. The ham was overcooked or undercooked. The glaze tasted bitter to him. Why didn't she know how to cook a good ham, a juicy turkey or whatever we were having for the main dish? By the time dessert came, if we made it to dessert, invariably a plate was thrown to the wall or the floor. He'd be boozed up and out of control."

"And then he'd beat her?" Flint moved yet again closer to her, trying to imagine navigating such violence and chaos as a child.

"It depends on what you consider a beating. Definitely he'd emotionally abuse her, telling her she was too stupid to live, a useless cow who nobody else would ever put up with. Sometimes it stopped at that, but other times he'd kick her and pull her hair, punch her down to the floor until his sick energy was finally spent. Then he'd go back to his recliner and brood for the rest of the day."

"And what would you do?"

"Crawl out from beneath the table or out of the pantry where I usually hid. I'd console my mother and then help her clean up whatever mess had been made. Of course, the violence wasn't just delegated to holidays. We never knew when he might explode."

"And this went on your entire childhood?" He couldn't imagine this being the background of the woman he knew, a woman who was always optimistic and a ray of sunshine in everyone's life.

"Until I was eighteen and left home. I got an apartment nearby, hoping it could be an escape place for my mother when things got too rough for her, but she never came. She just stayed with him and continued to endure his abuse."

"Why didn't she leave him?" Flint asked, even though he knew what the answer would probably be, the same answer that so many women in domestic abuse situations gave when asked why they stayed.

Nina gave him a wry look. "You've been in law enforcement long enough to know how many women stay with their abusers. She loved him. There were always those amazing honeymoon periods between the blowups when he'd bring home flowers and treat her so well. When things were good between them they were so good. She constantly told me he was a good man who just had a little anger problem."

She shook her head once again and released a bitter laugh. "By that time I didn't know who I disrespected more, my abusive father or my mother who stayed despite the abuse."

"She never called the police? Never reported the abuse?"

"She called a couple of times and the same two cops always showed up. They'd take my dad away for a couple of hours or the night but he'd be home the next day." She looked him straight in the eye and there was censure in her voice. "You see, my dad was a cop, and his cop friends all covered for him."

Flint sucked in a gulp of air in surprise. Her father had been a police officer?

"Let's just say the whole experience left me with a bad taste for men in law uniforms," she added.

He thought of all the times he'd come into the diner and she'd been accommodating, but rather cool. It hadn't been Flint the man she'd been responding to, but rather Flint in his uniform as the chief of police.

"When I was twenty-five my father beat my mother to death." She said the words starkly. A new wave of shock flew through Flint. "He went to prison. I discovered my mother had named me beneficiary on a life insurance policy, and that was when I turned my back on Casper forever. For years I harbored such darkness and bitterness in my heart. I refused to celebrate any holidays. I never stayed too long in one place to build any kind of relationships. I was like a zombie, just going through the motions of life."

He could stand it no more. He moved so that he was right next to her, and he took her hand in his. Cold…icy, her fingers curled around his as if seeking his warmth. "And then you arrived here in Dead River," he said.

"With a new attitude," she replied. "For some reason when I decided to settle here, I also decided I had a choice. I could either go through my life being angry and bitter, or I could decide to be a positive, optimistic force as the owner of the diner."

"And you have been," he replied and squeezed her fingers a little tighter. "Nina, today wasn't your failure. You did everything right to make it a wonderful holiday."

She withdrew her hand from his. "No, it was my failure. It was my stupid hope for one perfect holiday in a town that has quickly lost all hope. It was my failure because I misjudged how broken this town is right now. I thought food and fancy centerpieces could overcome everything, and that was my biggest mistake."

She rose suddenly. "I don't want to talk about it anymore. I've told you more about my life than I've ever told anyone, and I'm exhausted. Although I'm planning on keeping the diner closed for a couple of days to get things cleaned up, I intend to be there in the morning. I'll call Charley to meet me there so you don't have to worry about me being there all alone."

He got up from the sofa. "I'd feel better if I knew there were more people there than Charley."

"Charley is perfectly capable of taking care of me. Not only does he punch like a prizefighter, he also keeps a gun in the kitchen."

"Is there anything I can do?" Flint asked helplessly.

She stared at him for a long moment. "Get Bittard behind bars so that I can get my real life back." She didn't wait for him to reply, but turned on her heels and disappeared down the hallway.

She took a long hot shower, as if the near-scalding water would not only wash away the food particles that might cling to her hair and skin, but could also wash away all the old painful memories that the debacle at the diner had wrought.

She hadn't wanted to tell Flint about her sordid past, but the memories of that time had pressed too close to the surface, and he'd been the only person she'd ever trusted to allow them release.

In fact, she was surprised by her depth of trust in Flint. She didn't believe he had a bad bone in his body. She'd seen him angry, depressed and frustrated and never had he allowed those emotions to evolve into anything ugly.

After her shower she got into bed and begged for sleep, but it remained elusive as the events of the day played through her mind. She had no idea how many days it would take to put the diner right again and have it ready for a reopening.

She only knew she wanted it done as soon as possible. Without the diner and the few customers who had remained loyal, she had nothing. She'd made the call to Charley, who had agreed to meet her in the morning at eight. It was already late, and she just wanted to fall into the oblivion of a dreamless sleep.

No matter how hard she tried to shut off her brain, it refused to turn off. Memories of her past continued to plague her, grief and anger at her mother and father battled inside her. She'd thought she'd put it all behind her years ago, but apparently those memories had festered inside her.

Still, there was no question that talking to Flint had been a balm to her spirit, a lancing of a wound she hadn't realized she'd carried for so long. She'd sensed

Flint's need to comfort her, his desire to pull her into his arms and hold her close.

And she'd wanted that so badly it had scared her. She'd consciously kept herself from falling into his arms, taking comfort from his embrace.

What she had wanted to do was pull him into her bedroom and make love with him, banishing all thoughts of anything but pleasure and passion. But she knew it would just be a mindless escape for her and would definitely give him the wrong impression.

While she believed she had healed from much of her childhood, she was still sure she could never fully trust any man except Flint, and she feared becoming her mother. She simply wasn't willing to entertain any thoughts of any lasting relationship with any man. She feared eventually it would be just another screwed-up holiday.

It was after two when she realized sleep just wasn't happening. She got out of bed and hoped she wouldn't awaken Flint if she sneaked into the kitchen and made herself a quick cup of tea.

She tiptoed down the hallway and into the kitchen, where she tried to be as quiet as a mouse as she pulled a cup of hot water out of the microwave before it dinged and then grabbed a tea bag and sat at the table.

The blinds were open and the moon was near full outside, streaming through the window and giving the kitchen a ghostly light. She sat in a chair farthest from the window, confident that she couldn't be seen by anyone outside in the darkness of the kitchen.

She sipped her tea and suddenly remembered Grace and Billy standing next to her behind the counter as the worst of the fight had been ongoing.

She looked up in dismay as Flint came into the kitchen. "I was hoping I wouldn't wake you up," she said.

"It's my job to wake up if I hear an unusual sound in the house. Can't sleep?" He walked over to the blinds and pulled them all closed and then stood next to the cabinets.

"My head just keeps spinning and spinning, and I can't seem to shut it off," she replied. "I was just thinking about Billy and how traumatized he must have been by what he saw."

Flint leaned against the refrigerator. "Grace is a good mother. She'll be able to explain it to Billy so that he'll be all right and will understand that what happened at the diner today was an unusual incident of a lot of grown men behaving badly."

"I hope so. I can't stand the thought of my little man being scared." She took a sip of her tea and then set the cup back on the table. "I'm sorry I dumped on you earlier."

"I'm not. If it's true that I'm the first person you told about your early life, then you've carried it around by yourself for far too long. To be honest, I've been waiting for you to completely open up to me."

He pushed off the refrigerator and took a step toward her. "The one thing I don't want to happen is for what happened today to steal away the smiling, positive woman you've become. You have the incredible ability to make people feel good, and I don't want you to lose that."

She shook her head. "I can't let that happen. I won't go backward. What I also can't let happen is keeping awake the man who needs to keep peace in a town where people are obviously more on edge than we realized and who has to investigate an attack on his sister and get two fugitives behind bars." Besides, she needed to escape the sexy scent of him that lingered in the air and the intimacy of the middle-of-the-night contact.

She finished her tea and carried the cup to the sink. "I think I can sleep now, and you should do the same."

Together they left the kitchen. "Thanks, Flint, for always being here for me."

"I've told you before, anytime…day or night. I'll always be here for you." He stepped toward her and delivered a kiss on her forehead that was both gentle and sweet and yet held a touch of fire. "Now sleep well."

"Good night Flint," she said, but instead of hurrying to her bedroom before she did something stupid like fall into his arms, she fell into his arms.

He instantly enfolded her and claimed her mouth with his as his hands cupped her buttocks and pulled her tight against him.

Desire crackled in the air as he slowly moved them from the hallway to the sofa, where he pulled her down on top of him.

Hot kisses, silken caresses, it would have been so easy to fall into making love with him again, and her desire to do so was so intense it scared her.

As his hand slid beneath her nightgown, she broke their kiss and stood up.

"I'm sorry," she said. "I just don't think this would be a good idea." She gave him no chance to reply but turned and hurried into her bedroom.

Heat still fired through her as she got into bed, a heat she thought would keep her awake for hours.

But she must have fallen asleep immediately, for

the next thing she knew she awakened to the scent of fresh coffee in the air and her alarm clock reading just before seven.

She jumped out of bed, grabbed a pair of jeans and a sweatshirt and hurried into the bathroom to get ready for the day. For the first time since she'd bought the diner, she dreaded walking in its front door this morning, knowing the utter chaos that would greet her. It would be a day of scrubbing and cleaning and trying to put things right after everything had gone so wrong.

Aware that she had told Charley to meet her at the diner at eight and that Flint needed to get to work, she didn't linger getting dressed.

"Good morning," Flint greeted her as she walked into the kitchen. "Coffee is ready, and I even made toast."

"Hmm, I'm impressed." She poured herself a cup of coffee, sat at the table and grabbed one of the slightly burned around the edges pieces of toast.

"Anytime you want a gourmet breakfast, just call my name," he replied teasingly.

It was exactly the mood she needed…light and easy after such an emotional, draining night and facing what she suspected would be an equally emotionally draining day.

"Your name isn't exactly the one that jumps onto the tip of my tongue when I think of gourmet cooking," she replied.

"But when you think of gourmet kisses, whose name comes to mind?" he asked with a wicked gleam in his eyes.

She couldn't help but laugh. "I never knew you could be so silly. I always thought of you as a serious, somber kind of guy who didn't have much of a sense of humor."

"Maybe it just took a special woman to tap into that hidden part of me," he replied.

"And maybe we should get out of here so you can get to work, and I can meet Charley on time." She refused to acknowledge how his words or the soft gaze of his eyes quickened her heart.

"You're right, we should probably head out." He downed his coffee in one gulp. "Charley doesn't strike me as a man who likes to be kept waiting."

"You've got that right," she agreed. She finished her toast, took a last swig of coffee and then they were on their way.

The closer they got to the diner, the more Nina's stomach twisted with dread. The vision she had of the place from the night before was nightmarish. It was as if all the fates from her past had conspired to destroy not only the holiday, but the diner, as well.

"Are you sure you're ready to face this today?" Flint asked, as if reading her thoughts. "You could always do this tomorrow or the next day and give yourself a little break away."

"It has to be faced sooner or later, and it might as well be today. Hopefully, we can get it all cleaned up and ready to reopen in the next couple of days. I don't just have myself to think about. I have staff who depend on this job to pay their bills."

"I wish I could be in there helping you," he said.

"You have your own job to do. Keep peace on the streets, catch the bad guys and take care of police business. That's way more important than cleaning up a diner," she replied.

He pulled up in front of the diner and as usual she waited for him to come around to the passenger door to escort her inside. In spite of any other dramas going on, she knew that Flint had not forgotten his first order of business, to keep her safe and sound from a killer who could be anywhere, a killer who wanted her dead.

She unlocked the door, and they stepped inside. Standing before them, dressed in uniforms and obviously ready to work were Molly, Grace and Wilma. Charley and Abe stood just behind them.

The diner smelled of cleanser and polish. The tables and booths were clean and set and it was obvious they had worked for hours the night before to make sure the diner was ready to open for business this morning.

Nina looked around in disbelief, and her eyes filled with tears as she gazed at the people who had cared enough about their jobs, about this place and about her to go to so much trouble.

"Well, you look like you're in good hands," Flint said and looked at the others with obvious gratitude. "I'll see you later." He gave her shoulder a tight squeeze.

He left and Nina's tears became more profuse. Molly and Grace rushed to either side of her. "Don't cry," Grace said. "For goodness' sake, the last thing we wanted to do was make you cry."

Nina gasped out a laugh. "These are happy, grateful, loving tears," she exclaimed as she swiped at her cheeks.

"We didn't want you to have to come in here this morning and face the mess," Charley said, his voice gruffer than usual.

"But you all must have been here all night," Nina

said, moving away from Molly and Grace to sit at one of the stools at the pristinely clean counter.

"With all of us working together, it didn't take that long," Wilma said. "You do so much for us, Nina. We wanted to do this for you."

"We're family here," Grace said. "And family helps family."

Grace's words expanded Nina's heart. Yes, the people who worked for her here, this core part of her staff, were her family.

And she told herself that it was all the family she would ever need.

Chapter 12

While Flint was happy for Nina, and the fact that her staff had really stepped up for her, by the time he reached the station he fought off a healthy dose of frustration.

It had been almost a month since Nina had witnessed the murder of Jolene Tate at Hank Bittard's hands, and yet in a quarantine town, there had been no sightings of the fugitive other than the near encounters in the woods.

Hank certainly remained his priority, but he'd also like to get some cuffs around Jimmy Johnson's wrists and get back the family ring to give Molly some closure. He also remained upset about the attack on Gemma and would like to get some definitive answers about who had been behind it.

He walked into the station and was greeted by Patrick, who sported a faint shiner on his left eye. "Heck of a row yesterday," he said cheerfully.

"Looks like you got the worst of it," Flint replied.

Patrick grinned. "I think I see a bit of a bruise on your lower jaw."

Flint reached up and touched the slightly tender area where he just remembered he'd taken a fairly powerful punch. "Bruised but not beaten, right?"

"We should have arrested somebody," Patrick said.

"Where would we have begun? It was like a flash mob of scared, overstressed people all striking out at each other. I was just glad to get them out the door and see them all go home."

"Nina must be completely devastated."

"She was last night, but she got a nice surprise when she walked into the diner this morning. The staff stayed last night and got the whole place cleaned up. You'd never know anything crazy happened by seeing the place this morning."

"That's nice. That's the real Dead River spirit at work, or at least it was before the virus and everything else that's gone wrong."

"Are you trying to cheer me up?" Flint asked drily.

"Ha, I can't even think of something to cheer myself up," Patrick replied.

"I don't know, you looked pretty cheerful flirting with Grace yesterday."

Patrick's cheeks colored slightly. "I wasn't flirting, we were just getting to know each other a little better."

"It's okay if you were flirting, Patrick."

He grinned. "Okay, maybe I was just a little bit. I think she's attractive, and from talking to her, I like her."

"She's a good woman," Flint replied. "Now, let's get everyone into the conference room and compare notes, see where we are with everything," he said.

"I'll gather everyone up," Patrick replied.

Flint stopped by the coffee machine, poured himself a cup and then headed to the conference room where unfortunately, he didn't expect any exciting breaking news from any of his men.

It took only minutes for those who were in the station to join him in the conference room. Most of the officers had already hit the streets to do their daily patrols, but there were a few of Flint's most trusted men in the room.

"Mike, how's the head?" Flint asked.

"Apparently hard since I didn't even have a mild concussion," Mike replied with a grin.

"So, what have we got?" Flint asked.

"No recent reports of robberies in or around the area," Officer Sam Blair said. "No sightings of either man anywhere. It's like they've both vanished into thin air."

"Are we sure they didn't somehow slip out of the woods and through the quarantine?" Patrick asked.

"No way," Flint said. "The guards around the town are deadly serious about nobody getting out or in. I heard one of them shot a deer the other day because he thought it was a person trying to escape. The CDC is determined to keep this virus and all of us contained."

"So, our fugitives still have to be in town somewhere," Mike said.

"I still believe Hank is in the woods. He strikes me as the kind of man who could survive on very little. Jimmy, I'm not so sure about. Once we took his things from the lean-to shed, I think he possibly moved into town and is holed up with some friend we don't know about," Flint said.

"But the last time we checked those woods, it was Jimmy's hidey-hole that we found," Patrick reminded them. "It's possible he just found another hidey-hole that we don't know about."

"True, but it's getting downright cold out, and Jimmy doesn't strike me as a kid who likes roughing it for too long," Flint replied.

"Yeah, I can't imagine how he's surviving without his video games and electronic devices," Patrick said, disgust dripping from his voice.

"Maybe we need to do a house-by-house search for both of them," Mike suggested. "With people staying in their houses because they're afraid they'll get sick, maybe Hank is holding somebody hostage in their home."

Flint winced at the very idea. "We just don't have the manpower for that kind of search. We're having a hard enough time just checking out sheds and abandoned buildings and keeping people from fighting on the streets."

"We all know he's just waiting for a chance to get to Nina. Maybe we could somehow use her as bait," Mike said.

"No way," Flint growled out. "No way, no how. You can't come up with a plan good enough for me to agree to it. Not on my watch." There was no way he wanted any hint of a failed operation where Nina's safety was concerned.

"I keep thinking that one of them is going to surface where somebody will see them," Patrick said. "Everyone in town knows we're looking for them. They'd got to be cold and hungry. Eventually they're going to have to break in someplace again or get closer to town. All it would take is one person to see one of them and call us."

"I just can't figure out why that hasn't happened yet," Mike added.

Flint frowned. "The whole town is paranoid. I think we got a good look at that yesterday at the diner. I'm not sure that even if somebody saw one of them they'd call us. The tenure of the town right now is one of isolation. I don't think anyone wants to get involved in anything with anyone else."

"So, what's our next move?" Patrick asked, his voice filled with the frustration that burned in Flint's very soul.

"I don't know." It was a painful admission for Flint to make. "I guess we just keep on doing what we're doing…beating feet, keeping our ears to the ground and hoping we catch a break."

Flint paused as his cell phone rang. He listened, trying to tamp down his excitement and then gave instructions and hung up. "This might just be our break. That was Dana. She's been sitting on Ralph Dane. He just left his parents' house, dressed in winter clothes and carrying a couple of grocery bags and what looked like several blankets. He was just getting into his car when she called. I told her to tail him, and we'd catch up to her."

All four men were out of their chairs. "I drove my wife's car today. Maybe we should take it because Dane won't recognize it," Mike said.

"Sounds like a plan," Flint said as they grabbed their coats and then headed for the door.

His phone rang again. It was Dana giving them the direction Ralph was heading. "It sounds like he's headed to the woods," Flint said as he took shotgun position and Mike slid behind the wheel. Sam and Patrick took the backseat.

Flint tried to tamp down his excitement. They had been here several times before and had only hit dead ends. But the fact that Dane had personal ties to Hank and appeared to be headed to the woods with groceries and blankets was definitely promising.

It didn't take them long to catch up with Dana, who was driving an old Chevy, and about a mile down the road in front of her was Ralph Dane's red Jeep.

Flint called Dana. "Back off and let us pass you. We don't want him to get suspicious since you've been following him since he left his house."

She slowed down and Mike passed her, still keeping Ralph in view but not following so close as to be obvious. "Let's hope this kid is leading us directly to Hank," Patrick muttered from the backseat.

"I definitely got the feeling when we spoke to Ted Garrett that Ralph was Hank's little punk, and he's probably the only person in town Hank might trust," Flint said. His finger itched to be on the trigger of his gun, and his handcuffs begged to be wrapped around thick wrists.

Nobody spoke for several minutes as they continued to hang back just far enough to keep Dane's vehicle in sight. It was impossible not to entertain a bit of anxious anticipation, but it was definitely tempered by too many disappointments in the past.

"He's definitely headed toward the woods," Mike said, his fingers flexing around the steering wheel. "We're out far enough now that there's no other place for him to go."

Maybe this was finally the big break they'd all been waiting for, Flint thought as a new burst of adrenaline filled him. Nina's staff had given her back her diner this morning. Wouldn't it be great if he could finally give her back her sense of safety, if he could finally give her back her life?

And he'd hope and pray that her life without fear, without danger, would somehow include him.

But he couldn't think about that now. His only goal was to get Bittard behind bars so that a killer would have no more opportunity to act again.

Ralph pulled into the small cutout in the road where Flint and his men had parked the last time they'd been here on a chase.

"Drive on by," he instructed Mike. "We'll park up ahead and double back." Flint's adrenaline spiked higher. This had to be it. They'd worked so hard and had come so close, this finally had to be the time to put Hank back in jail where he belonged.

They found a place to park up the road and they all got out of the car. "I imagine Ralph is meeting somebody fairly close to where he parked. Dana said he's carrying blankets and grocery bags. He won't want to walk too far with that load," Flint said. "We'll head back to where he parked and start from there."

He didn't have to tell his men to go in quietly or to be prepared for anything. Before they left the car he called Dana and had her park her vehicle so that Ralph's Jeep was blocked in by hers.

"We go in as two teams of two," Flint said. "Keep your eye out for our suspects, but make sure you have an eye on each other's backs." He glanced at Mike. "We don't need any officers down. Mike and I will go back to Ralph's car and start the search from there, and you two start from here and work in the general directions of Ralph's car."

The four parted ways and as Sam and Patrick disappeared into the brush, Mike and Flint headed back to where Ralph had parked his car.

They moved quietly, hugging the edge of the woods until they were close to Ralph's Jeep, then they entered the woods.

As usual, they went in quietly, heading forward with only about eight feet between them. Flint kept his gaze divided between his surroundings and Mike. The last thing he wanted was another situation where one of his officers was injured or ambushed.

A month ago the woods had provided better cover with the last of the autumn leaves still clinging to the branches. Now those leaves were gone, forming piles in some places too high to walk through, but also giving the men better visibility as they continued onward.

Flint pulled the collar of his coat up closer around his neck as a cold wind blew through the trees. How could anyone possibly survive a harsh Wyoming winter out here?

They reached the old shed where Jimmy had been holed up, but it was now empty, as was the Miller house. Flint still didn't believe that Ralph would have ventured too far away with the load he'd been carrying. He had to be someplace nearby, and hopefully Hank was with him.

Despite the cold breeze, Flint's hand was sweaty on his gun as tension began to build with each footstep he took. Why else would Ralph be out here with blankets and food if not to meet his old buddy?

This had to be it, Flint's moment of success. Certainly talking to Nina about the trauma in Cheyenne had helped him absolve himself of some of his guilt, but not all of it. He needed this to be his moment of final redemption. He needed to make sure Nina would be safe. He needed Bittard behind bars.

There was a rise just ahead of them, and Flint knew on the other side was a fairly deep ravine. He held up a hand to stop Mike as he thought he heard the faint sound of a male voice coming from over the ridge.

Every muscle in Flint's body tensed as he imagined Ralph and Hank hunkered down in the ravine wrapped in blankets and sharing food. He took several steps closer and now distinctively heard Ralph's voice.

"I made the sandwiches special from the turkey my mom cooked yesterday," Ralph said. "I thought you'd like a little mustard and some lettuce. Are you warm enough? I brought two blankets in case you needed them."

Flint motioned Mike closer to the edge of the ridge. Mike nodded, letting Flint know he heard the voice and was ready for action. Taking a deep breath, gun at the ready, Flint jumped over the ridge.

He landed on his feet in the ravine about three feet from where Ralph sat next to a young, mousey-haired girl who instantly screamed.

Ralph jumped up to his feet, his eyes wide in alarm, but quickly sank back down to the ground as he saw

Sam and Patrick coming down the ravine from the opposite side.

Mousy-haired girl hadn't stopped screaming since the moment Flint had hit the bottom of the ravine.

"Would you please shut up," Mike said to the girl, obviously as frustrated as Flint that it wasn't Bittard sitting next to Ralph. She snapped her mouth closed as tears began to form in her pale blue eyes.

"What in the hell are you two doing out here?" Flint asked. "You both almost got yourselves shot."

Ralph put an arm around the girl, who was shivering as tears continued to fall down her cheeks. "Jeez, this is my girlfriend, Melody. I didn't know it was a crime to plan a little picnic with her."

"In the winter in the woods?" Patrick asked. "Woods where we believe two fugitives have been hiding out? What in the hell is wrong with you?"

"I can't exactly take her to my parents' house. They have stupid rules and don't let me have girls there," Ralph said sulkily.

"And my parents don't like Ralph so we can't see each other at my house," Melody said. "And we're afraid to let anyone in town see us together so we've been meeting here."

"How old are you?" Flint asked, his blood still boiling with the fire of defeat.

"Seventeen," Melody sniffed.

"Why aren't you in school?"

"We're out for Thanksgiving holiday until Monday. Are you going to arrest us?" she asked fearfully.

Flint turned his attention to Ralph. "Have you ever heard of statutory rape?"

Ralph jumped to his feet once again. "Hey, it's not

like that," he protested. "We aren't having sex. I know the law and besides, I respect Melody too much to go there when she isn't old enough."

"You respect her so much you've got her out in the woods in the cold for leftover turkey sandwiches," Patrick said drily.

"I'm going to be eighteen in two months," Melody added as if any of them cared.

"How about you two lovebirds pack it up and go home," Flint said. "I'm in the mood to arrest somebody even if it's for littering."

They watched as Ralph and Melody quickly packed up their things and then followed them to Ralph's car. "Do you need a ride home?" Mike asked Melody.

Melody nodded. "A girlfriend dropped me off here."

"I'll take her home," Ralph replied.

"Dana, escort Ralph to Melody's house and then see Ralph back to his parents' house," Flint instructed.

It took only minutes for the four lawmen to be alone and start the trek back to where they'd parked the car. "I really thought this was it," Patrick said with disgust as he holstered his gun.

"I was so sure it would be Hank down in that ravine with Ralph," Mike agreed.

"Just another damn dead end," Sam said, summing up the situation succinctly.

Flint got into the passenger seat and stared out the window. It was rumored that by Monday or Tuesday Dr. Colleen Goodhue would finally arrive.

If she was as good as her reputation, then within days or weeks she could discover a cure to the virus and the quarantine would be lifted.

Tick-tock. Tick-tock. The sound of time running out filled Flint's head.

There was no question that Jimmy Johnson would take the Colton heirloom ring and run as far and as fast as he could away from Dead River. Flint would never get the precious ring back.

Tick-tock. Tick-tock.

If the quarantine was lifted, he wasn't sure what Hank would do. He didn't like the idea of a killer heading for new hunting grounds, and in all honesty he wasn't sure Hank would immediately flee.

He had unfinished business here. Flint wished he could figure out a motive for Hank to have attacked Gemma. Did he somehow believe that Gemma had seen something she shouldn't have? Knew something she shouldn't know?

According to Gemma she'd never had any dealings with Hank and had no idea what he might have against her. The only possibly feasible motive Flint could come up with was that Hank had attacked her in an effort to have Flint call off the dogs.

Definitely Nina was a dangerous loose end for Hank. If the quarantine was lifted would he run or would he stick around to make sure that he took care of the eyewitness to Jolene Tate's murder?

Even if he did head out of town, there was nothing to keep him from coming back in a week or a month or even a year to make sure that Nina could never testify against him.

If the quarantine was lifted before Flint got Bittard behind bars, then Nina would have to be afraid and look over her shoulders for the rest of her life.

Tick-tock.

* * *

It was Monday afternoon and the diner was empty, as it had been for much of the holiday weekend. The few people who came in were the most loyal of her customers, and although on Friday and Saturday the talk had been of the debacle of the Thanksgiving Day celebration, she was grateful that by Sunday it seemed to be old news.

She'd sent home Molly an hour ago when the lunch rush had been anemic at best, and now she sat next to Grace at the counter, sharing small talk to pass the time until Billy would arrive after school.

"I feel so bad for Flint," Nina said as she ran a finger around the rim of the teacup in front of her. "He's so discouraged, and I wish there was something I could do to help him."

"I'm sure you help just by being there in the evenings for him," Grace replied. "At least you have your mojo back."

"My mojo?"

"Your sunshine, your smile, your general optimism about life," Grace replied. "I was afraid you'd lose it after Thanksgiving."

"I'm not sure anything can steal that away from me forever at this point in my life. I made a conscious decision a long time ago that it was much easier to be positive than negative."

"And I'm sure that's part of why Flint is in love with you," Grace replied.

"Don't say that," Nina protested.

"But you know it's the truth."

"No, he's not in love with me. He's in love with the idea of me, of the life we've shared for almost a month. He's in love with somebody sitting across the table from him in the mornings and talking with him in the evenings."

Grace shook her head firmly. "You're wrong, Nina. It's you. He's definitely in love with you."

Nina's heart squeezed tight. She didn't want to hear it. She didn't want to believe it. She didn't want to feel the truth in her heart and soul.

"Even if it is true, sooner or later I'll be out of Flint's house and hopefully, he'll be able to find that special woman he's looking for who wants marriage and a family. But that woman is never going to be me," Nina said.

"That's too bad because you two are pretty terrific together," Grace replied.

They were good together, Nina thought, but they'd been living a pretend life under extraordinary circumstances. It had been a matter of chemistry and close proximity, but that didn't make her Flint's special woman.

Grace took a sip of her tea and then gave Nina a little secretive smile. "I got a phone call yesterday from Officer...Patrick Carter. He asked me out on a date."

Nina gave her a playful slap on the shoulder. "And you're just now telling me this?"

"I've been kind of savoring it all day. He asked me out to dinner on Friday night."

"And, of course, you agreed," Nina said.

"I told him yes as long as I can find a babysitter for Billy that night."

"I'll babysit Billy. Bring him over to Flint's and we'll show him a good time," Nina offered immediately. "We'll have a homemade pizza night and it will be good for all of us."

"Are you sure Flint wouldn't mind?" Grace asked tentatively.

"Flint would probably welcome the distraction. Besides, he adores Billy almost as much as I do, and personally I'd be thrilled to see you with Patrick."

Grace laughed. "It's just a first date, not a lifetime commitment."

"Trust me, I have a good feeling about this," Nina replied and took a sip of her tea. "I wouldn't be surprised to see a spring wedding."

Grace laughed again. "You're too much. Besides, I refuse to get married in a town under quarantine."

"From everything I'm hearing, the CDC specialist is due to arrive sometime tomorrow, and there will be no more postponements of her arrival."

"That's good. We need her here as soon as possible. How's Flint's grandmother doing?"

Nina frowned. "Not well. Flint thinks it's just her sheer willpower alone that's keeping her alive. I just hope Dr. Goodhue gets some answers in time to save her." Nina's heart squeezed as she thought about Flint having to endure the pain of losing the woman who raised him.

By the time Nina had lost her mother to her father's hands, there had been little grief left inside her, only a weary resignation that what she'd always believed and feared would happen had finally happened.

A couple came through the door, and as Grace got up to take care of them, Nina remained on her stool and sipped her tea, her thoughts on Flint and the weekend that had just passed.

They had almost made love again. Saturday night. It had been a moment of suppressed desire that had begun with a simple kiss and had nearly spiraled out of control.

Although she had desperately wanted to make love to him again, that was exactly why she had stopped things before they went too far.

She was determined that at the end of her protective custody she would give him exactly what he needed from her, and that was her walking out of his life.

There was no question that it would be difficult, but she knew in her heart that it was the right thing to do. She had to walk away from him so he'd have room in his life to find the right woman, the one who could fulfill all the dreams he had for himself for the future.

Having served the couple their drinks and turned in their food order, Grace returned to the stool next to Nina and checked her wristwatch. "Another ten minutes or so and our little munchkin will be arriving."

"Maybe I'll surprise him today and already have his treat on his table waiting for him." Nina jumped down from her stool. "I've got a couple of big fat brownies for him today."

Nina headed behind the counter where several of her daily desserts were kept. While she plated the brownies and poured a glass of milk, Grace disappeared to the kitchen to pick up her order for the couple.

Nina put the goodies on Billy's table and then returned to the counter to wait for his arrival. She knew Flint wouldn't mind having Billy as a little houseguest for a while on Friday night. In fact, it would probably be good for him.

She mentally began to put together a grocery list for the best, most fun homemade pizzas ever made.

She knew it was going to take a lot more than making pizzas to keep an energetic kid like Billy occupied.

They couldn't plan anything outside. Not only had the nights gotten too cold, but Flint would never allow her to spend any time outside in the open where she'd be a target for Hank.

Maybe she could come up with some sort of treasure hunt inside the house, with clues to discern and tricks to perform in order to win the prize.

She smiled. Yes, she liked the idea, and she'd insist that Flint participate. She'd have big-guy clues and little-guy clues and two prizes to be won.

"You look like a cat who just swallowed a canary," Grace said as she resumed her seat next to Nina.

"I'm just planning out my big date with my little man on Friday night and hoping that you and Patrick have as much fun as we're planning."

"I have to confess, I'm a little bit nervous. I mean, I haven't been on a date in years."

Nina smiled and patted her hand. "You'll be fine. Just be your wonderful self, and he won't stand a chance against your charms."

"We talked on the phone for almost an hour, and the more I found out about him the more I liked him," Grace confessed.

"Like I said, he will be overwhelmed by your sexy, gracious charms."

"Speaking of charms, I wonder where my little charmer is," Grace said as she checked her watch. "He should have walked through that door already."

"Calm down. He's only like two minutes late. He might just be walking a little slower today, taking the time to smell the roses."

"Roses in Wyoming at the end of November?" Grace replied drily. She scooted off the stool as the man at her table indicated they were ready for their check.

While Grace took care of the customers, Nina walked to the front door and poked her head out, looking down the sidewalk in the direction Billy would come from his bus stop at the next corner. There was no sign of him.

"I'm sure he'll be here anytime," she said to Grace, whose forehead was creased with a worried frown.

"If he isn't here in the next five minutes, he's so grounded," Grace replied. "I've told him a million times not to dawdle on the way home from the bus stop. I've told him to come directly here."

"Maybe the bus is running late today for some reason or another," Nina replied. "You can't ground him for a late bus."

Grace grinned. "If you had it your way, I'd never ground him for anything."

"He's just too cute to be grounded," Nina replied with a smile.

When another ten minutes had passed and there was still no sign of Billy, neither Grace nor Nina was smiling. Ten minutes usually was nothing more than a blink of time, but when waiting for a child to be safe and sound where he belonged, it felt like an eternity.

Grace paced the floor, occasionally looking outside while Nina found herself scrubbing down the counter that was already immaculate.

"Maybe I should call the school," Grace finally said. "I suppose it's possible he missed the bus or maybe there's another reason why he isn't here."

Charley stepped out of the kitchen, his features as grim as Nina had ever seen them. "I just got a phone call from a buddy. He said he heard a rumor that one of the school buses was hijacked by an armed man wearing a ski mask."

Nina sucked in her breath as Grace gasped and stumbled in alarm. Grace grabbed the back of a chair as Nina walked around the counter to stand next to her.

"Did he know what bus?" Grace managed to ask. "Did he have a bus number?" Nina held her breath.

"Bus three," Charley replied.

Grace groaned and fell into the chair, her eyes wide with terror as she stared at Nina. "Heaven help me, that's Billy's bus."

Chapter 13

Nina's heart fell to the floor. "Did you get any more information?" she asked Charley, trying to tamp down her own frantic fear.

"Just that apparently he was driving the bus west toward the woods," Charley replied.

"I've got to go," Grace said frantically as she struggled to stand from the chair. "I've got to go find my son."

"Get your keys. I'll drive you," Nina replied.

"But you can't leave here without Flint," she protested.

"Flint will have his hands full. I'm going with you. We need to get Billy back safe and sound." Nina knew she was taking a chance by leaving the diner, but it was a chance she would take for the little boy who owned so much of her heart.

Grace grabbed her coat and keys and Nina pulled on the black coat that Flint had bought for her and then they ran for Grace's car.

Nina drove as Grace was too distraught. "Why would a man take a school bus? Why would he do something so heinous?"

Nina didn't reply. She didn't have any answers and knew that Grace didn't expect her to have any. But the same questions flew through her head.

Was this some kind of desperate bid to get out of town? Was Hank Bittard the man who had taken the bus and hoped to use the children as hostages to get him a pass out of the quarantine?

What about Alma, the bus driver? Was she all right or had he hurt or killed her? Alma had been a bus driver for years. Nina could only hope that the caring woman so devoted to the children hadn't done something to sacrifice her own life.

If it was Bittard, would he be capable of hurting a child? As she thought of how he'd pulled the rope around Jolene's neck, she fought off a shiver of terror. A man like that could hurt anyone.

She ignored the speed limit, and she certainly wasn't the only vehicle on the road speeding in the direction of the woods west of town.

She pulled over to hug the side of the road as her rearview mirror showed her a patrol car, cherry light spinning and siren screaming, approaching from behind her.

As the patrol car went by she saw Dana McGlowen behind the wheel. Hopefully, all the police in Dead River were responding to the call of children in trouble.

"Billy is a smart kid," she said to Grace, who was

now silently weeping. "He won't do anything to draw attention to himself. I'm sure he'll be just fine."

Grace didn't reply, and Nina wasn't sure how much she believed her own words. It was impossible to know how a little boy would react under such terror. It was impossible to know for sure why this was happening.

Only an evil person could commit such a crime. Only true evil could prey on innocent children. By the time they reached the edge of the woods, cars were parked helter-skelter along the side of the road.

Several patrol cars were also parked, although she saw no officers in the near vicinity. Nina and Grace got out of the car, and in the distance was the sound of chaos.

Male voices battled with female cries and children crying. "This way," Nina said and grabbed Grace's hand to pull her toward whatever action was happening.

They hurried through the brush and piles of dead leaves, and a surge of optimism jumped through Nina as she saw the splash of the bright yellow of the bus against the dark browns of the woods.

There was too big a crowd gathered for them to be able to get as close as they wanted. Officers Mike Harriman and Dana McGlowen were trying to control the crowd, while the children remained seated in the bus as they waved their hands out open windows and sobbed for their parents.

Seated next to Mike on the ground was Alma Castor, the older woman who had been driving the bus for years. She held what appeared to be a handkerchief to a wound on the side of her head and blood had dried in a path from the injury down one cheek to her chin.

"The danger is over." Mike yelled to be heard. "The hijacker has fled and Chief of Police Colton and several other officers are hunting for him." The crowd quieted to listen, and Grace reached for Nina's hand and squeezed tight.

"The children are all safe, and we're going to unload the bus in an orderly fashion," Dana said. "We'll let the students off one at a time. If a parent is here, then the child will be released immediately into their custody. If no parent or legal guardian is present, then the child will remain with us until we can contact the appropriate person."

Thus began an agonizingly slow process. As each child was taken off the bus and reunited with a parent, Grace's hand squeezed Nina's tighter. Her visceral need to have her son in her arms was transferred to Nina, whose stomach was in a million hard knots.

They were too far away to see the children still on the bus, and as the beginning of dusk moved in, the wooded area took on the shadows of night and made it more difficult to see how many were left.

Dana turned on the school bus lights, which cut a swatch through the encroaching darkness as the bus continued to be emptied and the crowd around it grew smaller.

"There can't be that many more left on board," Grace said frantically. "Why hasn't Billy come off yet?"

"It will be just our luck that he'll be the last one off," Nina replied, but the knots in her stomach twisted tighter. It appeared to her as if there were only a couple of children left. Billy had to be one of them.

Grace dropped Nina's hand and moved closer to the

bus. Now that the crowd had greatly diminished, she managed to get right up to the side of the bus. She rose on her tiptoes to peek through one of the windows. She moved frantically from window to window and then back to Nina, her eyes wide and filled with horror.

"He's not here," she cried out. "Billy isn't here." She turned to Mike and Dana with wild eyes. "My son, Billy, rides this bus and he isn't here." She pushed past Mike and took a step into the bus. "Billy!" she cried and when there was no response, she half fell off the bus.

Nina ran to her side, her heart beating a rhythm of terror as she kept Grace from falling to the ground.

"He took one," Alma said, her features a study in torture. "The gunman, he took one of the kids with him but I didn't see who it was. I tried to stop him but that's when he hit me and I fell to the floor. I'm sorry. I'm so sorry. I tried to protect them all."

"Billy. He has my Billy." Grace fell into Mike's arms and began to weep.

"Does Flint know about this?" Nina asked, fighting against the horror that filled her heart.

Mike nodded. "He didn't know who, but he knew a child had been taken." He patted Grace's back awkwardly. "Don't worry, Grace, Flint and his men will find them and get your son back safely."

"You stay here with Mike and Dana," Nina said to Grace.

"What are you going to do?" Grace asked amid tears.

"What I'm trained to do," Nina replied. She walked out to the road where she knew she could get the strongest cell phone signal and made four quick phone calls to the people who were trained to work search and rescue with her.

They would arrive with high-power flashlights, ropes and other equipment that would not only help in searching through the ever-growing darkness, but also might prove handy in navigating the uneven terrain.

She knew that Flint and his men would be doing everything in their power to find the man, who she could only believe was Hank Bittard. But the woods were vast and the search team could help in the effort.

Although the search team would do nothing to confront Hank and Billy, if they found them then the team could call in a specific location for the officers to respond to.

As she waited for the team to arrive, her heart cried out in fear, in anguish. Billy. She fought back the burn of tears. Why had he taken Billy? He had to be so scared. If she thought about the boy too much she'd drop to her knees in despair and be no good to anyone.

Once the other members of the search and rescue group arrived, she'd have Mike contact Flint to let him know the team was working the area.

The last thing they needed was an accident where one of the good guys got hurt by another good guy. She leaned down and picked up a handful of rocks and worked them in her hand like worry beads as she anxiously waited.

Flint would probably be angry that she was out here, but he'd have to just get over it. There was no way she could have just sat in her diner and done nothing when she'd heard that children were at risk. And now that she knew Billy was the missing child, nothing and nobody would make her leave here.

She didn't want to be out here hunting for a child she loved. She wanted him seated in the diner eating a brownie. She wanted him at a pizza party she'd planned, enjoying his contagious giggles.

She wasn't afraid of coming face-to-face with Hank Bittard, not if it meant somehow saving Billy. She'd give her life for that little boy with his laughing eyes and infectious happiness.

The minute Flint got word about the hijacked school bus, he urgently mobilized every one of his deputies. It had been Alma who had called in, letting him know that the bus had been taken over by a masked, armed man who had driven it into the woods and then grabbed a child and disappeared.

His blood had chilled as he thought of those children, terrified by a gunman who, according to Alma, had jumped on the bus as the last student had gotten on.

It hadn't taken them long to locate the bus, where they found Alma seated inside with the door locked and bleeding profusely from a head wound.

Alma refused medical treatment for her injury and had also refused to leave the scene until each and every child was safe and united with their family.

Confused by the blow to the head, traumatized by the entire event, she'd been unable to tell them which child had been taken. After the armed man had left, she'd locked herself in with the rest of the children and had done her best to keep them as calm as possible.

There was little question in Flint's mind that the gunman was Hank Bittard, although the motive for this particular action was murky to Flint.

Did he really believe that by using a child as a hostage he might be able to get himself out of town? Out from under the quarantine? This had been a bold, reckless move that nobody had seen coming.

At the moment, motive didn't matter. What mattered was finding the bastard and getting the child safely away from him and then taking Hank down once and for all.

He and his men had fanned out from the bus, all of them aware that this was more than just a wanted killer on the loose, but a hostage situation with a young child. They were armed with guns and flashlights, but had been given orders not to fire unless they had a clear shot at the man and were confident the child would not be harmed.

It was after darkness had fallen that he got a call from Mike that the search and rescue team had arrived and had begun to work the woods in a grid pattern on the south side. Mike also informed him that Billy Willard was the child who had been taken.

Flint's blood froze at the news that the little hostage was Billy, and then a new fear filled him. "Is Nina here with search and rescue?" he asked.

"Yeah, she is," Mike replied with a touch of reluctance.

Flint silently cursed. He'd hoped she would have sense enough to stay at the diner where she'd be safe. Now he not only had to worry about the safety of Billy, but Nina's safety, as well.

He nearly stumbled over a half-exposed vine as a new thought struck him. Had Billy been a random choice for Bittard to grab, or had the murderer somehow known of Nina's special relationship with the boy? Had he known that taking Billy would force a mistake on Nina's part? That she would come out here to help and ignore her own safety?

If this had all been a ruse to pull Nina out in the open alone and unarmed, then it had worked. With this thought in mind, Flint continued the search with an additional urgency.

Now he had two people at risk in the woods, in the dark, and a killer he feared would stop at nothing to achieve whatever goal he desired.

As he walked along, he could see flashlights cutting through the darkness on either side of him. He didn't dare call out to Billy, afraid that if the boy tried to answer, Hank would hurt him. He'd also told his men not to call out to Billy. He feared that if Billy tried to respond, he'd be punished in some way.

It was eerie, men and women silently creeping through the woods, their flashlight beams appearing like ghost lights in the darkness. And someplace out there was a little boy and a woman he loved.

Despite all the years in law enforcement, Flint found it impossible not to second-guess what Hank's intention might be. If his goal was to use Billy as a hostage to get out of town, then they should be moving toward the opposite edge of the woods where he could seek freedom with his gun and a kid.

He could kill a CDC guard, and others might be afraid to respond in kind if he used Billy as a shield.

If his goal was to encounter Nina, then he could be anywhere, just waiting for an opportunity to use Billy to lure her close and then shut her up forever.

Flint should be livid that Nina had put herself in the potential path of danger, but it was difficult to be angry with her knowing that it was her love for Billy that had brought her here. It was simply who she was at her very core.

Still, he wished she was at the diner, serving up a meal to customers rather than in these woods where evil had peaked and still ran rampant.

He walked a few steps and then stopped to listen, but each time he stopped he heard nothing to indicate that any of his men had encountered Bittard and Billy.

He moved toward the south, in the direction where the search team had indicated they were working. He would feel a hell of a lot better if he could get Nina in his sight.

He knew there was no way he would be able to convince her to abandon the search and get out of here, but he'd feel a little bit of relief if he could get her close enough to him that he could keep a watchful eye on her and make sure she wasn't the one who encountered Bittard.

Pausing by a thick tree, he pulled out his cell phone and checked in with each of the men. They all had radios, but had agreed to use their phones because they were quieter.

Thankfully, there were only a couple of places on the far outer edges of the woods where the cell phone service was weak. He managed to touch base with everyone, unsurprised that none of them had stumbled on Bittard and Billy.

He thought about calling Nina, but not only did he not want her distracted, he also couldn't be sure that she had her phone set to vibrate. A ringtone in the woods would be like a spotlight on her back. He couldn't take a chance of doing something that might draw any attention to her.

He knew how the search and rescue team worked and took some comfort in the fact that they stayed in visual proximity to each other. They were trained not just to look for lost people, but also to make sure none of them became lost.

Failure.

The word whispered through his head and for a moment, he leaned weakly against the tree trunk. He had a child in danger and a known killer who would love to silence Nina forever.

Failure. It burned deep in his soul.

He pushed himself off the tree with a surge of determined resolve. In this particular case, failure was simply not an option.

Chapter 14

Nina held tight to her flashlight in one hand and the rocks she'd picked up off the side of the road in her other. The flashlight beam was strong and steady in lighting her way while she worked the rocks in her hand with nervous energy.

To her right she could see the flashlight beam of a fellow search and rescue member and beyond that, another light from another volunteer as they worked methodically in moving forward and checking every space they passed.

She tried to keep Billy out of her head, but it was impossible. As time passed and the darkness of the woods grew more profound, it was difficult not to think of Billy's terror.

She could only hope that he was a valuable pawn in whatever game Bittard was playing and therefore wouldn't be harmed. Grace wasn't the only one who would be shattered if anything happened to her son.

Her vision blurred with tears as she thought of all the plans she'd made earlier in the day for a pizza party and treasure hunt. Memories of his hugs, of the little boy scent of him only made her tears more profuse.

Her tears weren't just for herself and Billy, but also for Grace, who had to be completely crazy with fear by now. Her heart ached for her friend.

Had Billy just been a convenient target? The kid sitting close enough to the door to grab as Bittard had exited the bus? Or had Billy been specifically targeted because somehow Bittard knew of Nina's love for him?

At this point it didn't matter. All she wanted was Billy safe and back in his mother's arms where he belonged. If that meant Nina would have to face her demon, then so be it. She would gladly face off with Bittard to save Billy.

It felt as if they'd been in the woods forever. Time no longer existed as the team moved slowly, methodically and in a gridlike fashion.

Why hadn't anyone spotted them yet? She knew that in addition to the search and rescue crew, there had to be at least a dozen officers searching, as well.

Where are you, you murdering creep? And where was her sweet Billy? Was Hank on the run, or was he holed up someplace just waiting for her to show up?

She never saw the ravine. All she knew was that one minute she stood on firm ground and the next minute she was airborne. She hit the hard earth below and rolled, banging into thick roots, small saplings and finally coming to rest on her back with the wind knocked out of her.

Surprised to discover that she had both her flashlight and the rocks still in her hands, she remained on her back until she finally caught her breath.

Only then did she slowly get to her feet. Her hip ached from making contact with something, and her blouse was torn at the elbow, but she wasn't about to let a few aches and pains stop her.

Thank God she had managed to keep hold of her flashlight, she thought as she began to walk down the jet-black ravine until she found a spot where she could pull herself up the embankment. When she did, she realized that she'd rolled far enough down the ravine that she'd lost the other members of the team.

She paused for a moment to get her bearings and someplace nearby heard the sound of soft crying. She flashed her light in the general direction she thought the sound had come from.

"Billy?" she called softly. "Billy, is that you? It's me, Nina."

A beam of light hit her in her eyes as a deep voice rumbled with laughter. "Well, if this isn't a big slice of perfect on a plate for me."

He lowered his light from her eyes, letting her see that he stood about six feet in front of her and he had Billy by the back of his jacket and pulled tight against the front of him. His features were hidden beneath the black ski mask he wore.

"I knew you'd show up out here sooner or later, and I was afraid I'd have to wander around all night before I finally found you, but here you are, like a plum dropped off a tree right at my feet," he said.

"Let him go," Nina said. "He's just a child. He has nothing to do with this." Her heart beat so hard her ribs ached, and she couldn't be sure if it was from her fall down the ravine or the fear that pressed tight in her chest.

"He's the kid who got you here." He yanked Billy closer. "Everyone in town knows how you dote on this kid. I figured he was a good worm to get you hooked."

"Don't be ridiculous," she scoffed. "He's nothing but a sniffling, irritating kid I've got to put up with because his mother works for me." She didn't look at Billy, and hoped and prayed he understood the reason for her saying such a thing.

"Doesn't matter one way or the other to me what you think about him. He got you here, and that's all that's important to me."

"Hijacking and terrifying an entire school bus of children was a terrible thing to do," Nina replied angrily.

"It got me what I wanted, here with you, and if you even think about screaming or doing anything to draw any attention from anyone else, I'll snap this kid's neck like a dried twig."

Nina didn't think it was possible for her blood to grow colder, but it did as she knew he was capable of just such an act of violence.

"You should have just kept driving on by that night and minded your own damn business," he said, his voice deepening with anger. "That two-timing floozy Jolene Tate got exactly what she deserved. She played me for a fool one too many times."

"Just let Billy go. This is between you and me. He has nothing to do with any of it. He's just an innocent child. I'm here now, and you don't need him." Nina tried to keep the utter desperation out of her voice.

Billy was the only person who mattered out here. All she wanted was for him to get away and live a wonderful life, and if things went bad for her, she hoped Grace would remind Billy that he'd once had a favorite auntie who had loved him dearly.

Hank didn't appear to have a weapon, although she could only assume he had a gun tucked somewhere on his person. He held the flashlight in one hand and Billy with the other. But Nina couldn't underestimate his muscular strength. He could easily follow through on his threat to break Billy's neck. She needed to get Billy away from him. "Let him go," she repeated.

Her mind whirled and she kept her focus away from Billy's face, knowing that to see him so scared might have her make a mistake, and she had no room to make any mistakes. Both of their lives depended on it.

Her heart pounded so hard she was afraid she would be physically ill, but she had to stay strong. She had to save Billy. If she managed to save herself, all the better, but right now her sole focus was getting Billy to safety.

"You know if you let him go, I can get Chief of Police Colton to get you out of town," she said. "He knows the CDC guards, and he can get one of them to let you slip by. You could be out of the entire state by tomorrow."

His eyes narrowed and glittered from the mask's eye holes in the beam of her flashlight as if he was contemplating her words. "All I have to do is make a phone call," she pressed, "and I swear you can leave this town forever."

"There's only one little problem with that. First of all, I don't believe you and secondly, you're a problem for me whether I leave town or not. No matter where I go, I'm a murderer, and you're the witness that can put me behind bars in any state in the country."

Nina took a step closer and saw the terror in Billy's eyes as he whimpered. "Then let him go and take me," she said. She took another step closer, her heart beating frantically.

There had to be a way not to just save Billy, but to save herself, as well. She just wasn't sure what it was at the moment. She only knew this standoff had to end with Billy getting away.

"What are you waiting for? Let him go. I'm the one you want, and I'm right here in front of you."

She saw his fingers loosen their grip on Billy's jacket and knew she only had one chance to take action. "Run, Billy," she cried as she threw the handful of rocks at his captor's face.

The rocks hit him hard in the face, and he cried out as Billy shot away from him. "Come on, baby," she said to Billy, and when he was in front of her, she turned to run, as well.

She only managed to take several steps before the man grabbed her by the ankle, tripping her to her hands and knees. "Keep running, Billy," she cried as she kicked backward in an effort to get free.

"Just keep running and don't look back." Hopefully, he would run into one of the search team or one of Flint's men, and he would be taken to Grace.

Screaming like a banshee, she used her free leg to kick backward again and again, finally rewarded with a grunt and the release of her trapped ankle.

She scrabbled forward and finally made it to her feet. Although she tried to run as fast as possible, she felt his hot breath on the back of her neck, smelled the scent of his sour sweat and knew in desperation that she was not going to be able to outrun him.

She screamed again as he grabbed her by the shoulders and once again pulled her down, this time turning her over and straddling her.

She slammed her flashlight as hard as she could into the side of his face, but he instantly wrangled it out of her hand and tossed it aside.

Bucking and kicking in an effort to get free, she also screamed at the top of her lungs, hoping somebody, anyone, would hear her cries and come to help her.

The screams were cut short as he wrapped his big hands around her throat and began to squeeze. She gurgled for air and it was at that moment that Nina knew she was going to die.

As the breath was slowly squeezed out of her, myriad thoughts flew through her mind with near impossible speed. She took comfort in knowing that Billy was safe and would be reunited with his mother, and that Grace would do everything in her power to make sure he eventually forgot his horrible time in the woods.

Her heart ached as she thought of Flint, who she knew would embrace her death as yet another failure despite the fact that she'd chosen to be out here knowing full well what the end result might be.

She hated that he would carry the burden of her death along with Madelaine's in Cheyenne. Neither were his fault, but he was the kind of man who would shoulder the guilt.

Finally, she wished she had made love to Flint one more time. She should have never denied herself or him that pleasure. At this point, what difference would it have made if they'd made love once or twice?

She tried to pull Hank's hands from her throat, but as he squeezed tighter she didn't have the energy to begin to break his grasp.

Tears weeped from her eyes and when they fluttered closed she was grateful. She didn't want the last vision she had on this earth to be of the man who killed her. Instead a vision of Flint filled her head, bringing with it a sense of peace and love.

A guttural roar came from someplace nearby and a dark figure flew out of the woods and suddenly, Nina was free as Bittard was knocked off the top of her.

She coughed and choked as precious air filled her lungs and then crawled to where her flashlight had been thrown. Grabbing it she focused the beam on the two men who were grappling on the ground.

Flint. She'd never seen him look so savage as he fought to gain control of Bittard. They wrestled on the ground, rolling back and forth as each tried to take control of the other.

She shone her light directly in Bittard's eyes, and that gave the advantage that Flint needed. He got to his feet and pulled his gun.

"Put your hands in the air and turn around," he commanded. As he handcuffed the perp, he glanced at Nina. "Are you okay?"

"Fine." She reached up and rubbed her throat. "I'm fine now."

Patrick Carter came rushing through the darkness, his gun in one hand and a flashlight in the other. "Everyone okay?"

"Everyone is fine," Flint replied and yanked the ski mask off. He frowned as Patrick's light played on his prisoner's face. "This isn't Hank Bittard."

Nina looked at him in stunned surprise. "Then who is he?" she asked.

"His name is Brett Logan," Patrick said. "He's a regular down at the Dead River Bar where Jolene used to hang out with Hank and a group of other lowlifes."

"Jolene was nothing but a piece of trash, a two-timing bitch," Brett spat. "I paid the rent on that house for her and bought her food and clothes and then she had a revolving door of men coming in and out when I was busting my ass at work to pay her bills. She got what she deserved, and I'm not sorry about what I did to her."

Nina's head was reeling. There was no question that Brett shared common physical features with Hank. They both were tall with a muscular build. They both had dark hair and eyes and similar facial features, and apparently, they both were cold-blooded killers.

"Patrick, you want to do the honors and take the prisoner in?" Flint asked.

"It would be my pleasure," Patrick replied.

"And call off the search. We're done for the night," Flint added.

He walked over and pulled Nina into his arms. She went willingly, unaware until this moment that despite her coat she was icy cold. She huddled against him as he held her fiercely tight.

"I should lock you up for coming out here alone," he murmured gruffly into her ear.

"I couldn't stay away, especially when I found out it was Billy who had been taken off the bus. Is he okay? Did somebody find him?" she asked worriedly.

"He ran into one of the search team members and was being taken back to the bus and Grace." He held her even tighter. "God, woman, you never fail to amaze me. I think if I'd been a minute later you would have been dead, and yet your first thought is for Billy's welfare."

"He's my little buddy," she replied.

He released her and took her by the hand. "And we need to get back to the bus. Grace and Billy will be frantic about your safety."

Nina's flashlight led the way through the darkness. "I can't believe that all this time we thought it was Hank who had killed Jolene," she said.

"It was a scenario that made sense," he replied. "And I can understand the misidentification. Hank and Brett look a lot alike, and knowing that Jolene was a witness to Hank murdering his boss, it just seemed right that Hank was the perp."

"I wish it had been Hank, then you'd have him in custody and one of your worries would be gone."

"Trust me, right now I'm still trying to process seeing Brett on top of you with his hands around your throat." He squeezed her hand. "At least the worry of your safety is finally gone."

"How did you find me?" she asked.

"I heard your screams, and when you stopped screaming, I swear my heart stopped beating." He choked with obvious emotion on the last words, and his hand squeezed tight around hers once again.

"But all's well that ends well. At least you got the threat against me in custody, and I don't have to worry about being on Hank's radar. I doubt if Hank even knows who I am."

Bright lights ahead radiated on the yellow bus, and

Nina dropped Flint's hand and ran toward where Grace sat on the ground with Billy in her arms.

"Nina," Billy cried and jumped up to run to her. Nina knelt down and caught him and wrapped her arms around him as Grace joined them. The three of them hugged and cried together for several moments.

"Billy, you know I didn't mean those things I said about you being a sniffling brat," Nina said as she knelt down in front of him.

"I know, you just had to say that stuff to get me away from him. You saved me," Billy said, his arms wrapped tight around her shoulders. "You were so brave, and you saved my life."

"Actually, I wasn't so brave. I was totally scared," Nina confessed and stood.

"I'll never know how to thank you for what you did," Grace said, grateful tears chasing down her cheeks. "Billy told me all about it. You're my hero forever."

"I'm definitely no hero, and you don't have to thank me," Nina replied. "I'm just glad it's all over."

It was at that moment she realized it truly was over. With Brett's arrest, the danger to her was gone. She no longer needed to be in protective custody. She was free to move on with her life with no fear.

She looked over to where Flint stood with several of his other officers. With everything that had happened, he'd be tied up here for hours.

She turned to Grace. "Would you mind dropping me off at Flint's?"

"Not at all," Grace replied.

Nina walked over to Flint and touched his arm to get his attention. "I'm exhausted, and I know you have things to attend to here. I'm going to have Grace take me to your house if that's all right."

"Of course it's all right." He dug a set of keys from his pocket and removed one. "This is to the front door." He handed her the key. "And you can rest assured that you're safe now whether I'm there or not."

"That will be a novel feeling," she replied. "I'll see you later or if I'm asleep when you get home, I'll see you in the morning."

He nodded, and she turned to walk back to where Grace and Billy awaited her. As she walked she couldn't help but wonder if Flint understood that this was the beginning of their goodbye.

Chapter 15

It was almost three when Flint finally got home, weary to his very bones. Instead of bunking on the sofa, he headed for the master suite. As he passed Nina's doorway, her scent of peaches and vanilla drifted out to him and twisted his heart as he thought of that moment when he'd seen her on the ground being strangled by Brett.

His heart had momentarily stopped before he sprang into action. There was no question that he'd been disappointed that the man he had in custody wasn't Hank Bittard, but he was grateful that the threat to Nina had finally been neutralized.

Of course, it was a double-edged sword. She was free now, free to decide what was next for her without needing him for her protection. What he hoped was that she'd stay with him; that she could believe that she was the special woman to share his life, and that he was the man she wanted for the rest of her life.

Over the next couple of days they'd sort out their personal relationship, he thought as he grabbed a pair of clean boxers and headed into the bathroom for a long, hot shower.

He kept his mind blessedly blank as the scent of the woods washed away and was replaced by the fragrance of his minty soap. Hot water pummeled tense muscles until they began to relax, and the adrenaline that had driven him from the moment he'd gotten the news about the hijacked school bus finally began to ebb away.

He got out of the shower, dried off and pulled on his boxers and then opened the door to the bedroom, stunned to see one of his bedside lamps on and Nina in his bed.

He froze in the bathroom doorway. "What are you doing in here?"

She held the sheet up in front of her, but her bare shoulders let him know she was naked. "I've been living here all this time, and I'd never seen your bedroom," she replied.

"And what do you think?" he asked as any weariness he'd carried into the house disappeared.

She looked around the room. "I like it. The heavy dark wood is masculine yet welcoming, and the blue and black bedspread is lovely. The sheets smell like you." She looked back at him.

"What are you doing, Nina?" It hadn't been that long ago that they'd nearly made love on the sofa and she had stopped things before they could progress.

While he knew what he wanted at this moment was

to crawl beneath the sheets and make love to her, he wasn't really sure if Nina knew what she wanted.

It was after three in the morning, and it had been a traumatic evening and night for both of them. Even now in the dimness of the room, he could see the darkened bruises around her neck. Was this really the time and place for her to be making this kind of decision?

"I thought you were asleep when I came in," he said.

"I've just been dozing off and on since Grace brought me home," she replied.

"Nina, you're giving me mixed messages. It was a no-go a week ago, and now you're in my bed," he said with a hint of frustration.

"Can't you get into bed and hold me and make love to me and there be no message?" she asked. When he didn't immediately reply, she released a deep, long sigh. "Flint, I've never known such fear as I did tonight, and when I got here all I could think about was having you hold me, having you warm all the cold places that invaded me in those woods."

The fact that she was naked in his bed stirred him on one level, but her words stirred him on a completely different one. His heart twisted as he thought of her fear, of how very close she'd come to death. The evidence of that fact rode her throat in a necklace of bruises.

"I've always told you whatever you need, whenever you need it, I'm here for you," he said. And with those words he got into bed with her.

He barely got beneath the sheets before she was in his arms. He'd spent the entire night assuring parents that things were under control and seeing to it that Alma was finally transported to the clinic.

As Nina shivered in his arms, he realized he'd calmed and taken care of everyone except her. She'd nearly been choked to death and then had come here alone to deal with the emotional aftermath.

Eventually, he'd need to get an official statement from her about what happened between her and Brett before Flint had arrived on the scene, but there would be time for that tomorrow.

Right now his sole job was to hold her until she warmed, hold her as closely, as tightly as she wanted all night long if that's what she needed from him.

She didn't speak, nor did he. Their only communication was the sound of their heartbeats mirroring each other. If he could make a wish, it would be that he could have her this close to him every night for the rest of his life.

He thought she'd fallen asleep when she finally spoke. "When Brett was on top of me and strangling me, I had only two thoughts in my mind."

"And what were they?" he asked as he caressed one hand up and down her bare back in a soothing motion.

"The first thought I had was that I was so grateful that Billy had gotten away and was safe." Her voice was a soft whisper in the crook of his neck. "And the second thing I thought was that I was sorry we hadn't made love another time. I thought I was going to die with that regret."

Her words made his hand pause in its stroking of her back. There was no question that her words inspired a burst of heat to fire through him, even though his goal had been merely to soothe her.

He had no idea what her intention was concerning any future for them together. He had no idea of her feelings for him, although her actions and her gazes appeared filled with love to him.

"Anything you need, Nina," he repeated.

She nuzzled his throat with her lips and then shifted positions so that their mouths met in a gentle, tender kiss that set the mood for their lovemaking.

There was no frenzied, lustful energy, no frantic grope and grab. They moved together silently, lovingly, and when they were finished, she almost immediately fell asleep in his arms.

He remained awake long after, with the scent of her clinging to his skin and the warmth of her cuddled against him. He hadn't told her he loved her. His love had burned in his heart, and he'd tried to show her in every way possible, but he hadn't actually spoken the words aloud to her.

Would that change her mind about her own future? Would she trust in his love enough to realize she was the woman he wanted to build a family with, the woman he wanted to spend the rest of his life with?

More important, did she love him enough to realize that he was the man to change her mind about her solitary path through life?

She'd had enough love in her heart to put her life on the line for Billy. Did she have enough love in her heart for Flint to bind her life with his?

He fell asleep without an answer.

He awakened to the scent of fresh coffee and something cinnamon, indicating to him that Nina was already up and working in the kitchen.

While it was nice to have somebody cook for him, he'd be perfectly content if Nina never cooked for him again, as long as she was the first person he saw in the mornings and the person he held as they fell asleep each night.

He took a long, hot shower and dressed in his uniform, knowing that there were plenty of loose ends that needed to be tied up today after the action last night.

He also knew that despite the trauma of the night before, Nina would want to go into the diner as usual. At some point he needed to get an official statement from her on exactly what had transpired before he'd pulled Brett off her. He figured he could either go into the diner sometime this afternoon or he could write up a statement that night after dinner.

Despite the fact that nothing had changed that had plagued him before—Hank Bittard was still on the loose, Jimmy Johnson was hiding out somewhere with the precious Colton ring, the investigation into Gemma's attack hadn't advanced and the town was still under quarantine—a new optimism rode in his heart as he entered the kitchen.

"There's my hero," Nina said brightly.

"And right back at you," he replied as she pointed him to the table. As he sat she carried a cup of coffee to him. "Something smells delicious."

"Cinnamon coffee cake," she replied. "It should be ready in just a few minutes." She leaned against the counter and picked up her coffee cup. "Busy day today?"

"It's going to be a killer day of paperwork," he replied.

"We conducted a lot of interviews last night, and they all need to be typed up. Speaking of paperwork, at some point I need to get a complete statement from you. I can either come into the diner this afternoon, or we can do it this evening after dinner."

She set her cup down and opened the oven door. "Why don't we plan on doing it sometime this afternoon at the diner?" She used two hot pads to remove the coffee cake from the oven and set in on a nearby cooling rack.

"Works for me," he said agreeably. "How does around two o'clock sound?"

"Perfect. That's always the slowest time in the diner, and we can go back in my office and get it done." She turned back to the counter and cut the coffee cake. She ladled two large pieces on two plates and then joined him at the table.

"We've still got a ton of people to interview today and tie up all the loose ends concerning Jolene's murder," he said.

"It helped that Brett confessed he killed her in the presence of three witnesses," she replied.

"He was even crowing about it later in front of everyone when he was locked up at the station. We won't have a problem building a case against him not only for Jolene's murder, but also for kidnapping and attempted murder of you. He won't see the light of day for years to come."

"Success," she said with a smile.

"One success, but many challenges ahead," he replied.

"I was hoping that on the way to the diner today we could swing by your office and pick up my car." Her gaze didn't quite meet his. "I've already packed up all my things and have them ready to go."

Flint gazed at her, stunned. "Go? Go today? But

where do you plan to go? You have no house. It's silly for you not to stay here." His heart had begun to beat an unexpected rhythm of dread. He wasn't ready for this, especially after last night.

"I'm going to stay in the back room of the diner for a week or two until I find an apartment to rent." She still refused to meet his gaze. "Flint, we both knew I was only here until the threat to me was removed, and when it was I would be gone."

"But what about last night?"

"Last night was beautiful, but it doesn't change anything," she replied.

"Nina, I don't want you to be gone." Flint's heart felt as if it might beat completely out of his chest. "I want you here, Nina. I want you here always. I'm so in love with you."

For the first time since she'd sat at the table, her gaze met his. Her beautiful hazel eyes were filled with pain. "Flint, I told you from the very beginning that I'm not the marrying kind, that I have no intention of being an always kind of woman with a husband and a family."

"That's what your mouth has said, but I don't believe that's what your heart is saying," he replied. "Nina, you were willing to die for a little boy. That's not a woman who doesn't want a family. I've felt your love for me in a million different ways since you've been here with me. You can't make me believe that you aren't in love with me."

"It doesn't matter. None of that matters." She got up from the table. "It's time for me to move on…alone. It's the choice I made for myself a long time ago."

A hollow emptiness filled Flint, along with a desperation to understand…to change her mind. "But why would you make that choice? You're a woman meant to be loved, to be cherished, and I know I'm the man to make you happy for the rest of your life. Is this because I'm a cop? Because in your childhood cops let you down? I don't have to be a cop, Nina."

"Don't be silly. I know you aren't like those men from my childhood. You were meant to be a lawman, Flint. This town needs you as chief of police."

"And you don't need me?" he asked, aware that he had no dignity left as he faced her. "Trust in me, Nina. Trust in us."

Her features closed in, letting him know he could talk himself blue in the face but she'd shut down. Maybe he'd been mistaken about her love for him after all. Maybe he'd only imagined it because he'd wanted it so badly.

"I'm sorry, Flint," she finally said.

He couldn't force her to be his special woman, not if she didn't believe it herself. He couldn't talk her into believing that he was the special man for her, not if she didn't feel it.

It was over, and he had to accept that. It certainly didn't hurt any less. He felt as if he'd spent a long time waiting for the woman who would lift his spirits with her smile, warm his heart with a simple touch and make him laugh when he thought he'd lost the ability. He'd found her and yet he was denied her.

"Eat your coffee cake," she said.

"I'm not hungry." He shoved the plate aside. "Let's head out of here. I've got a lot of things to attend to today."

She pulled his house key from her pocket and set

it on the table. "I've got my things packed up and by the front door."

Flint got up from the table, and within minutes her things were in his trunk, and they were on their way to the police station where her car had been parked since the night she'd witnessed Jolene's murder.

They didn't speak on the way. Flint had nothing more to say, and in any case his aching heart felt too big to talk around.

Nina stared out the passenger window, apparently disinclined to break the awkward silence as easily as she'd broken his heart.

When they reached the station he helped her load her things into her car trunk. "Depending on how busy I get today, it might be Patrick who comes to the diner to take your statement," he said.

He wasn't sure he was ready for the awkwardness of sitting with her in her office to take her statement. His utter devastation was too fresh, his heart far too vulnerable.

"Thank you, Flint, for everything." Her gaze held his and in their whiskey-colored depths, he could swear he saw regret and the simmer of love.

False images, he told himself. The wishful thinking of a foolish man in love. "I'm just glad we got the bad guy, and you don't have to be afraid anymore. Now all I need to do is get Bittard and Jimmy behind bars."

She reached out a hand as if to touch his arm, but then dropped it to her side. "You'll get them, Flint, and with Dr. Colleen Goodhue set to arrive sometime this afternoon, it won't be long before the town will be back to normal again."

He nodded. "Goodbye, Nina."

"I'll see you later." She got into her car and after three attempts, finally got it started and pulled out of the parking lot.

Flint watched until her car disappeared from sight, a hollowness sweeping over him. The town would never be normal to him again. His life would never feel normal without Nina in it.

With a frown he turned and headed into the station. He had fugitives to catch and the job of keeping peace. That's what he needed to focus on, and he needed to forget the woman who had captured his heart and then thrown it away.

Chapter 16

The first thing Nina did when she left the police station was drive to the discount store where she bought a comfortable bed pillow and a thick blanket for the cot in the storeroom where she would be sleeping until she made other arrangements.

It felt odd to be out shopping without Flint by her side, and she steadfastly tried to shove thoughts of him and the conversation they'd just shared out of her head.

Still, his words of love rang through her ears and constricted her heart. The shock on his face when he realized she was leaving, the anguish in his eyes when he'd realized he wasn't going to change her mind, ripped pain through her.

She'd never meant for him to fall in love with her, and she'd never meant to fall in love with him.

Yes, she could admit that she was in love with Flint,

but she'd had years of believing she was best off alone, of seeing her future in that way, and her love for Flint didn't change her mind about her solitary path through life. She'd finally learned to be in control of her own life and the idea of any change terrified her.

The storage room not only had tall metal shelving for foodstuff and paper goods, but also gray metal lockers where her workers could lock up their personal belongings.

Besides the cot, there was also a small stall shower, which was rarely used, but would provide her the ability to shower during the time she spent here.

Charley was the only one at the diner when she arrived and carried her things into the storeroom. He followed her into the room.

"I heard there was quite a bit of excitement last night," he said.

"Enough excitement to last me for the rest of my life, but the good news is Flint arrested Jolene Tate's killer, so I'm now a free woman who no longer needs to be in protective custody." She attempted a cheerfulness as she tossed the pillow and blanket on the cot.

"So, you're moving in here?"

She shrugged. "My house was burned to the ground and it was time for me to leave Flint's, so I figure I'll bunk here for a while."

"Surely Grace or one of the other waitresses would be glad to put you up," Charley said.

"I know, but to be honest, I'd rather be here. I need a little alone time to process everything that's happened to me in the past month. I'll be fine back here," she assured him.

By the time she had stored her things, Grace and

Molly had arrived for the morning shift. "I just wanted to let you know that Patrick and I agreed last night to postpone our date on Friday. To be honest, I'm not ready to have Billy out of my sight. If I'd had my way I would have kept him out of school today, but he insisted he had to go because he had to tell everyone what had happened to him. I figured it was best to keep things as normal as possible and let him go."

"He's doing okay?" Nina asked worriedly. The last thing she wanted was for Billy to carry scars from his ordeal through the rest of his life.

Grace smiled. "He's probably doing better than any of us. When we got home he wanted a bowl of ice cream, and he told me that even though he was scared as soon as he saw you, he knew you were going to save him, and then Flint saved you and all's well that ends well."

"The offer still stands for me to babysit Billy if you and Patrick change your mind. The only difference is I'd have to watch him at your house instead of at Flint's. I moved out of there this morning." Nina refused to acknowledge the squeeze of her heart.

"Already?" Grace frowned in obvious dismay. "But I had hoped…" She allowed her voice to trail off.

"There was no hope. There never was any hope," Nina said firmly. "And now it's time to get to work and get things ready to open for the day," she added.

Surprisingly, there was a brisk morning rush, prompted mostly by people wanting to gossip or find out about what had happened the night before. Parents came in to talk about the fear they'd had for their children, and others came in to listen to their tales.

Still, no matter how busy she was, no matter how

many customers she served and chatted with, she couldn't stop thinking about Flint and the month she had spent with him.

There had been an easy magic between them that she knew was rare, but she told herself over and over again that didn't make it right for her. She was right to let him move on. She had her life here.

The lunch rush was equally robust, keeping the waitresses running from table to booth to accommodate everyone's needs. Nina found herself giving a condensed version of what had happened in the woods with Brett over and over again to interested customers.

The mood in the diner remained positive, as if it didn't matter what bad guy had been arrested, but only that one had been.

Nina fought to stay positive, to keep her happy smile in place, but it was an effort. She didn't understand why following her own path could make her feel so sad inside.

At two o'clock Patrick showed up to take Nina's official statement of the events of the night before. They went into her office where it took almost an hour for her to give him a blow-by-blow account of her encounter with Brett.

Talking about it brought back all the emotions, all the fears she'd experienced while it was happening, and she wished it was Flint taking her statement. Thankfully, she managed to keep control of those emotions.

When they had finished, Patrick took a seat at a table Grace was serving, and Nina prepared Billy's after-school treat…a chocolate cupcake and the usual glass of milk.

When he came through the door she gave him a

big hug and then sat at his table with him. "How was school?"

"Awesome," he replied and licked the side of his mouth where a dollop of frosting had clung. "I was totally the center of attention. Everyone wanted to know what happened when that man took me into the woods."

"And what did you tell them?" Nina asked.

"I told them that it was scary, and he dragged me around by my coat and talked mean to me, and then you found us and even though you knew that man wanted to hurt you, you made him let me go and told me to run." His dark eyes gazed at her in obvious hero worship. "I told everybody at school that you were the bravest person in the whole world."

"I told you last night, I didn't feel very brave. I was scared, too, but I didn't want anything to happen to you."

"That still makes you the bravest person in this whole town," he replied.

"And you're still my favorite little man," Nina replied.

She visited with him a few more minutes and then left the table so he could get to his homework.

She sat at the counter and watched Patrick and Grace interact, Grace's cheeks slightly pink, and Patrick looked animated and engaged.

She knew exactly what Grace was feeling, the flush of excitement and the flutter of her heartbeat. Nina had felt that way each evening at five o'clock when Flint had walked through the diner door to take her home.

But this evening there would be no handsome lawman appearing to take her to the house that had felt like home for almost a month.

There would be no more dinners of light flirting and conversation and laughter, no evenings drinking wine and feeling the simmering sexual tension that was undeniable between them. She would never again know the warmth, the sense of safety, that she'd always felt when his arms were wrapped around her.

She'd consciously walked away from all of that.

She was glad when dinner found the diner relatively full, and she kept her focus solely on making sure her customers were well-fed and happy. This was her life, and her staff and the customers were her family, and she continued to tell herself that this was all she needed.

By the time the diner closed down for the night she was exhausted. She took a quick shower, got into her nightgown and then got beneath the new blanket on the cot.

A small security light shone on the gray lockers and the hum of the walk-in freezer provided a white noise that should have been soothing, but instead she found it irritating.

She burrowed deeper beneath the blanket. She'd never felt alone before, but at this moment she felt more alone than she ever had in her life.

Tears began to seep from her eyes, tears she didn't understand and couldn't control. She'd made this choice to leave Flint and his love of her own free will. So, why was she crying?

She thought of Billy telling her she was the bravest person on earth. She'd faced down a killer to save him. If she was truly one of the bravest people on earth, then why was she so afraid of Flint's love and of her love for him?

Yesterday had been one of the busiest, the longest and the most painful days Flint had ever endured in his life. There were more interviews to conduct, reports to type up and no matter how busy he stayed, there was a simmer of heartache that ripped at his soul.

Patrick returned with the report from Nina and as Flint read it, his heart had quickened with the utter terror she must have felt when she first encountered Brett with Billy.

He'd had Patrick type in the report and then at three-thirty in the afternoon, the only good news of the day showed its face.

CDC expert Dr. Colleen Goodhue had finally arrived in a large white trailer that hopefully held the specialized equipment and whatever else was necessary for her to find the cure for the Dead River virus.

Today had been another busy day and by five o'clock, Flint was ready to head out. As he drove home he tried not to think about how differently he'd be feeling right now if he was headed to the diner to pick up Nina. Instead he was headed into a silent, lonely house where he'd believed foolishly that love had blossomed.

He parked his car in the driveway and walked out to his mailbox to get his mail and as he headed back to the house, he reminded himself to close the window in the spare bedroom.

He'd opened it the night before when he'd come home to a silent house that smelled of vanilla and peaches. He'd needed to get her scent out of his house and out of his head, and he needed to figure out how to drive her completely out of his mind.

It had been another day of highs and lows. No signs of the fugitives, no further answers as to who had attacked Gemma or why. To make matters worse, the weather had made its final shift toward winter, with gray skies and a bitter, frigid wind that seemed to reflect his mood.

The high of the day had been a new optimism among everyone he spoke to in town due to Dr. Goodhue's presence at the clinic. Her arrival had brought hope to the people of Dead River. Every place Flint had gone that day people had talked about the renowned doctor finally finding a cure and the quarantine being lifted.

Flint just hoped she managed to come up with something that would save Gram Dottie, who remained unconscious and barely clinging to life.

As he approached his front door, a sense of dread flew through him as he thought of Nina's absence. She'd not only filled the house with warmth and laughter, but she'd filled his heart. And he thought he'd filled hers, but he'd obviously been so wrong.

He unlocked his front door and stepped inside, greeted by the scent of something delicious cooking. He stopped in his tracks, his heart banging against his ribs as he tried to figure out why she would be here cooking for him.

Was she cooking him a pity meal? A final thank-you dinner? Did she not realize having her here again was sheer torture? And how had she gotten inside anyway?

He took off his coat, hat and holster and set them on a chair and then moved on wooden feet toward the kitchen. One step inside and he saw her at the stove, stirring a big pot.

She didn't appear to be aware of him, and he took a moment just to look at her, to notice how her jeans fit so neatly down her legs and cupped her buttocks and how the forest-green T-shirt showcased her beautiful auburn hair.

But instead of stirring any desire in him, her very presence whipped up more than a little anger. "What are you doing here?" he finally spoke.

She looked up at him, startled. "Oh, I didn't hear you come in." She gazed back at the pot on the stove. "It just felt like the perfect day to make a big pot of chili. Don't you think so?"

He felt like he'd entered an alternate universe. "How did you get in here?" He still didn't understand why she was here or what was going on, and that tinge of anger inside him hadn't dissipated.

She set her big spoon down and turned to face him. "You had a window open. It was like an open invitation for some dummy to break into the chief of police's house." She paused a moment. "So, are you going to arrest me for breaking and entering, or are you going to eat chili?"

He moved to the table and sat down. "Right now I'm not inclined to do either," he replied. "What I want to know is what kind of games you're playing with me, Nina. You've been giving me mixed messages since the moment you moved in here. I thought we finished it all when you moved out and told me you want your life back."

She turned down the burner under the pot of chili and then leaned against the counter and gazed at him with an expression he couldn't begin to discern. "No games, Flint. The last thing I want to do is play games with your heart or with my own."

She left the counter and moved to sit across from him at the table. "I went to bed last night on the cot in the back room of the diner, but instead of sleeping, I found myself doing a lot of soul searching."

Flint remained silent. He'd said everything he had to say to her the morning before, when he'd professed the depth of his love for her, and she'd walked out.

She laced her fingers on top of the table and stared down at them. "I thought I'd put my childhood all behind me, that I'd endured my personal hell and had come out stronger on the other side with no scars to show for the experience."

Her eyes darkened as she looked up at him. "The first hint I had that there might be a few scars was when I was so attracted to you when you first started coming into the diner, but was so put off by your uniform. I found myself wondering if you were like the lawmen of my youth, men who covered for my father's crimes, who saw to it that he never faced any charges and always brought him back home to continue his abuse."

"And so you worried that I was the same kind of dirty cop," he replied, unable to hide his offense at her words.

She nodded miserably. "But it didn't take me long to realize you were nothing like those men, that you were respected and trustworthy and honorable. That night in the woods, I saw a savage side to you, but I wasn't afraid because I knew you were that way to protect and defend, not to abuse and hurt."

Flint wondered where this conversation was going.

Did she just need one final cathartic spilling of her past and her emotions?

Despite the chili scent that filled the air, he could smell the fragrance of vanilla and peaches. Did she not realize that having her in the house, sitting across from him, was a particular kind of torture?

She raised a hand up and shoved a strand of her hair behind her ear. "Yesterday when Billy came into the diner, he said that I was the bravest person on the face of the earth."

"You were very brave in those woods with Brett," Flint agreed.

She shook her head as if to dismiss his words. "Billy's words kept playing again and again in my head and what I couldn't figure out was if I was so brave, then why was I willing to turn my back on your love, to turn my back on the love I have for you in my heart?"

"Did you come up with any answers?" he asked and tried to ignore the sudden acceleration of his heartbeat.

"Enough answers to have an epiphany of sorts," she replied. "It was on the day that my father murdered my mother that I made two promises to myself. The first was that I'd never celebrate a holiday again, and the second was that I would never marry or have a family of my own. I managed to go a long time before I broke my first promise, and we both saw how my plans for a perfect holiday were ruined."

"Nina, there are no perfect holidays," Flint replied. "No matter how well you plan, a drink gets spilled or a bowl gets overturned. An uncle gets drunk or an argument breaks out."

"But you had perfect holidays with your family when you were young," she protested.

"I didn't tell you about the Easter that Theo ate so much candy he threw up for two hours, or the Christmas when Gemma didn't get a doll that wet her diapers and threw a massive temper tantrum. I can't tell you how many fights Theo and I had about who got the wishbone from the turkey. Nothing is perfect, Nina. We just try to make everything as perfect as possible."

She nodded thoughtfully. "I've been scared about celebrating holidays and then when I finally decided it was time, it all fell apart so badly. I was afraid that if I took a chance on my second commitment to myself and allowed myself to believe that home and family were truly possible for me, it would all be ruined like my holidays."

Tears misted her eyes. "I appreciate you explaining all of this to me," Flint replied, unsure what else to say.

"I'm not finished," she said and quickly swiped at her eyes. "And then all I could think about was my time here with you, and how I've never known such happiness before in my entire life. I thought about how much I loved Billy and that I could easily love a child of my own…a child of yours."

Joy flooded Flint's heart at her words. "So, you're willing to give us a chance?" he asked tentatively, not wanting to misunderstand exactly what she was saying.

"I'm willing to go all in," she replied, a shimmering light filling her eyes. "I love you, Flint Colton, and I want to build my life with yours. I want to share my morning coffee with you across from me and the last thought I have before I go to sleep with you."

She looked at him expectantly, and then continued, "And if you don't get out of that chair and come and hug and kiss me and tell me that you still want those things with me, I'm going to scream."

Flint was up and out of his chair and had her in his arms before she could take another breath. He kissed her long and hard, with every ounce of love he harbored in his heart.

When he finally stopped the kiss, he gazed down at her soberly. "I can't promise you perfect, Nina."

"Perfection was a childhood fantasy, but I'm not a child anymore, and I don't want to live my life alone without love, without family. I want it all, Flint. I want it all with you."

He kissed her again and knew that he had found his special woman, the one who would bring laughter and love to him for the rest of his life.

Epilogue

Flint sat at his desk and stared out the window where snow flurries whirled in the air. He felt ridiculously optimistic despite the fact that it was the beginning of a new month and nothing had changed.

Well, that wasn't exactly true. What had changed was that the night before he and Nina had eaten chili and talked about their pasts, but more important, had talked about their future together here in Dead River.

Any thought he'd had of giving up his position was gone, for Nina had given him the confidence to continue his work.

They hadn't talked about weddings and babies in the near future. Instead they'd agreed to take things slow and steady. She would continue to live with him, and he knew they would only build on their love for each other.

Afterward they had gone to bed together in his master suite and made love and had fallen asleep in each other's arms. He'd been greeted that morning by her cheerful smile across the table, and that had definitely started his day off right.

The icing on the cake had been a phone call from Gemma that morning telling him that Gram Dottie had regained consciousness, although they weren't allowing any visitors at the moment. Still, the knowledge that she was better had filled his heart and soul with an additional layer of happiness.

He stared at the stack of files next to him, and his thoughts turned somber. Hank Bittard remained on the loose, as did Jimmy Johnson. They had come to dead ends when it came to the attack on Gemma.

His personal life might be finally in order, but he still faced a number of professional issues. With Dr. Colleen Goodhue now in town, a cure for the Dead River virus could happen sooner rather than later and that would end the quarantine that kept Hank and Jimmy trapped within the town's limits.

At least with Brett behind bars, he'd managed to clear up Jolene's murder and free Nina from fear. More than anything, he wanted to get Bittard behind bars before the quarantine was lifted, but he no longer feared the murderer would stick around town when that happened.

Hank had no reason to stick around Dead River when the quarantine was lifted. He'd run as fast and as far away as he could in an attempt to elude the scene of his crimes. If that happened then Flint would just have to live with the fact that a criminal got out of his jurisdiction.

He still wanted Jimmy Johnson and the Colton heirloom ring back where it belonged, but he couldn't be sure that would happen before the quarantine was lifted.

Just as he'd finally come to peace with the fact that the tragedy in Cheyenne hadn't been his own personal failure, he knew he couldn't control the circumstances of when a cure for the virus might be discovered.

There were still many challenges ahead for the people of Dead River and for Flint, but he knew he could meet each one as they came along, especially with Nina by his side.

* * * * *

THE COLTONS: RETURN TO WYOMING
Don't miss a single story!

A SECRET COLTON BABY by Karen Whiddon
HER COLTON LAWMAN by Carla Cassidy
COLTON HOLIDAY LOCKDOWN by C.J. Miller

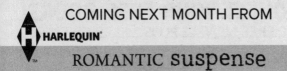

REQUEST YOUR FREE BOOKS!
2 FREE NOVELS PLUS 2 FREE GIFTS!

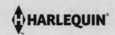

ROMANTIC suspense

Sparked by danger, fueled by passion

HRS13R

SPECIAL EXCERPT FROM

 HARLEQUIN

ROMANTIC suspense

Returning to Dead River is anything but welcoming for Dr. Rafe Granger, who lands himself in the middle of an epidemic…and discovers a connection to the powerful Colton family he never anticipates.

Read on for a sneak peek of

COLTON HOLIDAY LOCKDOWN
by C.J. Miller

Dr. Rafe Granger would never escape this rotting purgatory. His return had brought with it a terrible series of events: an unidentified virus was claiming victims by the dozens, the virus research lab had been trashed and a murderer had escaped the local prison and was adding to the terror and paranoia of every person in town.

Rafe entered the clinic through the single metal entry door. The smell of smoke hung in the air. Behind the reception area, the clinic's patient files had been pulled from the shelves and littered the floor. The culprit had done much worse to Rafe's office and the lab.

Dread pooled low in his stomach. What had been taken? The most critical work had been stored in the lab.

Rafe checked over his protective gear, pulled it on and entered the lab, noting the lock was broken on the door. Anger and frustration shook Rafe to his core. The inside of the lab was a disaster—tables overturned, equipment thrown to the floor and petri dishes and beakers smashed on the ground. But the most alarming thing was what had been done to the samples. The small refrigerator they'd been using to store the carefully labeled Vacutainer tubes was open and emptied.

Rafe let loose a curse he almost never used. This situation was beyond all repair.

He felt a hand on his back and whirled around, coming face-to-face with Gemma Colton, one of the clinic's registered nurses.

"Where are our samples?" Gemma asked, sounding shocked and panicked. Her green eyes were filled with concern. As many times as he had looked into those green eyes, the vibrancy and beauty of them struck him every time. "Who would do this?"

"Not sure. But that virus is deadly on the street," Rafe said.

"We already have an epidemic and now we have to worry about someone running around with vials containing the virus," Gemma said, her voice shaking.

Rafe heard shouts and banging from the clinic. He and Gemma exchanged looks. What else could go wrong?

Don't miss COLTON HOLIDAY LOCKDOWN by C.J. Miller, available December 2014 wherever Harlequin® Romantic Suspense books and ebooks are sold.

ROMANTIC suspense

Heart-racing romance, high-stakes suspense!

BETH CORNELISON
brings you the next installment of
THE MANSFIELD BROTHERS miniseries
THE MANSFIELD RESCUE

Available December 2014

A single father discovers the price of revenge and the power of love...

After his wife's murder, Grant Mansfield vowed to stay true to her memory and to protect their children. But fate has other plans. His temporary houseguest, injured smokejumper Amy Robinson, has him burning with a white-hot attraction. And the single dad's nightmare comes true when his older daughter is kidnapped.

Grant is just the man the adventurous Amy never knew she needed, his children the family she never knew she wanted. Before she can rescue his lonely heart, the handsome widower must become a hero. Only Grant can rescue his little girl. But time is running out...

Don't miss other exciting titles from BETH CORNELISON's
THE MANSFIELD BROTHERS:
PROTECTING HER ROYAL BABY
THE RETURN OF CONNOR MANSFIELD

Available wherever books and ebooks are sold.

www.Harlequin.com

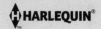

ROMANTIC suspense

Heart-racing romance, high-stakes suspense!

LONE STAR SURVIVOR by Colleen Thompson

Available December 2014

A soldier's memories are more dangerous than anything he's encountered in the line of duty

"Killed in action" a year ago, US Army captain Ian Rayford shocks everyone when he stumbles half-dead onto his family's Texas ranch. Suffering from post-traumatic stress disorder, his former fiancée, a psychologist specializing in PTSD, arrives to help Ian recover. But not everyone wants her to unearth the dangerous secrets he's carrying.

Now engaged to another man, Dr. Andrea Warrington fights her feelings for Ian even as she helps him remember how much they once loved each other. Yet the closer Ian gets to his past, the more someone else has to ensure the treacherous truth stays buried.

Don't miss other exciting Harlequin® Romantic Suspense titles from Colleen Thompson:
LONE STAR REDEMPTION
THE COLTON HEIR
PASSION TO PROTECT

Available wherever books and ebooks are sold.

www.Harlequin.com

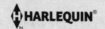

ROMANTIC suspense

Heart-racing romance, high-stakes suspense!

LETHAL LIES
by Lara Lacombe

Available December 2014

Trusting the man she loves could cost her her life

Putting her faith in someone who lies for a living isn't the
safest thing Dr. Jillian Mahoney has ever done. But to stay
alive, she has to believe the undercover agent—who's
kidnapped her to prove his innocence—isn't a traitor to the
FBI. And to help him, she must deny their intense attraction as
they run from two vengeful killers.

Her captor, Alex Malcom, *has* lived a life of lies—some worse
than others. Still, there's one truth he's reluctant to disclose
to Jillian, the woman of his dreams. One that could stop their
relationship cold.

Don't miss other exciting Harlequin® Romantic Suspense
titles from Lara Lacombe:
FATAL FALLOUT
DEADLY CONTACT

Available wherever books and ebooks are sold.